I0730465

Itinerant Soul

Don Alcock

Turtle Publishing

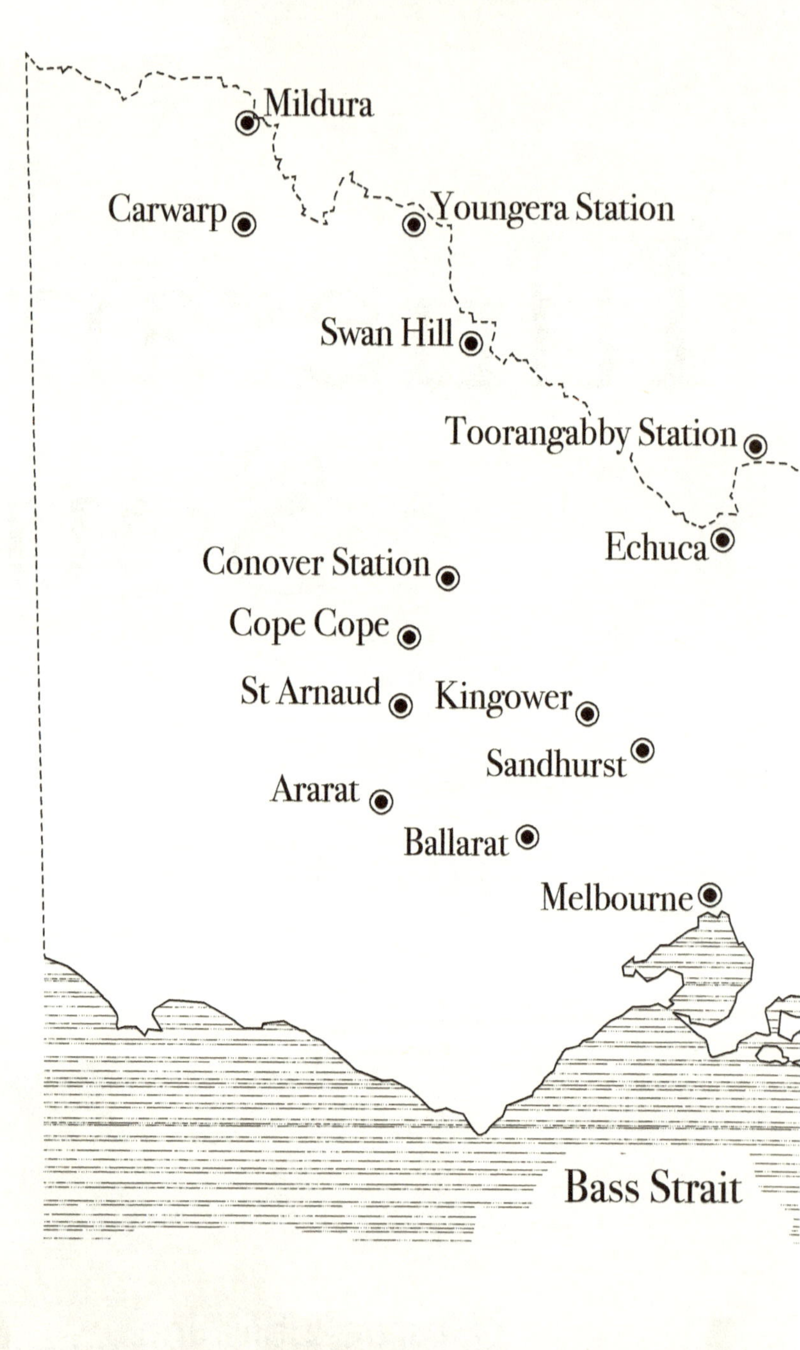

Mildura
Carwarp
Youngera Station
Swan Hill
Toorangabby Station
Echuca
Conover Station
Cope Cope
St Arnaud
Kingower
Sandhurst
Ararat
Ballarat
Melbourne
Bass Strait

Victoria 1860s
Belsar's Journey

Copyright © 2025 Don Alcock

All rights reserved.

No part of this publication may be reproduced, stored in a retrieval system, or transmitted in any form or by any means–electronic, mechanical, photocopying, recording, or otherwise–without the prior written permission of the author. Any unauthorised use of this material may result in legal action, including criminal prosecution and civil claims for damages. For permissions and enquiries, please contact the publisher.

Don Alcock has asserted his moral right to be identified as the author of this work under the Copyright, Designs and Patents Act 1988.

This book is a work of fiction based on real names and dates, with creative license taken by the author in the development of the narrative. While inspired by actual events, the story, and interpretations are fictionalised.

Citation

Location map of Victoria Artist: Graham Bliss

First published by Turtle Publishing 2025

ISBN: 978-1-7642441-0-7 (paperback)
ISBN: 978-1-7642441-1-4 (ebook)

TurtlePublishing

*As all historians know, the past is a
great darkness, and filled with echoes.
Voices may reach us from it; but what
they say to us is imbued with the
obscurity of the matrix out of which
they come; and try as we may, we
cannot always decipher them precisely
in the clearer light of our day.*

Margaret Atwood

PREFACE

How do you untangle a story about past lives; those who have died, their voices lost? Not the prominent or wealthy – their episodic memory saved in books and biographies. Nor the recent, still in our hearts. I mean the distant past – a time of forgotten lives, of illiterate survivors, lost echoes we hear no more. Unknown souls and common folk, pioneers who came before us and lived just long enough to bear children. Humble, uneducated men and brave, hardy women who struggled to eke out a living among the poor and desperate. Seamen, lumpers of carts, drovers, convict wives, children in unmarked graves. Hopeful emigrants and tragic miners, forgotten in time. How do we hear *their* voices?

In one way, we carry them inside us – in our DNA and epigenetic inheritance, passed down through generations. Can we recall their history and understand their lives? There are clues, of course, in faded documents, in library archives, many digitised – birth certificates, census records, old newspapers, shipping registers, crew lists. Traces of lost voices.

An old photograph, frozen in time. A family story, distorted, soon to be forgotten. An heirloom, a wedding ring or lock of hair. Lists of names and dates in registers of births, deaths and marriages. Who were they, these lost voices? How do we find their hearts, put flesh on the bones of their lives, and tell their stories?

This novel is a biographic imagination of a true story. The events, dates, voyages and locations are accurate, and almost every character is real. From the squalor of Liverpool, young Richard Belsar survived and carved out a life as a merchant sailor and carpenter. He crossed vast oceans and explored far-off ports in Newfoundland, Portugal, West Africa, America, and Van Diemen's Land, before crossing paths with Elizabeth Carter – a domestic servant – in the goldfields of Victoria.

Together, they became itinerant workers on sheep stations before making a home for their family along the Murray River. They loved, overcame hardship, found great joy and suffered tragedy. Both Richard and Elizabeth survived. In many ways, they survive still.

Liverpool, 1830

There are two things to remember when you're being hunted by a violent street gang. Run like the clappers and do the unexpected.

Standing at Sweeny's corner with three ruffians in front of him and two behind, the chase began. Fear and adrenaline made Richard Belsar take off. Taken by surprise, he almost forgot to run, to think ahead, to find obstacles and use cover. He scanned the street. A row of paling fences next to a coal yard, a small crowd of dock labourers sauntering past, a horse and cart on the cobbled street, earthworks at Wapping Station. Duck and dart. Never run straight. Dodge and weave or they'll run you down, especially the older brutes. If you get outflanked and surrounded, you're screwed. If caught, bullied and mugged. Bashed for the sake of a halfpenny, or just for the fun of it.

The guttersnipes, older boys known as the Rat Pack, chased him down Watkinson Street, near where he lived. Like a fox being chased by a rabid pack of hounds, he sprinted past sallow-eyed cellar-dwellers emerging from their grimy basements, then slid under a slow-moving dray laden with goods from the docks.

The Rat Pack were gaining, hot on his heels. He could hear their hoots and cries as he sprinted under the iron rail bridge at Chalenor Street, which led to the docks. 'Run rabbit!' they shouted. They howled their tribal call, 'Yawp, yawp!' In desperation, he put on a burst of speed along the Park Lane Goods Station coal yard. Above him, on a steel bridge overpass, a steam train thundered past, belching smoke and fibres of cotton into the air, rattling on its way to Manchester.

Richard was fast and agile, running down narrow cobbled lanes, darting between sweat-stained men hauling trolleys of wheat, around wagons loaded with barrels of salted fish, nearing the King's Dock, where his father worked. He eventually slowed in the crowd and caught his breath, taking in great gulps of air, spitting out gobs of phlegm laced with cotton dust. He had escaped the rascal gang yet again.

He knew every inch of the slums and docks – his kingdom and playground. Four miles of enormous and magnificent stone walls and Georgian buildings along the Mersey River. So many berths and piers, crowded with tall wood sailing ships: the huge Salthouse Dock, the massive Prince's Dock, the royally named King's and Queen's Docks. Granite barriers, timber swing bridges, high stone breakwaters, swinging gantries with cranes, thick oak sea gates, designed to deal with an armada of trading ships, all waiting to gain access to the bustling inner docks.

Richard, now 15, had explored Liverpool's docks and warehouses since he was a young boy, fascinated by the constant procession of tall ships and strange, foreign cargo. He watched majestic square riggers being warped in and out by pilot boats and by hardened men hauling tow ropes at the wharves. He knew the wet and dry docks – timber yards, shipwright's huts, filthy market stalls, chandleries, fancy merchant houses, goods warehouses, and roperies – places where he could hide or where he could be seen. He could outrun guttersnipes and roughnecks trying to chase him to steal a penny or pick a fight. He knew their ugly faces and city territories. The dockside gangs, the Park Lane pickpockets, the thugs and nibblers from St James Street. He knew the sons of the dock labourers who worked with his old man. The strong ones, the tough ones, the weak ones.

He found his old man lumping bags of raw sugar off a schooner recently arrived from the Americas. A tall man, square-shouldered and red-faced under his flat cap, wearing a black linen shirt and thick wool canvass breeches. His old man was yelling at his team to move faster, unpacking and lifting heavy canvass sacks of wheat by shoulder onto horse-drawn wagons, to be stored in Clarke and Co. warehouse, where he worked. His old man turned around, annoyed by the boy's distraction, his piercing blue eyes glancing down.

'What?' he said, scowling, tipping his head slightly, signalling the boy to approach.

Richard skipped cautiously to his side. 'Whencha home tonight, Pa?' he said. 'Ma needs you so she can go see Father Glover at Saint Peter's. She told me to fetch you.'

'Did she, now? Knowing it's Friday,' he said. 'Time for me ale at the end of me shift. Twelve long hard hours. *Mien Got*, that woman expects some, she does.' He stared coldly at Richard, shifting his gaze back to the men, weighing up his choices, then decided. '*Nein*, you'll 'ave to look after the bairns t'night. Feed 'em and put 'em to bed. I'll be home whenever I get there. Now *pissen auf.*'

'But Pa, it's my boat time!' Fridays were his only free time to visit *Venteux*, a French ketch captured in the last war, grounded and abandoned on the Mersey's muddy bank. There, each week, Richard learnt about boats from Ben Farquar, a retired sailor who taught him to hitch knots, repair torn canvass, read the degrees of a compass, splice a rope and caulk split timbers on a deck. The old seaman, looking like a Chelsea pensioner in his tattered blue jacket and white breeches, limped around *Venteux* with a wound he never spoke of.

Whether Ben Farquar had been a former British Royal Navy captain like he claimed, or that *Venteax* was a rotting wreck lying beached in the Mersey's fetid, stinking mud, Richard didn't care. The wrinkled old seaman, missing three fingers and an eye, told grand and wonderous stories of his days at sea, occasionally spitting phlegm while he smoked his clay pipe. Ben was a pensioned navy man who'd seen the Battle of Grand Port in France. Now he was reduced to being a ship's caretaker until *Venteax* was either sold or salvaged for wood, living in a cabin inside its dilapidated hold.

'*Gehen* home,' John Belsar ordered in his guttural Prussian accent, one he could never shake. He put his hand in his pocket. 'Ere's a shillin' for potato and herring at Smith's stall. Git on now, boy!' A coin spun in the air and was grabbed before it fell to the ground. Richard knew not to answer back or push him. The old man had a hot temper and sometimes hit him. He sometimes hit his ma.

His old man half raised his arm – only a mock test, with no intended malice. Richard dodged the clip he might get and ran off, leaving his pa to yell at his men some more to continue hauling bags onto the company wagon. His pa was a strong man, powerfully built. A stevedore hired for his strength. Merchants respected him because he worked hard, drove his men hard and wouldn't steal. John Belsar knew all about loading and unloading cargo from merchant ships. How to unpack sacks of sugar or wheat without spoiling it. How to carefully stow pig iron or bins of coal inside the tight confines of a ship's ballast. Or lift sacks of coffee by a boom and winch, so porters and carriers on the dock could weigh and mark for storage inside huge warehouses that lined Liverpool's port. He knew sloppy stowage or poor unloading could damage cargo or spoil goods – even sink a ship in rough weather, killing profit for the ship's owners.

Richard pushed his way through the noisy, bustling crowd that always lined the docks – the yelling hawkers, swaggering seamen, layabouts, bludgers and drunks – and came to a row of stalls that fronted Sefton Steet. He could feel the simmering tension around the markets; there was always competition and frustration in the rabble. Occasionally, fights broke out among the haggling buyers and sellers, or between stall owners and costermongers. To Richard, it was a normal, everyday occurrence, just like the gangs on the street. Everywhere around the docks, everywhere in the city itself, someone was trying to take advantage of someone else.

He passed several drays unloading their cargo of raw sugar inside a stone-walled warehouse and ordinance building, and heard the hammering shouts of the auctioneers, the grinding of wheels, the sounds of the angry men. There was a constant commotion of small traders and hawkers vying for custom: costermongers selling watercress and onions, butchers hacking up sheep trotters, merchants trading gin, fishmongers plying vats of jellied eels – among the cacophony of sing-song chants there was a smell of rotting waste, piss and horse shit.

Richard bought a pound of potatoes, six herrings, and a cut of bacon from Smith's stall for his family meal tonight. He pocketed the potatoes and wrapped the fish and bacon inside a hessian cloth, then walked cautiously back to his home in Lawrence Cottages on Watkinson Street, three blocks away from King's Dock, alert for any gang thieves. The streets, by then, seemed empty and clear. Tonight, at least, the family wouldn't go hungry, he thought. His sister, Ellen, would help prepare their meal, ready for his ma's return. Now 11, she should be back from her job washing and drying bed sheets at Mrs O'Dwyer's boarding house.

There was always gossip in the streets, about the city and its port. It moved from house to house. It flowed faster through the inns and markets than it did by newspaper and the town criers, or from Sunday priests at the pulpit. Labouring men complained about their work, or lack of it. They railed against the swell of immigrants taking their jobs. They decried Liverpool as the Black Spot on the Mersey, full of disease and overcrowding. The poor were everywhere as Irish emigrants, ex-navy seamen, and people fleeing war-torn Europe flocked to the city. Families lived in damp cellars or two-room houses, many in squalor. Even city officials and church leaders had begun to condemn the growth of filthy conditions in the slums.

So far, Richard's old man was doing alright. He arrived after Napoleon's war, an emigrant from Prussia, battling against the swell of ex-British navy men discharged from duty, all seeking work at the docks, part of the post-war slump. He started as a carter, hauling goods around the docks with a horse-drawn cart, then became a stevedore, and now ran a team of six men contracted with Clarke and Co.

He found regular work – no longer battling crowds of casual, hungry men, begging for a day's hire each morning at six am. Tall and strong, standing head and shoulder above the rest. He drank, had learned to speak English, married an Irish girl, fought to get noticed by the company foremen.

He insisting the children be baptised Catholic, yet he wasn't much of a believer. He swore and cursed when he got frustrated or upset, unable to find the right words to express his emotions, often exploding in a sudden rage, especially about money. '*Schiesse*, I got not a rap. No goddamn silver coin left in me damn pockets.' It was worse when he drank liquor. He became sullen and moody, reddening in silent rage.

Richard never saw anything soft about his pa. When he came home from the docks he seemed to fill their small kitchen: massive, solid, a great rock of a man. He sat at the head of the table. His big, rough hands, flat on the wood, waiting for his meal to put down in front of him. His moods would often swing from silence rages of frustration to drunken melancholy, when he would reminisce about his youth. The Old Country this, or the Old Country that.

'Escaped the ruin of Stettin, I did,' he said one evening at home after a few too many drinks of ale at Squires Inn. He stared into his frothy glass, slumped in his chair, lost in thought, recalling scattered memories of the past. Richard listened intently at their small kitchen table, fascinated by pa's earlier life. He'd been a sailor. Stories of seafaring adventures and bloody battles.

The old man waxed on, mumbling in a mix of Prussian and English, about his childhood home in the land of Pomerania, his long-dead dead family, Napoleon's war of invasion. 'Old Stettin. Such a peaceful place. We had a little *bauernhof*, a farm. Boney destroyed the town when the Frenchies invaded in 1806. Our *saudumm*, our piss-weak army collapsed. *Shiza Wehrmacht!* Just lay down their weapons and surrendered. *Widerlich!* I was a *troppen* and escaped.'

'You fought in a war?' Richard asked.

'I did. We all did. More a slaughter.'

'What happened? After?'

'After my regiment was *getötet*, wiped out, I got a berth as a *deckhelfer*. Ended up here, for God's sake. *Ich hatte das glück*. One of the lucky ones to escape. Liverpool's not bad, though *abstossend*. How you say? Squalid. Pommen was better.'

Yet Liverpool was exciting to Richard. A place of constant wonder. Impressive public buildings being constructed everywhere, some looking like palaces. The huge stone balustrades of Customs House, the giant dome of the Town Hall, the tall spire of St Nicolas cathedral. A new iron railway to Manchester had been built that could carry hundreds of passengers and tons of freight. Richard had seen its first steam locomotive arrive, standing squeezed in the crowd. They called it the 'Rocket'. A big black metal monster, belching steam, pulling open carriages filled with rich men and gaudy dames. It was sight to behold.

But it was the docks that fascinated Richard most. Whenever he could, he'd walk to the docks and watch the ships move up and down the Mersey. Great big ships built of oak and pine, powered by wind on sails of flax canvass attached to masts and yards, supported by hemp rigging. Graceful brigs, fast schooners, three-masted barques, and sturdy brigantines, all crewed by hardy Jack tars and filled with strange and exotic cargo. He saw wheat arrive from New York, beaver pelts from Quebec, cotton from Pennsylvania, tobacco from Virginia, timber from Newfoundland. All kinds of goods: corn, leather, cheese, and tallow, loaded from King's Dock. From Duke's Dock came ships filled with fruits from the Mediterranean, wines from Portugal, olives from Italy, dates from Persia. At North Dock, tea from China, coffee from Cuba. Queen's Dock unloaded palm oil from West Africa. It was as if the world, and all its riches, chose Liverpool as its epicentre.

Richard couldn't wait to join his pa as a lumper, hauling cargo to and from ships. He loved everything about the Mersey and the docks. It was his world, all that he knew – including stories of its dark history. About Liverpool being the largest slave trading port in Britain. He'd heard the tales from the men at the docks about the transatlantic trade. Who in Liverpool hadn't? To a poor 15-year-old, they were the facts of life. Slave trading had brought immense wealth to the city, they said. It was the difference between the haves and the have-nots. How the privileged had become wealthy. How else did they pay for all their grand buildings and mansions? For over half a century, wealthy merchants and city officials had prospered enormously in buying and selling human lives.

Yes, Richard wanted to become a lumper and to earn an adult wage. But he knew in his heart that one day he'd be a merchant sailor and leave Liverpool.

Watkinson Street

Richard started work at 12, like most children in the city. His school years had been short: four years at Saint Peter's Priory, a charity school run by one of the Catholic priests. Just long enough for him to learn his letters and numbers. Simple reading, writing and arithmetic, mostly done by rote. He could read several verses from the Bible and scratch out the Ten Commandments on a slate board. While he could recognise and understand most words and write letters and notes, lengthy reading or writing didn't come easy. He learnt how to add, subtract and multiply mostly from spending money to buy food or by playing games with copper coins on the kitchen floor.

It was his pa that took him away, soon after his twelfth birthday. His pa had no regard for a full school education, or the priests for that matter. The earlier a boy could find work, the better. 'Time to earn a shillin' for your ma,' he said. 'Time to earn your keep, son. Work hard and do the boss's favour. I can't always be 'ere for you.'

'A shillin'?'

'Aye. You get three shillin', threepence a week.'

'Doing what?'

'Picken' oakum.'

Richard worked at the Seel Street Ropery.

He began by picking hemp, pulling apart pieces of old rope. Sitting on the stone floor with other boys untwisting rough, broken rope, separating it into piles, first picking it into strands, then picking apart individual fibres with his fingernails until they bled. Hard, frayed rope, covered in dirt, rust, and grease.

When he turned 13, Richard worked at 'the ropewalk' on Seel Street. His job was to turn the large wheel that twisted long strands together to make lengths of new rope. The older boys made the younger ones drag lines of rope strands along the length of the narrow street, then, when instructed, Richard would turn huge machine wheels at one end to pull in and twist the strands tightly together into rope cables of different widths. In winter, the boys worked 40 hours a week, in summer up to 50 hours, rain or shine. All for three shillings and threepence a week.

Richard hated it. He hated the cruelty of the ropewalk and he hated the older men. Linesmen walked the line with a switch rod, and if a boy was too slow or if the rope twisted the wrong way, they cut the boy's backs.

One of the new boys, Billy Baker, an 8-year-old urchin from Toxteth who had only just started at the ropery and was next to Richard, almost lost his hand when it got caught in the cable. As the boys started to tighten the strands, twisting and pulling the thick rope into a hard, taught line, Billy's shirt sleeve got caught and it dragged his hand into the twisting cable. He screamed in pain as it shredded the skin almost to the bone. All he could do was try to pull his mangled hand and fingers away from the thick, twisting rope, which made it worse.

'Stop the wheel!' yelled Richard. 'Stop it, for Christ sake.' But it was several minutes before the linesman could run to the wheel and stop it. By then Billy had been dragged several yards and his hand was covered in blood, the flayed skin hanging on the rope in globs, and he slumped on the ground, whimpering and crying in pain.

'You there!' snapped a linesman, glaring at Richard. 'Aye, I'm lookin' at you. You're at fault! Keep the lit'luns in order, damn you. Show 'em how to do it.' His switch stick flicked onto Richard's back which stung like a whip.

By the time the supervisors took out the tension in the rope and eventually released Billy's hand, the poor boy was almost unconscious. His eyes rolled had back in his head and his body went limp. The men bound his hand and carried him away. Then the linesmen, flashing the switch sticks, told everyone to get back in line.

'A lost hour! All because of one foolish lad. Watch for the twist, boys! Watch the wheel.'

The boys got back to their work.

Time moved slowly at Lawrence Cottages in Watkinson Street. John and Ann Belsar tried to make the best of their meagre earnings, but times were hard. In the moody closeness of the slum cottages, where large families lived side by side, surrounded by neighbours and enveloped by the stink of sewage, where privacy was a rarity, the Belsars struggled to make ends meet. They would often argue about things Richard didn't comprehend, and when they shouted, he left the house and walked the streets.

The docklands, between Park Lane Station and Parliament Street, near where they lived, was always packed and overcrowded. Rows of densely populated courtyard houses flanked by narrow alleys which, in summer, would receive a pungent brew of odours that wafted from the estuary. Congested, it was dark and damp, with wastewater and sewage from privies draining onto streets.

Richard slept upstairs in one room with his three brothers and three sisters, biding his time until he could afford to move into a boarding house. Being the eldest, he bore the brunt of the chores for the household. More and more he began to crave his independence. He resented being told to change straw in the mattresses, collect water from the well, haul coal for the fire, empty the slops bucket. He began to dislike attending Sunday Mass with his family and having to sit through the long sermons from the bible, about how not to sin and how to behave. All he thought about was going to sea.

Still, he loved his ma – a smart, tidy little woman, Irish to the bone, and she loved him, more so since the loss of Johno, her firstborn, on his maiden voyage in the Irish Sea. In her terrible loss she was now more protective of Richard than ever, doubly afraid she'd lose him to the sea as well.

'You're the eldest now, my lovely boyo. You can't leave me yet,' she told him whenever he mentioned leaving home. 'I need you here. Promise you'll stay. Another year, at least.'

'I'm leavin', ma.'

'Why? Where'd you go, son?'

'Far away from here as I can.'

'But why?'

'To see the world.'

Which sounded fantastical but it surely had possibilities. Hadn't he seen the ships, heard about the places they came from, watched the Jack tars that filled the docks. To a boy with dreams, it was just a matter of time.

He grizzled having to pay her board from his measly weekly earnings. 'A shillin'. It ain't much,' she told him. She gazed lovingly at him, sometimes late in the evening, after cleaning up the family meal, humming nursery rhymes she used to sing when he was a child. 'Jack Sprat could eat no fat, his wife could eat no lean. And so, between them both, you see, they licked the platter clean ...'

His ma was a strange one. Born and raised in Ireland, she arrived in Liverpool as a 15-year-old seeking work as a domestic servant, a 'slavey', and poor as a church mouse. She had found employment with a family that owned a small tailor's shop on George Street, where she worked until she got married. Strong-willed and superstitious, she believed in both a Catholic God and in mythical fairies. She believed in the spirit world and prayed to *Cailleach*, the Celtic goddess of wintery and stormy weather, to keep her sons safe, should they go to sea.

Each morning, as Richard put on his wool jacket and left for work, she blessed him with one Irish saying or another. 'May the road rise to meet you. May the wind be at your back, the sunshine on your face.' Or she'd close her eyes and whisper as she kissed him on the cheek, 'May God bless you and keep you safe.' Often, she blessed him in Gaelic, '*Go raibh míle maith agat!*'

Ann Belsar attended Church in Liverpool more fervently after her marriage. She often helped the local Catholic priest, the aging Father Vincent Glover at St Peter's Priory, near where they lived. Father Glover was well-loved by the Irish immigrant congregation, and he served the community well.

Ann attended Mass two, sometimes three-times a week, often arriving early to hand out prayer sheets and she stayed afterwards to clean and tidy up. Even though she couldn't read a word of the bible, she loved listening to Father Glover with his fiery sermons and holy words to the faithful. He'd kept the congregation safe, hadn't he, holding them together during the cholera riots of the early 1830s. His sermons were published in the newspapers and helped to quell the street riots.

In many ways Ann was in awe of him. Father Glover was a kindly, educated man who cared for the sick and needy. He had visited their house after poor Johno died and had prayed with her, holding her hands and calling for Johno's salvation and eternal rest. His prayers, his pastoral visit, made her feel special to be blessed and kept the poor boy's spirit in God's gentle hands.

Everyone said Father Glover was a liberal man, an intelligent man, a learned man of God. Ma knew he must be good for the family. He even opened a small parish school for children a few years back, and Ma made sure hers attended, at least for a few years, so they could learn their letters and numbers. Even the girls were allowed to attend. Ma said they needed lessons in morality and must learn to adhere to the Lord's Commandments.

Their small house was cramped and crowded, like all on Watkinson Street. Three girls and four boys, one still a babe, clinging to ma most of the time. Ellen, the eldest, the wild one who raced about like a banshee, playing like a tomboy, talkative and fearless, chasing whatever few pennies she could earn by washing sheets and clothes for their neighbours. Then came Adelade, aged 11, the sickly one, catching colds each winter. Everyone could see she would become a beauty. Dark-eyed and fair-skinned, she was a true Irish maid. But Ma said she had been born with a weak chest.

Then there was Mary, who had just turned 10. Ma said she was the smartest one; she already knew her letters and could recite the alphabet. She could write everyone's name, scratching them on the pavement with chalk or etching them onto their brick walls with a nail. She ran about with a chalk stick in her hand, daring everyone to ask her to write or draw something. She could even write the surnames of neighbours in their street.

John was next, aged seven, named in memory their lost brother Johno. He was a big lad, strong and fearless, like Richard, with a thick head of dark blond hair and blue penetrating eyes. Agile and daring, he shadowed his older brother around the streets and alleyways trying to prove his worth; he had already won his first street fight against a rival boy from Kitchen Street. He loved to draw pictures of ships on brick walls with chalk stone and constantly asked Richard about different types of rigging or how sails worked with the wind. He too wanted to become a merchant sailor. It was all he could think of.

'But not on a fisho. They stink to high heaven. I'm going to cross the Atlantic on a merchant ship,' he said. 'I'll get an apprenticeship with a trader.'

Next in the family came James, aged six, then Lewis, aged four.

The children's future predetermined by their education and circumstances. All were destined to become domestic servants, dock labourers, or seamen. Acorns didn't fall far from trees in Liverpool in the mid-19th century. If they survived, that is.

Ben Farquar on the *Venteax*

Despite his work at the ropery, Richard still managed to visit Ben Farquar on the *Venteax* when he could. Not every week, but often on a Sunday afternoon after he attended morning Mass. It was his precious time, being away from family chores and from the harshness of the ropery.

He loved the simple, unburdened companionship with the old seaman. He felt he could relax, doing odd jobs if he wanted or just sitting and watching ships glide up and down the Mersey. There were no orders, no demands, no reprimands. A gentle voice every now and then, hearing stories of far-off lands, adventures at sea, and life aboard ships.

Old one-eyed Ben looked more like a pirate than a navy man with his eye patch. He pottered about, usually working above deck, often showing Richard something, who then tried to copy it. How to caulk a timber with tar and oakum, how to carve a peg screw, how tie a clove hitch.

'Watch lad. Tie it like this,' Ben said, holding a hemp rope with his gnarled hands. 'Loop right around the pole, loop left around the pole, then up through the hole.' Richard copied the action, saying the rhyme as he went, and pulled the hitch tight.

'Show me more,' he asked. It was like a door had opened into a new world. Full of technical puzzles and wonder, a skill to help him go to sea. The way ropes could hold fast or pull loose. How rigging held ships together. He learnt all kinds of hitches: Cow hitch, halyard hitch, mooring hitch, anchor hitch.

'Practice in your spare time,' Ben said, and threw him a length of rope to take home. 'Now, help me caulk the deck.'

Richard watched as Ben took out several tools from his kit sack and laid them on the deck. A wood mallet and five long iron spikes, each with a flat end, some wide, some narrow. 'These are caulkin' irons,' Ben said. 'Startin' irons and harden' irons. Every good ship carpenter has 'em. And here's oakum. Suppose you know all about that. Now, watch as I go along the seam.' He laid out a length of oakum, soaked in pine tar, between two deck planks, then started to tap it along the seam.

'Two taps to run the oakum in, smooth as you go. Work slow and follow the seam. Here you go.' Ben handed the mallet and iron spike to Richard, who looked at each in awe. He felt the weight and power in his grip, their complete usefulness for any ship. He bent down and studied the job at hand, concentrating on the seam, on the fibrous oakum, its length and width, wanting to get it right. He positioned the iron on the oakum above the seam and tapped twice, then again. Tap-tap, tap-tap. It filled the seam perfectly. After six feet of caulking, he looked up at Ben, expectingly.

'Good job, lad,' Ben said. 'Now come back along the seam with a narrow iron an' tap it more, good an' deep.' The oakum seemed to roll in with a gentle tap. Richard learnt not to tap too hard, or too soft. There was an art in it, Ben said. Packed too tight, oakum swells with water and bends the wood. Too weak and it comes out.

The old caretaker's job was to keep the wreck careened and ensure it didn't sink. Its hull needed constant attention to fill gaps in between drying timbers, especially those above the waterline on the muddy bank. He also had to keep scavengers away, especially at night – scamps and prigs who tried to steal whatever they could.

'Here, show me your hands, boyo,' Ben said as Richard was fumbling to tie a loose line. They were blistered and bleeding, with split fingernails. 'Aye, that aren't good. Pickin' oakum, no doubt. Let me get you something.'

He went below and found a small bottle with a cork stopper and a cotton cloth. 'Rub on this ointment. Me special elixir. Alcohol, spices and whale oil.' It stung but Richard kept rubbing it over his sore, bloody fingers and hands.

'That'll help clean and toughen them,' Ben said. 'Keep it. Use every day for a week.' The ointment seemed to work and his hands began to heal.

Two weeks later, on his next visit to *Venteax*, Richard arrived to find everything was about to change.

As he climbed the gangplank, he saw Ben packing his kit bag, stowing clothes and tools.

'What's happening, Ben?' Richard asked.

'I'm leaving, matey. Old girl's just been sold. Salvage team arrives tomorrow to break her apart. Towing her downriver to dismantle her. Save what they can. They'll keep the hull but rip out her guts at the shipyard.'

'No! Not the *Venteax*! What will you do?' Richard was heartbroken, not so much for the ship as about his feelings for Ben. He was being evicted from his home – the only one he had. 'Where will you go?'

'Oh, I'll head to London, I expect. Got a sister there. Can't live on me pension, pittance as it is. I got no one else here. So, I'm off, lad.'

A swell of emotion rose from inside Richard's chest which gripped him by the throat. He barely got the words out. 'I don't want you to go, Ben. I'll... miss you.'

'I'll miss you too lad. I enjoyed your visits. But me time's up. Here, take me hand and say farewell like a man.' Ben took Richard's small hand in his and shook it, then pulled him into an embrace. 'Goodbye, lad. Fare thee well. May you have fair winds and following seas.' It was his way of saying goodbye, a sailor's farewell.

Then he turned, picked up his kit bag and walked down the gangplank, leaving Richard standing alone on the deck. Ben raised his hand once to wave but didn't turn around.

When Richard turned 16, he started work at the docks, finding casual jobs where he could. Pa told him he was now old enough to deal with bullyrags on his own, especially bruisers that were always found in work gangs.

Richard was given all kinds of hard-collar labour work. Holding horse-drawn wagons while they were being loaded or unloaded, shovelling out coal and lifting pig iron, packing vegetable crates for costermongers, hauling puncheons of rum for grog merchants, manhandling bags of raw sugar, lumping wheat from inside the holds of ships. He often joined the job crowd each morning at seven am, jostling in a semi-circle of 50 or so tired men outside the sheds, trying to be picked for a day's hire.

Winter was worst, standing in cold rain with the broken-down tradesmen, failed shopkeepers and drunks, struggling and cursing to get a few days' work at the docks. He was lucky to have his pa point him out every now and then, whispering in the boss's ear, and he got to be known as a reliable lumper, unloading ships coming in from the British colonies.

Richard was tall and strong; he could earn up to four shillings a day. What he loved most was moving about the ship's decks, exploring this exciting world from afar, talking to seamen about where they'd come from, what they'd seen, touching and smelling rich aromas of cargo like coffee, sugar, tobacco and rum. Tall ships with their bounty from all parts of the world. He tasted oranges from Seville and bacon from New York. He smoked his first cigar with tobacco from a place called Carolina. He met sailors of all colours and races: blacks from Africa, Chinese coolies, lascars from India, French marines. He listened to their stories and knew this was his future. *I'm going to sea, soon as I can,* he thought.

Richard learnt how to swear and how to drink. One evening, he was invited to join his work crew at Squires Inn after a day's heavy lumping coal. It was his first time in a bawdy house.

'A pint for me and the lad,' one of the men said, and tossed some coins onto the bar. The waitress pulled the ales and handed tankards over, all frothy and dark. 'Down the hatch, quick. First one clears the throat. Washes the grit away.'

'Another round!'

After three pints of ale, he felt his cheeks flush, and the men laughed when he grimaced and swallowed the dregs. 'That's the way boy, bottoms up. It'll put hairs on your chest. Here's another!'

He stood by the men, laughed when they laughed, trying to fit in. He copied their stance, feet apart, looking relaxed, loud and confident, hardened backs. He tried to keep up with them, drink for drink, but found he couldn't. He offered to buy a round, but they shouted him down. They laughed at him, but he didn't notice.

When he returned home that night, after vomiting in the alley, his mother cried when she saw him, 'God help us! He's taken to the demon drink. At such an age.' She slapped his face, pointing her finger at him and yelled, 'When your Pa's back, he'll tan your hide! I'll not have it, you hear me?'

Embarrassed, Richard knew he couldn't argue back, just as he knew he'd keep drinking. He was now a labourer. He earned an honest shilling and he was going to be a sailor. He wasn't going to spend his life at the docks. He went to bed, head spinning.

So, the story of Richard Belsar's life at sea begins. His surname, like that of his father and his family, is sometimes spelt differently on crew lists, marriage certificates, census and electoral rolls, and court records. It's been recorded over the years as Belsar, Balser, Balsen, Bellsir, Belsen, Belsor, Belcher, making it difficult to track him down.

You can imagine harbour clerks and government officials asking his name for their logbook or ledger and Richard saying it in his broad, Lancashire accent, not knowing or caring how it was spelt. This makes the search for him difficult as it takes us around the world, to remote ports and British outposts. Merchant seaman records are thin with many black holes. What difference does documentary evidence make in this story? These people – Richard, his brothers and sisters, his father, his mother – were once as real as you and me. So too are the crew he sailed with, and the ship captains, and later, fellow convict prisoners. So are the landowners in far-away places at the edge of the world who cross his path and touch his life. His story, and theirs, are real.

There is the marriage licence of his parents – John Christian Ballsall, mariner, and Nancy Basson, spinster, held at their church, St Peter's Priory, Liverpool, on 22 May 1811. They both made their mark 'X'. John and Ann couldn't read or write. And there's Richard's baptism record at St Peter's Priory, marked on 20 November, written by hand, *Was Bapt Richd, Son to John and Ann Balser. Witness John Balser and Betty Bradly (born Nov 13).* Richard's brothers and sisters were all baptised at St Peter's Priory, their names etched in ink.

These people once lived and loved, worked and found happiness, suffered pain and hardship. They struggled and, fortunately, most survived.

First Voyages

Richard first day at sea began in the Irish Sea, a life governed by confusing orders, ship's bells and brutality. He boarded at the crack dawn at Wapping Dock, wearing a threadbare jacket and patched trousers, carrying his whole world in a bundle of cloth. The ship, a trading schooner, carried a cargo of coal, which he'd helped load the previous day.

'Hey, lackey,' the first mate ordered. 'Move arse and help unfurl the topsail. We're puttin' out to sea. Look lively!'

His first climb aloft was in heavy seas under a stiff southwester. Richard stepped over the gunwale and began to climb up the ratlines ladder, his heart racing. A stiff wind had come up, and the ship leaned at an angle, swaying like a pendulum, so when he looked down, it was a long drop into the icy sea below. *I can't swim,* he thought. *If I fall, I'll drown. Like Johnno. They'd never find my body.*

He clung to the ratlines for dear life, rising slowly, then closed his eyes and pulled his body close to the ropes, and prayed. 'Keep climbing, fucker,' someone yelled below him. It was another mate, pushing around him, nimble and fast. Richard had seen him on the docks before. A small boy, wild-haired and skinny, several years younger than him. 'Up we go. Follow me.' Richard took two deep breaths and started to climb again to the top yard.

'Put your feet on the footrope. One arm around the yard. Move along. Use the other to unfurl,' the boy said, pitching his voice hard into the wind. 'I'll go out first.' He seemed to glide effortlessly along the footrope, sliding along the top yard, to the very end, hair blowing freely in the wind. He untied the ropes and looked back, grinning, waiting for Richard to clumsily untie his ropes. The boys on the other side of the yard were both waiting. Then the top sail caught the wind.

'Away!' the boys screamed, and the men on deck below began to haul the lines, adjusting the sail, and the ship turned against the wind. They were away. Despite his fear, Richard felt the exhilaration of the ship at sea.

He lived in the fo'c'sle in cramped quarters, sleeping in a hammock among sweating men, squeezed together, swinging with the roll of the ship. They cursed and told stories of strange lands and fearful seas.

They ordered him to fetch pans of soup, wash their filthy clothes, called him a cocksucker for being slow to learn. They bullied and laughed at his ineptitude, along with another boy, an apprentice indentured for four years, on his first voyage. He knew seasickness in the dark, cramped hold as the ship rolled and pitched in the swell. He knew cold – more than anything he had felt on land – from the bitter wind on deck.

He discovered the rhythm of the ship, tacking and jibing, and the use of each sail. He learnt the names and uses of each rope – so many. If he didn't break or hold ready, he was cursed or hit over his shoulders. Halyards, sheets, cables, shrouds, warps, jackstays, ratlines.

He watched older seamen so he could copy their movement and learnt to follow the topman's order quick smart or be stung by a lash over his legs. Some men were kind and taught him how to set sails and fix a bearing in easy seas. The second mate explained the midship sails and rigging, and how to read the wind. He learnt to smoke a pipe and drink grog; that age-old tradition, part of each seaman's rations.

He wore loose canvas breeches, a white checked linen shirt, a knotted handkerchief at his neck, leather shoes, but no stockings. His pa gave him a thick jacket coated with tar for weatherproofing in case of foul weather. His hair grew long and was pulled back in a pigtail.

They took him to a whorehouse. He went with trepidation, drinking whiskey for Dutch courage. The men laughed at his clumsy ineptitude, slapping him on the back, urging him on. 'Here you go, matey,' one of them said. 'Take this lass upstairs.'

He was led to a small room, a dark cell with a musty-smelling mattress on the floor. The woman lifted her skirt, lay down and told him to kneel. His apprehension was obvious. 'First time is it, boyo? Ol' Susie will take care of you.'

It was over quickly, a sudden sensation of release, then she was wiping herself and pulling down her skirt. 'Good lad, how was that?' He mumbled something like good. She patted him on the head, then held her hand out for payment, his last remaining coins.

His early voyages were short, a few days out and back. Coastal traders to the Isle of Man or Greenock, shifting imported goods to other ports. He picked up deckhand work where he could on packet sloops that crossed the Irish Sea between Dublin and Liverpool in their hundreds. Working on deck in the rain, handling lines and pulling canvas, loading and unloading cargo: barrels of wheat, crates of eggs, boxes of linen, puncheons of whiskey, casks of herring. Even loading animals like pigs, horses, and sheep.

There were always Irish passengers aboard, pale and scared, poor men with their families seeking work in British cities as dock labourers and warehouse porters or simply passing through Liverpool as emigrates to the New World. He heard their stories of desperate hope for a better future, and forlorn despair in leaving their families behind. Many said they were heading to America's northeast as unskilled labourers in canal building, lumbering and construction work. 'Land and opportunity, boyo,' one Irishman told him, holding onto his frightened young wife, white with seasickness. 'Taking the wife and bairns to New York to dig the Erie Canal. We're starving back home.'

Richard learnt about wood ships: sloops, barques, cutters, brigs. Sailing them, loading them, repairing them, sleeping in them. Each had unique rigging. His training with old Ben Farquar, his work as a dock labourer, his size and strength, put him ahead of most boys, even some older ones. He was good with his hands and would sometimes help shipwrights back in port, honing timber with their carpentry tools. A day's woodwork paid more in shillings than it did as a dock labourer.

He learnt about oak, prized for its strength – the most popular timber of all. Elm was most a favoured wood for keels, while ancient pine from the forests of the Baltic or America was best for decking and spars. He knew how to use a caulking mallet to force old rope fibre called junk into gaps between timbers and seal it with hot tar. He could replace a damaged plank and fashion a broken spar with an adze, and 'fish' – setting a cracked yard with a splint – using a peen hammer and chisel.

However, shipwright work was hard to come by for the untrained or inexperienced. While some carpenters in shipyards worked for themselves, most were contracted with ship owners and companies, and therefore couldn't always hire new workers. Some had apprentices who needed constant supervision and training. Richard, not apprenticed or indentured to a ship owner, worked with the carpenters whenever he could, but mostly returned to dock labour, lumping and stowing cargo, to earn a few shillings for his wages. At port, he bunked in with other men at sailors boarding houses and dormitory rooms.

Borough Sessions

Richard spent more time at public houses after each coastal voyage. He enjoyed the banter of men, the taste of ale, the tobacco-smoked warmth inside bars away from the wind. His voyages were short, a few days along the coast to Inverness and back. Across the Irish Sea to Dublin or Belfast. *The Celtic Lir*, as his ma called it. He still worked as a lumper at the docks with Clarke and Co. when he couldn't find regular work on a ship.

After hauling sacks of grain or labouring for day and a night inside a ship's hold, with wages in his pocket, he wanted nothing more than to wash down the dust with a few pints of amber fluid at one of the local inns. Now he had a job – he was independent, his own man. In between voyages, he bunked at a boarding house at Canning Place, next to the docks. It was nothing more than a large dormitory for sailors, a cheap shelter with a canteen that served gruel for breakfast. But he could stay as long as he wanted.

Richard came back home on and off between his trips away. Sometimes, after a particularly cold or hard voyage, he came home simply for a hot meal and warm bed on the kitchen floor. A chance to seen ma and pa and to tease the girls, give them a small gift he may have picked up. Eggs or a switch of bacon. Nothing stolen; the consequence of getting caught by a watchful master was too great. He found as he was getting away more, he enjoyed the pleasure of coming home. The familiar comfort of the kitchen, with its smell of baked bread, and the noise of giggling children running about.

His family was growing. By November 1835, there were now eight mouths for ma to feed. The girls were getting older and, when not at home, worked as washerwomen and cleaners for their neighbours. Ellen was 18, Adelade had turned 16, and Mary, 15. There were five boys still at home: John, aged 13, James, 11, Lewis, 9, and Frederick, 5. Ma had another baby to attend to – Edward, aged two.

John, James and Lewis had become scholars at St Peter's Priory Catholic School, which had opened with the blessing of Father Glover, and the school had a full-time teacher. Ma made them attend four mornings every week. Father Glover told her the children needed to read and write, so they could learn the Gospel and raise themselves up from a life of poverty. 'Fear of the Lord is the beginning of knowledge, but fools despise wisdom and instruction,' he told her.

Ma constantly worried about the family, whether they got the fever of flux, when they were away from home. She knew her *búachaills*, her boys, would eventually go to sea, like most young men who lived at the docks. But she feared the sea like the devil itself. 'I know it, in me poor heart. My boys will keep leaving. They'll be lost to the sea,' she cried, voice shaking, clutching the wood crucifix to her bosom. She had an intense fear of the ocean. At the Priory, she heard terrible stories of shipwrecks, sailors drowning in dreadful storms, the beating of young boys by harsh masters. 'Oh, save us from fearful seas and brutal men!'

Richard sometimes looked at her prayer beads and crucifix, which hung from her neck or were held by her hands. She rubbed them constantly. 'Thank the Lord Father Glover is here to watch over and bless you when you're away. He prays for all our good lads when they're at sea.' She crossed herself, her eyes tightly shut, and said, 'Lord, bless those who go down to the sea in ships, who occupy their business in great waters, Amen.'

Richard tried to cheer her up with small gifts and words of assurance. 'Here, ma. Look. See this?' He pulled a round fruit from his coat pocket. 'It's from Spain, an orange.' He put it on the table and sliced it with his pocket knife, giving a piece each to Ellen and Mary.

'Aw, sweet,' Ellen said, sucking the juice, then began to chew the peel. 'Got more?'

'No, but there's something else.' He reached inside his coat and drew out several small brown packets covered in waxed paper. 'Got these in a trade on me last voyage. One of me shipmates loaded crates of them.'

He handed a packet each to the girls and tossed some to his brothers, who were eagerly watching.

'Chocolate!' they cried, unwrapping the paper and biting eagerly into their blocks. 'Ta, bro. What a treat.'

'Don't go eating it all at once,' Ellen warned with a stern look. 'Save some for later.' There were unwilling nods of accent, but they all obliged.

She's becoming more like Ma each day, Richard thought. *Miss bossy britches.*

It seemed his life was taking shape. He was an independent 19-year-old man, getting regular work crewing on ships or lumping cargo, enjoying an outdoor life, drinking with mates when he wanted, visiting different ports. He could come and go as he pleased. Young and strong and could look after himself well enough in a fight. Smart enough to make it on his own.

Later that week on Saturday 28 November, Richard took some ale at Mr Seel's public house, one of his favourite waterfront haunts, with smoke-filled rooms, stinking of stale beer, full of Atlantic traders and seamen just in from Newfoundland and the Canadian Provinces.

He'd been there most of the afternoon and was feeling warm and merry, quite drunk in fact. It was windy and freezing outside, coming into winter, and he'd had a hard week, lumping bags of wheat. As he was deciding whether to leave or have another ale, a young woman came through the door with a basket of trinkets, hawking them to sailors sitting at the bar. Dark-haired and attractive. She caught his eye and smiled, then approached Richard sitting at his table.

'Hello, my lovey, whatcha got there?' he asked. She wore a red shawl and jacket to keep out the cold and a bonnet and ribbon to tie back her hair.

She sat next to him and opened her wicker basket to show him her stock of wares. 'Razors, bracelets, braces, watch guards, rings, belts, buckles. All good quality. What's your need, deary? Help a girl out, would you?'

He glanced in, not really interested in what she had to sell, but he liked her smile and wanted to keep her talking. 'What's your name, darling?' he asked.

He could see caution in her eyes. Many women were careful around sailors. But she was street savvy, and she clearly decided to appear friendly. 'Mary Ann Welsh, if you don't mind, but that's Mrs Welsh to you.'

'Bet your man's a dock labourer, then. You should be home with him on this cold night, rather than on the streets.'

'Never you mind that, boyo. I do what I want when I want. You need to sober up and get a shave. Could be, under that beard, there might be a handsome face. Here's what you need.' She pulled out some razors to show him. 'This'll clean you up, good and proper.'

Richard rubbed his chin and examined the razors, uncertain if she was flirting or just a good peddler. He laid them down on the bar. 'How much?'

'Four shillings a pair.'

'I tell you what, Miss Mary,' he said carefully, trying to seem sober and not make her leave, 'How 'bout five shillings if you throw in the watch guard and those braces? But the thing is, I'll have to walk to me lodgings for the money, 'cause I spent me last penny here. Would you care to accompany me? It's not far.'

She looked at him carefully, clearly weighing up whether to go or not. 'I'll follow you, but I'll wait on the street. Not coming inside, you hear?'

'Let's be off then.'

They walked out along Baxter Court, chatting about this and that. She seemed friendly enough, more relaxed. She even laughed when he swayed casually into her side, putting his hand on her arm to regain his balance. Then he stopped. 'Now Mary, those razors. Were they long blades or short?'

She carefully opened her basket once more to show him, 'Long ones, silly.'

He laughed, teasing her, staring intently into her eyes. There seemed a moment of connection.

Then he did something reckless, something stupid, something he felt sure he would regret. He snatched the razors and watch guard chain, and ran off, laughing. 'Come on, Miss Mary, catch me if you can!'

She started to run but lost sight of him in the crowded street. Flustered, furious she'd trusted him. Damn him! She lost her razors and her payment, a day's earnings. Her only thought was one of revenge.

Mary went to another public house that evening and met a sailor named Thomas Wiltshire, who produced the same razors, saying he'd bought them for a shilling from a sailor. Mary explained the circumstances to Wiltshire and then went to the police station in a mood of outrage. She'd have her way, especially with a drunk sailor, she thought. How dare he take advantage of her? She gave information to a senior officer on duty that night, Captain Shannahan, who found and apprehended Richard at his boarding house.

The following day, at the police station, Thomas Wiltshire identified Richard who sold him the razors.

'He's the one. I know him. He sold me them razors,' Wiltshire said. The matter was closed. Richard told the officer that he knew nothing of the matter, that he was drunk on the night in question, but by then it was too late. His charge was written up and he was committed for trial.

The story of Richard's theft and conviction can be found online in the British Newspaper Archives. This article appears in the Liverpool Albion, 8 December 1835:

Impudent Robbery

A man, attired as a seaman, who called himself Richard Balsar, was on Wednesday, charged before Alderman Lawrence with the following theft. Mary Anne Welch stated that she was the wife of a licensed hawker, residing at 69 Cross Hall Street. On Saturday, November 28th, she was hawking braces, cutlery, trinkets, &c.: at about five o'clock, she went into the public house of Mr. Seel, where the prisoner, who was sitting there asked her what she had to sell. She replied by exhibiting to him her stock of wares. He took up and examined a pair of razors, and requested to know the price; she replied, four shillings; ultimately, however, he made a bargain to give her five shillings for them, with a watch-guard and a pair of braces. He then said that he had no money with him, but his boarding-house was in Canning-place, if she would accompany him so far, he would pay for them.

Complainant assented, and the prisoner led the poor young woman as far as Baxter-court, when he made a snatch at the razors and a guard chain, and, telling her to follow him, ran off with them through the court, which is, open at both ends.

At about eight o'clock, the complainant went into another public-house, and there a sailor, named Wiltshire, produced the stolen razors, saying, that he had bought them for a shilling. She instantly knew them and told Wiltshire of the circumstance which had occurred. She gave information to Captain Shannahan, who soon after apprehended the prisoner. Thomas Wiltshire identified the prisoner who sold him razors. The latter said that he knew nothing of the matter; he was very drunk the night in question, and this was all a plot got up against him. He was committed for trial.

Liverpool Borough Gaol

Richard walked along Great Howard Street with a group of 15 other prisoners, some wearing leg irons to prevent them escaping. It was a humiliation being among such a desultory and destitute group – worse, they walked along public streets where local residents would notice and judge them. Richard recognised several familiar faces here and there, some from his church, others from the docks. Some saw him, chained and going to gaol, and they turned, shaking their heads, and looked away.

'Move along. Don't dawdle,' yelled one guards, who poked the lead prisoner with his cane.

'Fuck off, shunter,' the prisoner replied. The the guard turned and hit him across his neck. Enough to bite hard and hurt. 'More o' that coming to you inside, you turd,' the guard said.

As they rounded the coal yard near the old canal, Richard saw one of his sisters standing next to a group of onlookers. Ellen recognised him and waved, an expression of concern in her eyes. She started to walk toward him, but the guard waved her off. 'No closer, dearie. Stand back, no contact with the prisoners.' She followed at a distance trying to catch his eye.

'How long you in for, Richie?' she called.

'Dunno. Don't tell ma or pa to visit me. Tell them to stay away. I'll deal with it.'

'Quiet boy! Silent or you'll feel me cane,' the guard yelled raising his arm. 'Keep moving.'

'Course I'll tell them. I'll get Father Glover to pray for you, too. He'll help.' She turned and ran back to the docks, back home to Watkinson Street. *Now everyone will know*, he thought.

As they approached the borough gaol, Richard saw its huge stone wall rising from the ground like an impregnable fortress, a masonry monster flanked with high watch towers and arched wood gates. They halted at the entrance and waited till the great gate opened, then were ordered to walk inside, entering the monster's mouth. Richard had never felt so distraught, feeling he was about to be swallowed and might never leave the monster's cold, thick walls.

Once inside, the guard separated men from women into different rooms, then told the men to strip and issued them with regulation clothes: a jacket, waistcoat, trousers, pair of shoes, a pocket handkerchief and a cap. They were given a blanket and ordered to move on.

Liverpool Borough Gaol was a miserable place, a monolith of stone walls, long corridors and iron gates. Richard marched in a single line behind several boys, looking around at the stone cells, trying to comprehend his new home. Inside were six large two-story buildings with cell blocks and work rooms and guard rooms, all surrounded by the main boundary wall, 20 feet high. A warren of masonry vaults and cells, each reeking of piss and shit from slop buckets.

Richard and the new prisoners were marched to a bare holding room to be classed. One of the turnkey supervisors, a bald-headed soldier with whiskery mutton chops, told them they would be separated according to their crime. Serious offenders charged with violent crime in one block, women offenders in another, debtors to be held together in larger rooms. As he read out their name, another guard moved them into their respective group.

He read the prison rules and the punishments: obey the supervisor's orders, work silently, wash clothes weekly, prepare meals, wash cell slop buckets, work daily to pick oakum, attend the Sunday service. Disobedience, failure to comply, swearing and slovenly work would result in harsh discipline – flogging, solitary confinement or half rations. Then they were taken to their cells.

As Richard entered his tiny cell and heard the iron door slam behind him, he looked around, trying to measure his space: about 12 foot long, 7 foot wide, 9 foot high. In a corner a small table and stool, a wash hand basin, a tin cup to drink from, a wooden spoon. He placed his blanket on his hammock and sat, wondering how he would cope.

The first nights were the hardest, the moans of sorrow and cries of despair seemed to echo off the stone walls. Boys calling for their mothers, shouts of impotent rage, fevered nightmares, muffled grunts of lust.

Each morning, Richard and 20 newly minted male prisoners were marched to a workroom filled with rope to pick oakum. They were told they had to pick five pounds of old rope a day. They sat on benches, a distance apart to prevent communication, and tried to whisper or signal with others out of earshot of the guards. They asked their names, where they were from. Some spoke of their crime, the injustice of being caught, the uncertainty of trial and fear of severe punishment. Others asked if they could get a message out or send word to a relative. Most wanted to know how long they would stay in remand, waiting.

Richard asked if anyone knew what happened to other prisoners – the thieves, the poor vagrants, even the women. No one knew much of anything. Some said they had no one on the outside, no parents or relatives to support them. That they couldn't afford a defence, let alone understand how to defend themselves, as few could read nor write. They simply waited for their trial, their fate in the hands of a magistrate and jury.

Who will defend me? thought Richard. He picked at old rope next to several young men, each charged with larceny of some kind.

In the grim room, they sought reassurance from one another; some measure of commiseration they could muster.

Thomas Spence, aged 17, said he'd taken clothes drying on a line. Two pairs of trousers, a shirt and a jacket. He hoped they'd go easy on him 'being a minor offence'. He said he took them because he was cold.

One of the youngest, Henry Reed, a small-boned, nervous boy of 14, wept while he worked. He told Richard he'd stolen some silverware and a gold chain from his master and feared the worst – hanging or transportation. He fenced the goods to his friend, who tried to hock them at a 'dolly shop', an illegal pawnbroker, but they'd both been caught.

'See, thing is, we been convicted a'fore,' he said, snivelling. 'We're done in this time. I'm damned for death and ruination.'

His friend, sitting nearby, the more callous of the two, a boy of 15 named Michael Nedley, boasted they'd both do the Deadman's dance on the gallows, 'Or be sent in a hell ship to the edge of the world. Worked like slaves until dead. Each way, the same end.'

'What are you in for? Nedley asked.

'Stupid prank,' replied Richard. 'Grabbed some razors in a drunken spree. A few shillin's worth. A paltry sum.'

'You'll live, then,' Nedley said.

Days turned into weeks, sorrowful and monotonous. Bells rang continually. The prison bell rang every morning at 5.30 when each prisoner had to rise, air their hammock bed, wash and begin work with another bell at 6am. Bells for meals. Bells for retiring hour at 8pm. The men laboured and picked oakum. They were fed gruel and bread, or weak soup and potatoes, and slept in their miserable cells. The only respite was being allowed to walk in an outside yard each evening for an hour of exercise. There, under the watchful eye of a guard, they talked quietly amongst themselves.

'Any news of trial?' Richard asked an inmate, an older man named Billy McCann, who'd been in gaol four months already and was rumoured to have killed a man.

'The turnkey in my block said at the next assizes, but the devil only knows,' McCann replied. 'I care not a toss. At least here, I'm still breathin'. And off the streets in this foul winter. Not so bad 'ere.'

Richard had been a prisoner for six weeks. He'd missed Christmas; he knew it had passed only because the gaol governor supplied each prisoner with a small fruitcake to mark the day. There was still not a word or visit from his family.

Then a rumour began to spread that some of the larceny felons would be brought to Liverpool Borough Sessions Court to stand trial on 18 January 1836. One morning, during muster call, one of the turnkeys called out the names in the workroom of those listed to attend the next day. Richard's name was among them.

Conviction

Richard and 20 other prisoners marched back along Great Howard Road in irons under police escort to the city courthouse, shivering inside their canvas jackets which gave little protection from a bitterly cold winter wind, which had whipped up from the Mersey like an Irish Sea southwester. It twisted through Liverpool's streets and laneways, bringing heavy falls of rain, and causing people to hasten inside for shelter.

The prisoners arrived, wet and weary, at the Assizes Court building in St. George's Place at the centre of the city, an enormous edifice surrounded on each side by rows of high, carved stone columns. Richard had seen it once before from a distance. He recalled how impressed he was by its grandeur and impressive beauty. One of the city's most opulent buildings. Now he was being taken inside to be tried, and he bore no thought whatsoever of its attraction.

The prisoners were taken to a partitioned room inside a courtroom and told to sit on wood benches to wait their turn to stand at the dock while their charges were read. Richard sat next to Henry Reed, the child thief, who was wide-eyed and shivering, more in fear than from the cold, looking like a scared mouse.

Richard looked around the room. It was cavernous, crowded with all kinds of people jostling about and wearing fancy, colourful clothes: police in high-breasted jackets, lawyers wearing wigs and gowns, officials in black coats, red-coated soldiers, merchants in formal suits with cravats and ties. At the rear, a clamorous mob of curious onlookers and worried-looking relatives huddled in together. Try as he might, he couldn't recognise anyone in the crowd, neither his ma or pa, or Father Glover for that matter, who he hoped might have come to say a word in his favour. He was on his own, his mind reeling from the spectacle, the weighted authority of the court, which pressed down heavily upon him, on each of his fellow prisoners, all who shared the same uncertainty as to their fate.

An official-looking man at the head of the room called for all to be silent. He said he was a bailiff who would enforce court rules, and that all charges, warrants and orders had been given to the magistrate, who he introduced as the Honourable James Clarke, sitting beside him at a mahogany bench. The magistrate, wearing a wig and black gown, shuffled some papers before looking up to address the court.

'I've looked carefully over all the depositions and do not see that there are any cases of great intricacy,' the magistrate said. 'I note you've all pleaded not guilty, and some have appealed for mercy. The court is aware of increasing rates of crime, of which I am appalled. So let us begin.'

As he read out each name and charge, a police officer led the prisoner to the dock to stand up so the jury could see them. Richard heard Henry Reed's name called and he was taken by a constable. The poor lad could barely walk; he was so overcome by fear, hands trembling, his legs almost gave way, with no one in the room to support him. He turned to look at his friend, Michael Nedley, sitting next to Richard, but got no sign of encouragement in return.

The magistrate read the charge – housebreaking and stealing a silver plate, value six pounds – and he admonished the boy for the serious nature of his offence. The jury foreman looked to and fro, seeking any dissent, before announcing one word: guilty! Reed was sentenced to 14 year's transportation. He was led away in tears.

'Next.'

The constable nudged Michael Nedley, who needed no help coming to the dock, and there he stood, chest puffed out, looking arrogantly across to the magistrate. His charge was quickly read, and the magistrate asked the jury, 'What say you?' Guilty! He was sentenced. 'Housebreaking and larceny of valuables worth over £10. Caught while fencing stolen goods. Once before convicted of felony. Age 15. For you, 14 years' transportation. As you appear the ringleader, let's see.' The magistrate pondered a moment and proclaimed: 'Next month in solitary confinement and twice to be whipped.'

Then Richard's name was called. The magistrate spent a moment reading the charge, then looked up from his high bench with cold, indifferent eyes. 'Richard Belsar, age 19. A sailor. For the crime of larceny, value of four shillings, one month's gaol.'

He was back in prison again.

Lawrence Cottage

Richard was released from Borough Goal in Great Howard Street in mid-February 1836, thin and emaciated, covered in lice and grime, and he returned to his parents' house at Watkinson Street. As he walked back, he felt forlorn and ashamed. He stared straight ahead, walking familiar streets and laneways, passing neighbours, acknowledging no one.

When he knocked on the door, his ma opened it and took several moments to recognise him, then started to cry, wringing her hands to her head. 'Sweet Jesus, look at you. Come in, boy!'

She grabbed him and held him tight. 'No one told us you were out. They told us nothing! We weren't even allowed to visit. Come, sit down, so I can look at you.'

'It's all right, Ma.'

'It's not all right, you hear?' she said, busying herself in the kitchen larder. 'Two months in that God-awful place! Skin and bone, you are. Here, sit while I cook up a meat pie and bread. Then we'll run a hot bath to scrub you clean.'

As he sat, he was assailed by his two younger brothers, Frederick and Edward, who ran down the stairs to him yelling, 'He's back, he's back!'

Edward the toddler climbed on his lap and Richard held him up high. 'Hey there, Eddie boy, you're big a lad now. You've grown. How old are you?'

'Nearly three.'

'And you, Freddie, just had your sixth birthday. Sorry I missed it.'

While they jostled and hugged, Richard's eyes kept turning to his ma, moving slowly around the stove and larder, her belly swollen with pregnancy underneath her dress.

'How long?' he asked.

'Oh, I expect it'll be in a few weeks,' she said. 'Another mouth to feed, God willin'. Maybe two inside of me, by the feel of it.'

'Here, sit down, Ma. I can do this. Don't strain yourself.'

He ate until he could eat no more. Slices of pork pie, bread and butter, boiled potatoes, turnips and sprouts, cheese and bacon rind. Two pints of ale. All the while, Ma boiled pots of hot water and spoke of family and church. James and Lewis, scholars at St Peter's Elementary School at Seel Street. 'First Catholic school in Liverpool,' Ma said proudly.

Father Vincent Glover had visited to give his blessing and pray for the girls, as there was a dark shadow about in the house. Adelaide and Mary were sick with fever or some kind of flux, upstairs, both asleep in the beds.

'I'll go see them after I wash,' Richard said.

He stripped off his filthy clothes and sat in a hot soapy tub outside by the laundry enclosure, washing and scrubbing his body with a bristle brush until some semblance of cleanliness returned. He cut his matted beard with scissors, tied his hair back in a band, then shaved his whiskers. By the time he returned to the kitchen, wearing Pa's old canvas trousers, a cotton shirt and a jumper, he felt refreshed but drowsy, struggling to stay awake.

Ma ordered him upstairs to her bed. 'Go and sleep for a few hours before the others get back. Get some rest.'

He was asleep as his head touched the pillow.

It was late afternoon by the time he awoke. Light was fading and winter's chill had started to creep inside the house. He rose from the bed and walked out to the next door, looking in at the girls, resting in their beds. They were awake but looked pale and weak. He was taken aback by how thin they were.

'Hello brother, you're back,' Adelade said. 'Come in, take my hand.'

He walked over and sat on the floor beside them. 'It's good to see you, Adelade. And you, Mary. I've been thinking of you these last two months.'

'Was it bad in gaol?' asked Mary.

'Awful bad,' he said. 'But it's over now. I'll be back on my feet in no time.'

'We prayed for you, didn't we, Mary? We prayed with Father Glover.'

'And here I am,' Richard said. 'Next time you see me, I'll give you another orange. Maybe more chocolate.' For he was intending to go away. Richard was desperate to find a berth, any berth, to escape from Liverpool, to get away as far he could.

They talked, but spoke of nothing really, just gossip: Pa's work at the docks, Ma's pregnancy, their friends at church, Richard's future. After a time, he could see them tiring from the conversation, their eyelids dropping. 'Now rest,' he said. 'I'll be back shortly with some soup.'

'Brother?' Mary whispered. 'You'll stay, won't you? With us. Here in the house?'

'Yes, Mary. I'll stay. And I'll help. A few days at least.'

Downstairs, Ellen had returned, and they sat at the table and talked of the hard winter, the cost of food, how the boys were doing at St Peter's Church school, the goings on in Watkinson Street, all the time avoiding Richard's time in gaol. Pa labouring with men at the docks. John learning to write at school.

Ellen had found work as a seamstress in a dress shop. 'Slave to the needle, I am. Slop work, but better than washin' sheets,' she told him.

The conversation all but stopped as pa walked in, slamming the door behind, sweat-stained and dirty, seeing the huddle in the kitchen around the stove.

'Well, look what the cat dragged in. Gaol bird's home!'

'Hello, pa.'

'Out today, I reckon. Skint and penniless. *Schön dich zu sehen!* Good to see you, boy! Here, *kommen, greet your old man!'*

Richard rose and embraced his pa, his apprehension and embarrassment melting away.

'This calls for *feiern* … a celebration,' Pa said. 'After supper, you and me, we talk together, eh? We share some ale at Kings Head. We need to make plans.'

'Now, don't you go gettin' him drunk. He's skin and bone. He'll get sick,' warned Ma.

They drank, of course. It was the old man's shout. Several ales, not enough to get drunk, but enough to get them talking freely. Pa said he could organise lumping work with his dock crew when Richard was strong and ready. 'At least earn some shillings till you find a ship.'

He could stay home and sleep in the kitchen on the floor until he could afford a boarding house. It was his family. He didn't have to knock on the workhouse door or sleep rough at night in the shipyard. They'd squeeze him in somehow, even with a new bairn – maybe two – on the way.

But Pa said he was worried about the girls, about their fever, that they were skin and bone, their coughing. He made a sign of the cross on his chest. 'Might be consumption. God help us!'

In mid-spring 1836 Mary and Adelade died after succumbing to consumption, a disease of the lungs. They died horribly, wasting away with profuse diarrhoea, and fits of coughing and night sweats. The girls, 15 and 17, once bright and lively, dark-haired and pretty, full of ma's Irish spirit, had become skeletons.

Pa paid what he could for a doctor to visit and treat them. All the man said was they needed good food, fresh air and rest. There was purging and bleeding, cod liver oil, vinegar rubs, inhaling of hemlock, all to no avail.

'It's in God's hands if they live or not,' the doctor told them.

Father Glover came to see them. He brought fruit and prayed for their souls, giving the family some hope. But in the end, wasted and weak, their bed wet with blood and sweat, they died in the night, two days apart. Final rites were given. Ma was distraught with grief and sat by their bodies for a day and night.

A pall of sorrow filled the house. Despite having just given birth to twins, a boy named Robert and a girl, Mary, her milk dried up and they had to call for a wet nurse. The girls were buried in unmarked graves at St Mary's cemetery in Merseyside.

Cholera, typhus and tuberculosis were rife in Liverpool and had crept insidiously from the docks several years before. Disease filled the streets and lanes, already filthy with sewage and nightsoil, and it made its way into overcrowded houses via contaminated food and drinking water. Most of the affected, particularly those who died, were poor: cellar dwellers, Irish immigrants, underfed children, homeless vagrants.

Despite the outcry by residents who screamed at officials and local authorities to do something, little happened. Most thought diseases and plagues were spread through the air by vapours and miasma.

Atlantic Crossings

In July 1836, Richard signed on the brig *Charles*, a square-rigged, two-masted merchantman bound for Newfoundland.

He had to leave Liverpool, a city, he felt, now infected by death and despair. He had to escape: the filth of the streets, his time in gaol, the gloom within his family home, the looks and judgement he got from workers at the docks. He made the decision soon after they buried his sisters. Get far away to the New World. Hadn't it always been his dream? He heard the stories, of course. He'd seen the traders arrive, he'd unloaded their cargo and talked to the crew: better wages, opportunities to rise above your station, exciting new ports to see, the chance to make a fortune. He would 'go foreign'. The were plenty of Atlantic merchant traders going to and from Newfoundland. Scottish and Liverpool merchants dominated the Atlantic trade to the busy port at Saint John, bringing out supplies and equipment in spring and summer, and returning with salted cod and timber to Britain. He learnt the *Charles* needed a crew and he signed the agreement of employment on what would be his first trans-Atlantic voyage.

He told his pa the day he signed. 'I'm leaving, pa. Tomorrow I'm away. Can you tell ma? I haven't the heart.'

'I'm glad for you, boy. We're a seafarin' lot, we are. I'll tell her.'

Then his pa did something unusual, something Richard had never known him do before. He extended his arms and embraced him, then blessed him, 'Fair wind, son. Go with God.'

'Here, take this.' Pa pulled out a coin from his pocket. 'My *glücks* cent . My lucky cent.'

'What is it?'

'A charm. Just a *pfennig*, I know. My pa gave it to me for good luck. Now I'm givin' it to you.'

Richard put it in his trousers pocket. 'I'll hold it dear, pa. I'll sew it in and protect it.'

The *Charles* was cleared for loading at Liverpool dock on 9 July with a full cargo: potatoes, barrels of pork, coal for smiths' use, pig iron, spades, nails and canvas. It departed in a fair wind on 26 July under the command of Master Harris, an experienced seaman and commercial trader, who had recently returned from Barbados with a cargo of raw sugar.

The *Charles*, with a crew of 22 men, cast off from Pier Head at Liverpool dock and headed slowly down the estuary. Richard worked on deck with the other seamen and followed orders on the double. The first day was energetic, getting to know the routine and the ship. On the ebb tide, the *Charles* moored at Black Rock and waited for a change in the wind. Then she set main sails and tacked south into the Irish Sea, before rounding the coast of Ireland and into the Atlantic.

The crew settled to their watches, the chief mate commanding the larboard side and the second mate the seaboard side, dividing their time on or off duty, on deck and below, every four hours. Richard took his orders from the first mate without question or hesitation.

There was little leisure time with constant sailing night and day. At daybreak, he washed down, scrubbed and swabbed the deck, filled the scuttlebutt with fresh water, coiled up rigging, until seven bells, when all hands had breakfast. There was cargo to check, running gear to repair, chafing gear to mend and constant sail changes – adjustments for wind: reefing, bracing, furling, making, and setting sail. The *Charles* made good time across the North Atlantic Sea route to Saint John in Newfoundland, arriving on 20 August 1836; a journey of 25 days.

Saint John's harbour was teeming with ships of all sizes and classes, a forest of masts at its dockside. There were basque whalers from America, brigantines from Scotland, French schooners, passenger steamships from Quebec, sloops and barges under anchor. Saint John carried a brisk trade with American states and European countries.

While ports along the Gulf shore froze up and the mighty Saint Lawrence River was locked with ice for half the year, Saint John's deep water port remained ice-free all year round. But first ships had to 'thread and needle' and pass between the narrows before entering the harbour.

As the *Charles* passed Pentridge Island at its harbour entrance, with its lighthouse and signal station, the harbour master welcomed her arrival through a loud hailer. 'Ship ahoy! Prepare for inspection!'

A pilot boarded, checked the captain's papers, and steered her to dock. It was Richard's first view of a foreign town that was to become his new home, for as long as he could afford it. He was astonished by the harbour's magnificence, its dramatic scenery, the bustling outpost set below a large mountain peak.

The *Charles* moored at one of the finger wharves near Water Street and the crew began to unload the cargo, which took several days to clear, then the ship made ready to stow a new load of cargo: 20 tons of salted cod fish for a voyage to Barbados.

Richard was discharged after the voyage for reasons unknown. Did he want to join another ship or simply stay on and explore a foreign port, a bustling town of immigrants he could relate to - and drink with. It was full of Irish Catholics, American whalers, Liverpool seamen, Prussian merchants, Scottish fishermen and public hotel owners of all nations.

Saint John in Newfoundland

Richard wandered up Nelson Street, past iron stores and rows of fish warehouses behind North Market Wharf. There were several British schooners and brigantines moored at dock laden with all kinds of produce to trade: tin pots and metal ovens, farming tools, ploughs, axes. The town of Saint John was a place of seething energy and opportunity. Men on soapboxes spruiked votes for the town election. Inns and bawdy houses sold liquor and sexual favours. Sailors and timber cutters drank in the street. Wagons loaded with pine logs were hauled by teams of bullocks. Shops promoted 'best Liverpool soap' and Irish malt whiskey. Signs advertised tobacco and gunpowder tea imported from New York.

Richard walked down the main street, feeling a sense of optimism he'd not known before. Everything was new and different. So unlike the grey slums of Liverpool. There were public liquor houses and coffee shops on every street corner. A Winchester gun and armoury stood next to the Town Hall building. Clothing shops and hardware stores. Warehouses of salted cod fish dried on racks. Timber yards and wainwrights, shipbuilding yards and chandleries, and merchant seamen everywhere in striped shirts and canvas breeches.

He passed a hotel with several women leering at him. One smiled enticingly. She seemed younger than the rest, not hard faced. There was a sincere look about her, and she had a natural complexion rather than a painted face. She was wearing a tight red coloured bodice to display her breasts, and a voluminous crinoline skirt. 'Oy, sailor. Want a good time? Come inside, will you? Buy me a drink.'

'Another time, lassie.'

He continued on, climbing a small hill that overlooked the harbour, where he paused to take in the view. It was spectacular, blue water surrounded by green hills. He could see the *Charles* below, getting ready to take on a load of timber for her return voyage home. If he wanted, he still make it back, walk down and re-join the ship. But the lure of Saint John was too great. With wages in his pocket, he was ready for a good time. He walked back to the town.

'Aye there, matey. You a Dickey Sam?' A familiar accent arose from a small group of seamen standing on the steps of a public house, all drinking tankards of frothy ale.

Richard knew his meaning – was a native of Liverpool? He turned and replied, 'That I am. Just in on the *Charles*. And you?'

'Liverpool lad myself. William Blanker's me name. Born and bred in Kirkdale.'

'Practically neighbours, then. I'm Richard Belsar. A Mersey man from the docks.'

'Come join us, Belsar. We're pickled and slewed. We plan to do some carousing.'

They played skittles and went on a bar crawl, drinking tankards of frothy beer at O'Rielly's in Duckwoth Street and glasses of stout at an inn on Water Street by the docks. They played dice games and gambled. Willian Blanker pulled three dice from his pocket for 'crown and anchor', a favourite game among seamen, and bet on the symbols as he rolled the dice on the floor. They played *pasglass* and passed a glass of ale to each other take a swallow from. Each drinker went measure to measure in one gulp and if he missed the line, he had to drink again to the next measure. After an hour Richard reeked of stale beer, his shirt front and sleeves sodden.

'Down, down, Dickie,' William laughed and handed him another glass to scull. Someone said there was a cock fight in the back alley, and they rushed out to watch. A large group of rough looking fishermen and dock labourers were standing in a circle, handing around money, yelling and pointing at both contestants, each holding a large rooster, which they threw into the cockpit to fight. Richard laid five shillings on one cock and won, and someone pressed a one-pound note in his hand. He could barely see the fight, let alone understand what happened. By the time he staggered back to his hotel, his head was spinning, and he fell on a lounge chair in the foyer, trying not to be throw up.

'Hello, sailor,' a voice called out in front of him. He looked up groggily, and saw the shape of a dress, a blur of red. Slowly, her face came into focus, and he recognised her. It was the same young girl, the one he'd seen earlier that day, standing there with her hands on hips. The fresh one with the alluring breasts. There she was, smiling, shaking her head from side to side.

'Eh, 'ello miss. I've 'ad a big night,' he muttered.

'I can see that,' she said. 'You're a right mess. Got a room here? Looks like you need to lay down. Before you fall down.'

'I do, upstairs. Give me a hand, love, will ya? I don't think I can stand.' He raised his arm to her outstretched hand.

Somehow, they managed to up the stairs. Somehow, they made it to his room. He could hear himself laugh, or was it someone else? Then things seemed to go blank, and he passed out. The next thing he knew it was morning, just before dawn, when he awoke with a splitting headache and foul feeing in his stomach; his mouth tasting like the litter of a chicken coop. As he rolled over to piss in the bedpan, he saw a girl asleep on his bed, sprawled over the blanket. She was partly dressed in a petticoat, her boddice undone and partially exposing her breast, with her legs splayed across the bed. Her long dark hair, covering the pillow.

'Jesus,' he said. He couldn't recall what happened. *Who is she?* he thought. *Did I screw her?* He couldn't recall anything. After bending over to piss in the bedpan, he stood there, staring at her. 'Eh, miss,' he asked, prodding her back. 'Wake up, will ya?' She didn't move so he prodded her again, harder this time. 'Wake up, miss.'

She stirred and rolled over, slowly opened her eyes and saw him standing in front of her dressed in a shirt, naked below. Then she covered herself. 'Oh, lord. What time is it?' She stood up and quickly started to dress. Arms and legs moving fast, lifting up her skirt, squeezing into her boddice, buttoning her waistband, stepping into her shoes. 'Oh, lord. I'm late,' she kept saying said. 'They'll see me, downstairs. I'm not allowed to stay. Lordy, I'm in trouble now.'

'What trouble?'

'I ain't allowed to stay overnight with clients.'

'I'm a client, am I? Nothin' happened, as I recall, which isn't much, I grant you.'

'Still gotta pay.'

'How much, just to sleep in my bed?'

'Ten shillings.'

'That's robbery! Nothin' happened. Two weeks wage, and I didn't even get the pleasure.'

''Ow do you know?' she said. 'Maybe it did. Look at you, no trousers.'

He smiled at her gumption. 'I hope you had your fun. Removin' my boots and clothes. At least you didn't steal my purse.'

He pulled out a ten-shilling note and waved it. She reached out and grabbed it and stuffed it down the front of her boddice, then, after a moment to rearrange her dress and hair, walked to the door.

'Pleasure's been all mine, sir, I'm sure,' she said, and closed the door behind her.

Richard remained in Saint John for four weeks, taking it in, drinking at inns, gambling, spending his last penny. It was easy to find another ship. He signed on to an Atlantic trader, the *Caledonia*, registered in Greenock, Scotland, which he joined on 17 September 1836. There he is, his name misspelt as 'Ballsir' in a crew list found in the British National Archives, listed in a crew of 32 seamen. Their names, ages, qualities, dates and places of joining the ship, time of leaving, all written on a page and signed off by the captain, Walter Greig.

The 105-ton *Caledonia*, a three-masted brig on a voyage to Portugal, had a cargo of cod fish, dried and salted and stored in barrels. Portugal was a big trading nation and consumed half of Newfoundland's cod exports at the time. The price of cod fish was at an all-time high. Merchants sold and traded cod in large, four-quintal wood barrels, each weighing 448 pounds, to markets in Lisbon and Oporto. Trading ships returned to Newfoundland with their holds full of port wine stored in casks. It is a lucrative two-way trade.

Richard gave his name to the purser, who wrote on the crew agreement: *Richard Ballsir, Age 20, Quality: Seaman. Last ship he served: Charles. Place of Birth: Liverpool.* Once again, he cared not a toss that his surname was misspelt.

The *Caledonia*

He was glad to be aboard, earning four times more than he made as a seaman contracted in Britain. He needed to earn something; his savings spent to the last penny. Not that he minded. He'd had the time of his life. Four weeks of drinking, gambling and playing up in bars and bawdy houses. But now, as sea again, he could let the wind clear his head.

The *Caledonia* slipped her mooring on a warm autumn morning and was warped out of Saint John harbour under the command of Captain Walter Greig, a Scotsman from Kirkaldy. The crew settled for another long trans-Atlantic voyage east. Sails were set, watch crews arranged, barrels secured deep in the cargo hold as ballast, ready to meet any storm and tempest. Older seamen, British Jack Tars and German *matrose*, eyed younger men with an element of scorn, quick to judge. They hissed and swore if they saw a mistake or a loose line. On board, men formed alliances, depending on their station, age or birthplace. Sailors quickly became shipmates.

'Eye up cocker, 'ow do?' said Robert Thompson, a young seaman from Lancashire. He was on the same watch and immediately recognised Richard's Liverpool accent. 'You'll love Portugal, boyo. I've been there before. Dark-haired Judies and port wine. Good wine too, rich and strong.'

'I heard about it. What's the taste?' asked Richard.

'Best ever! Comes down from the hills. Add a bit o' brandy to fortify. Sweet an' rich flavour. Never spoils.'

'Will Master Greig give us leave?'

'Two days, if we unload and trade well. Don't worry, matey. I'll show you around the city.'

The men worked hard on deck, stripped to their waists in the midday sun, sweating as the ship crossed the equator, constantly trimming ropes and sails for speed, adjusting the rigging to catch every breath of wind. After each watch, Richard and Robert went below for their rations of salted beef or pork, cheese, fish, ale and ship's biscuit. They ate lobscourse cooked in an iron pot – a sailor's stew of salted beef with vegetables and hardtack. At night, they drank their daily tot of rum.

They talked of Liverpool, where they'd grown up, their plans to see the world and one day test their courage sailing around Cape Horn, the most dangerous cape in the world. 'The true test of all good seaman,' Thompson said. 'Full of danger. Known as the sailor's graveyard.'

The ship made good time and caught the westerly trade winds, riding warm currents in the North Atlantic Drift. After they passed the equator, there was a stiff breeze, with fine weather and no squalls, and Captain Greig fashioned a disciplined crew. Almost three weeks with nothing but sun, wind and a brilliant array of stars at night. The two Liverpool boys became close shipmates.

The *Caledonia* arrived at Oporto in Portugal in early November 1836 after a voyage of 20 days. It moored at its south wharf, a few miles inland of the Douro River entrance. The wharf was surrounded by flat-bottomed boats with long oars and broad sails, each hauling barrels full of wine down from vineyards in the Upper Douro.

Oporto

The old city of Oporto, set high on the opposite bank, was a colourful maze of winding streets and stone buildings with reddish hues of terracotta tile roofs. After paying customs duty and a harbour fee at Customs House, Walter Greig negotiated the sale of the cargo of codfish, and the first mate ordered the crew to begin unloading the cargo.

Down inside the ship's hold, Richard and Robert Thompson sweated in the heat. Each barrel had to carefully raised with block and tackle, then rolled down ramps to Portuguese stevedores for stowage in company warehouses. The air underdeck was putrid. It had a sickening odour of salted fish and bilge water. They jostled the barrels in the tight confines, rolling them onto one edge, then attached them to netting and tackle. The netting rope pinched and tore at the skin of their fingers and hands.

'Damn this job. Dog's work.' Robert said. 'Why can't the fuckin' Portuguese lumpers do it?'

'Dunno,' Richard said. 'Somethin' to do with pay. I just do what I'm told.'

'Well, all I know is, I'm blowin' off steam when we're done. Getting' good an' pickled.'

When finished, the first mate signalled 'All clear! Clean on board!' Portuguese dock workers then started to load casks and barrels of port wine onto the deck. It was two days of backbreaking labour. The crew, exhausted and anxious for shore leave, took their half-wage to spend on wine and grog.

'Come with me, Belsar. Shave and wash, dress smart. I know a place for some fun,' Thompson said.

They took a small ferry to cross the river and entered Oporto's walled city, climbing its steep narrow streets, admiring the terraced gardens and small *quintas* that lined the shore. British influence was everywhere. The city was bustling with English traders, wine merchants, with red-coated soldiers and foreign sailors all about on the streets. Ever since the Peninsular War with the French 30 years earlier, there had been a resurgence in English trade and prosperity.

Richard and Robert passed a strip of seedy taverns, sunny outdoor cafes and vegetable markets, and came to an imposing two-story granite building called the British Factory House.

'A fancy British club,' said Thompson. 'Full of toffs and officers. I know the manager, a local named

Queiroz. He'll admit us. Follow me in. Just act like a toff.'

They entered the door, finding themselves in a busy coffee room full of English sea captains, clerks and well-dressed businessmen at tables reading newspapers. A sweaty, well-dressed Portuguese man greeted them. When he saw Robert, he raised his arms and smiled widely, showing a set of broken and missing teeth. 'Ah, Mr Thompson, you return. Welcome back! I see you have a friend. Come in, come in, follow me. Allow me to escort you to the members lounge.'

He led them across the coffee room and through an arched marbled hallway, past a large banquet hall, across a library room, to a quiet smoking lounge with a bar and two large billiard tables.

'Here, sit down, I get you drinks,' Queiroz said as he walked to the bar. 'Drinks on the house.'

As they sat, Richard leaned over and whispered, 'On the house? What's this all about?'

'Long story, Belsar. Relax an' sit back. I'll explain.'

They settled into lounge settees and took a moment to admire the room, with its large frescos and blue hand-painted tiles, or *azulejos*. As they began to drink wine and smoke pipes of tobacco, Thompson told Richard how, on his last voyage to Oporto, he'd broken up a scuffle in the street when he saw three sailors assault a young woman. They were obviously drunk and becoming violent, pushing her to the ground. Thompson saw them, boastful and threatening, trying to drag the frightened women into a dark alleyway. Her screams set him off.

'I ran at them. My blood boiled, it did,' he said.

'I moved in, hit one hard on the back of his head, knocking him down, then I pulled my jack-knife on the other two, swearing I'd cut their balls off, so they turned and ran. The grateful young woman, as it turned out, was Queiroz's daughter.'

'The man was in tears with gratitude when I delivered her and explained what happened. Strange though, the girl, Maria, seemed quite nonchalant with it all.'

Queiroz arranged for the barman to serve them drinks, anything they wanted. Sparkling Mateus rose, tawny port from Fonesca, spicy Madeira wine. When their glasses were empty the barman brought more. They smoked Virginian tobacco and played billiards, ate cheese and anchovies on crusty bread, talked of the sea. Richard raised his glass for a toast. 'Cheers to the working class, ol' chap.'

'To the working man!'

Later that evening, Queiroz returned to see how they were. He found them, sprawled in lounge chairs, intoxicated and happy. 'You like, eh? Good wine, good food?'

'We like, Queiroz. We do,' Robert said. 'But surely, you thanked me enough.'

'Now come, both of you. First, some coffee. Then, entertainment. Down the road. At the Europa Club. There will be much singing, dancing and ladies, all awaiting you.'

Richard and Robert Thompson remained on the *Caledonia* for its return voyage with a cargo of port wine, 2,500 miles across the Atlantic Ocean, back to Saint John.

The *Caledonia* made another voyage to Portugal, again with a cargo of salted cod, leaving Saint John on 10 November 1836 on a voyage to Lisbon. Richard sailed again as a seaman. The *Caledonia* returned to Newfoundland in December 1836 and Richard was discharged on 9 January 1837, along with his friend Robert Thomson. They had sailed a distance of over 10,000 miles.

Soon after, Richard decided to return to Liverpool. He'd been away almost seven months and was keen to see with his family before his next voyage. He left Saint John on a two-masted trading brig named *Sarah*, which arrived at Liverpool on 31 January 1837 with a load of pine timber.

Little had changed in their small house at Lawrences Cottages on Watkinson Street. Ma looked older and gaunter than ever, still grieving the loss of her daughters. She greeted him at the front door with her baby, Robert, crying in her arms. 'Ah, you're safe home! Welcome back, son. Come in. Will you be stayin'?'

'No Ma, I got a doss at Sailors Rest. Just a quick visit to see you,' he said, and bent down to kiss her cheek. 'How are you feelin' Ma? How's the family?'

'Well an' good. So be it,' she said, 'You're just in time to hear news 'bout your bro, John.' She yelled his name: 'John-o! Richard's 'ere!'

The lad came running downstairs, all legs and smiles. 'Hey there, bro. You're back.' They greeted each other with a hug.

'Aye but leavin' for a voyage to Africa. Look at you, Johno. Musta grown another inch or two. What's your news, then?'

'Got me a ship!' John told him he'd been indentured for five years on Thomas Harrison's barque the *Wilberforce*, a merchant trader. His apprentice papers had just been signed. He was to join the ship on a voyage to Maranham, a colony on the Brazilian coast in South America. 'Cotton trader, she is. I'll be an Atlantic man, like you!' he said proudly.

Ma frowned, worry lines creasing her forehead. 'Just 15, he is. Another off to sea. May God bless and protect him.'

Richard sat at the kitchen table, holding baby Robert and talking to John while Ma busied herself preparing dinner. He talked of his last voyage to Newfoundland, but more importantly, he advised John how to survive the trials at sea as an apprentice. 'Stick close to your master, John. Follow his every instruction. Don't question or delay. You'll soon learn the ropes. But beware at night in the fo'c's'le. There's some that prey upon young men. Always sleep with a jack-knife. I'll get one for you. And be prepared to defend yourself, if you must. Make the first move like I taught you.'

'I will, bro. I can look after meself.'

'Good lad. Best of luck. And write home when you can. You've got a better hand that me. I hope we see one another again, sometime time, eh? Some foreign port, maybe?'

After Pa returned home that night, the family shared a simple meal of mutton stew. They talked of trading ships, the docks, news at home, Richard's voyages, what he'd seen, where he'd been. His brothers, John, James, Lewis, Edward and Fred, listened intently to his stories of distant lands and new world cities. They lived in a port city, saw nothing but ships coming and going from around the world, it was all they knew. The boys dreamed of becoming mariners, like their brother.

At the front door that evening, as Richard bade his farewell and was about to leave, his pa wished him good luck – a sailor's farewell: 'Fair winds, and following seas, my boy.'

Later that night, in his cold boarding house bunk, Richard felt the ties of home unfurling; he looked forward to his next voyage. He was beginning to lose his connection to Liverpool, with its cold grey skies, its sickness and filthy streets, the slums set away from the wealthy areas. He was leaving his family bonds.

Richard Belsar was 23 and he'd already seen much of the world, more than most Englishmen. He was a seaman. He'd proved himself capable and was glad to leave the city.

A Horrid Hole

On Thursday, 2 March 1837, Richard signed aboard the *Kingston*, a 280-ton three-masted barque owned by two wealthy Liverpool merchants. The ship was on a voyage to collect casks of palm oil from West Africa.

Richard signed his articles of agreement with an agent at the docks one week before departure. He knew the terms: payment at the end of voyage, a possibility of bonus depending on its success, forfeiture of wages for desertion, behaviour in an orderly manner, obedience to all lawful commands of the master. He knew the rules, the fines, the discipline, the punishments on a ship. *I'm not going back to a stinkin' gaol*, he promised himself. *And hope to steer clear of the lash.*

The agent, a portly, florid-faced man with a look of contempt in his eyes, slid the ledger across the counter and read out each fine with a fat, tobacco-stained finger. 'Listen up, son, about the loss of wage.' He kept shouting and pointing the list. 'Not being on board ship at fixed time, two days! Striking a person, two days! Drunkenness, two days! Sleeping while on lookout, two days! You know the rest?'

'I know 'em. I'm not a apprentice cabin boy. Give it here.'

The agent handed Richrd an ink quill and told him to make his mark, 'Make your cross there, Jack.'

Taking offence, Richard took the quill. 'I can sign me own name.' He scrawled his name in large, flowing letters, slowly, deliberately, then flicked the quill so it spilled ink droplets across the page. 'There you go, see?' As he left, the agent swore under his breath. 'Fuckin' tars.'

The *Kingston* had a full crew of 23, including officers and three apprentices. The master, Captain William Kelly, was in command. It would be a long voyage. Ten months at sea. Months of sweltering tropical heat, heavy rain, possible piracy, threats of disease and violence, to the Gulf of Guinea, a place many seamen called a horrid hole.

Only two seamen – the ship's cook, a coloured man named John Ash, and the ship's chief mate, James McGowan – had served aboard *Kingston* on its previous voyage to West Africa the year before. Ash called it a 'murderous voyage of death and despair'. He kept to himself, mostly working and sleeping in the galley.

Readying a ship at port was a busy affair. Often sailors worked alongside stevedores to load water, wood and cargo, ensuring ships were secured and balanced correctly. Dock cranes lifted heavy goods by nets into the hold: casks of drinking water, staves and iron hoops to make barrels, sacks of meat and vegetables, timber for repairs, casks of gunpowder and trading iron, sail canvas and ropes. Ship owners shouted at officers. Officers shouted at stevedores and chief mates shouted at deck crew.

The *Kingston* was rigged as a three-masted barque, of which the mizzen mast was always fore and aft rigged with triangular sails set parallel to the axis of the ship, while the fore and main masts were square-rigged. After the ship was readied, Captain Kelly gave orders to get underway.

The *Kingston* slipped its mooring and warped from port on the ebb tide, then drifted down the Mersey River, before setting sails due west. The ship rounded Holyhead with a light north-easterly wind and turned south, outward bound into the Celtic Sea towards the coast of Spain. It continued south to the coast of North Africa, the captain constantly at the helm navigating the ship's position.

The crew settled into their watch duties under the watchful eye of the chief mate, James McGowan, an experienced 33-year-old sailor from Aberdeen. Day by day, they made good progress southwards with a prevailing trade wind.

In early April, the *Kingston* passed the Canary Islands, then changed course to head east toward Western Sahara, the wind warmed with tropical heat. As they sailed around Cape Verde and past the coast of Sierra Leone, and the sea lanes became busy with sailing traffic: British merchant traders, Portuguese schooners, Spanish frigates. They were on constant alert for privateers and black sails.

One morning muster, McGowan gathered the crew on the foredeck. 'This is the Slave Coast, lads,' McGowan told them. 'Countless men and women captured an' sold as slaves in the Americas and Jamaica. Now it's British dominated, our trading coast. Still, pirate slavers remain, so stay sharp. Our enemies still ply these waters under Spanish and United States flags.'

'Ever crewed on a slaver, chief?' Richard asked the mate.

'Not I,' McGowan said. 'Stinkin' filthy holds full of black flesh. But I've seen the trade markets here, and Jamaican plantations. Poor bastards. There's still slavin' aplenty where we're heading to, in Bonny. The blacks are slavin' each other.'

Richard knew the slave trade stories. Everyone who lived in Liverpool did, even after slavery's abolition in 1833. Seamen whispered tales of black servitude on decks, in public houses or lumping cargo together.

Much of Liverpool's wealth came from slavery. Virtually all leading inhabitants of the city, including former mayors, councillors and members of parliament, had invested in the slave trade and had profited from it. Rich merchants had built their grand mansions, even churches and public buildings, with profits from slavery. He'd grown up hearing about the slave barons, envying their wealth, seeing them promenade in fancy carriages in the streets. They were the ones who ran the city, brought in the sugar and cotton, built the big ships. That much power and wealth was beyond his comprehension.

When a lookout sitting in the crow's nest spotted two British Royal Navy vessels on the horizon he shouted to the men below, 'Ships-ho, off starboard!' Captain Kelly, standing at the helm, raised his spyglass.

British ensigns were flying aloft and they watched for a flag signal. Well-armed brigantines. Part of the West Africa Station on patrol. The anti-slavery fleet.

The two navy frigates passed close by, acknowledging the *Kingston* with a signal of clearance and a captain's salute. The crew waved as the patrol continued sailing north, looking for suspicious vessels to search and board. Well-fitted with cannon and musket, they hunted pirate traders who refused to abide by Britain's anti-slavery laws.

'See there!' Captain Kelly yelled at the men, red-faced, raising his outstretched arm. 'See our Royal Navy ships. See their might! We rule these waters.'

By late April, the *Kingston's* crew started to feel the change of the tropics. The sun became intense and glaring, burning their skin. They entered the windless doldrums at the equator, the ship veering around, trying to find a small breeze, making slow progress.

Sails often hung dead in the air. Men complained about sunburn, blistered skin, headaches. Several days the ship was becalmed, so they sat on deck, in the shade, listless, smoking and gambling. They slept on deck to get respite from the stifling heat below in the fo'c'sle. They told stories, drank their daily ration of rum, asked questions about the palm oil trade – how they would load it, how soon they'd get it.

The ship's cook, John Ash, came on deck and sat down among the men, which was unusual, given his taciturn nature. His hands were fidgety and he looked anxious. He told them a tale that shook them to the bone.

'I was aboard *Kingston* last year,' he said. 'Same trip to the Niger River to collect palm oil at New Calabar. A man named Charles Cain was our commander – a short, angry cove he was. He murdered the ship's steward.'

The crew looked aghast, especially the three young apprentices, this being their first voyage.

Richard, sitting closest to Ash, asked what had happened.

'We were lying 10 miles off the coast,' Ash continued. 'The steward, a big, coloured man named Louis Handsford, pumped some rum from a puncheon in the master's cabin. Said he was getting it for the men. He got caught and there was a scuffle. He knocked Master Cain down then all hell broke loose.'

'Oh, Lord. Hittin' the captain,' one of the crew said.

'Bad, I know. But Cain exploded in furious rage. He called some of the natives alongside in canoes to come aboard, Kroo men, to drag Handsford up on deck. Then Cain came at him with the cat, 12 knotted tails, and struck him endlessly about the body. He cut him viciously, again and again and again. When he could do no more, he ordered the Kroo men to strike him with their sticks. "Pay him off," he said. "Lay it on and kill that black son." It was murder, it was.'

'What came next?' asked Richard, knowing how it would end. He'd seen the cat used before, flaying the skin off a man's back.

'The beating went on for half an hour or more. Poor man kept crying out, "Oh Lord, I'm a dead man" as we watched in horror. There were four Kroo men laying into him endlessly. He kept saying, "Not me head. Not me eyes!" Then the captain ordered the chief mate to cut up a lead line into pieces, thick as your finger, two feet long, and the Kroo men flogged him with those. He died horribly, face and head cut and swollen and bloody, then the captain walked around kicking him, cursing, even after he was dead. We didn't do anything, in fear of our own lives. He died right there, on the deck right by your feet.'

Richard stared at the deck in silence, shocked and disgusted., imagining the scene as it was: the covering man, his body bloody and broken, writhing in agony. He could almost see the stain shadowing in the oak timbers at his feet. He'd seen and heard brutal things before, but none as bad as this. 'What happened to the captain? Was he charged?'

'Aye, he was. Two merchant ships were alongside, the *Heyworth* and the *Ann*. And a man-o'-war lying inside the bar. Their captains came aboard and took statements from the men. But Cain sailed us back to Liverpool, silent and moody. He swore he'd kill any man who spoke out against him. It was a hell ship, it was! I feared for me life 'cause of me colour.

'We got back. He was charged, went to court. Only got two years for manslaughter! He should have been hanged, I say. I was one of the witnesses in court. Got off lightly he did, 'cause he had friends in high places.'[1]

---

1 The story of Louis Handsford's death by Captain Charles Cain, 'Murder on the High Seas', and the subsequent criminal court case, was published in the Yorkshire Gazette on 10 February 1838, and in the Liverpool Standard newspaper.

One of the apprentices, George Lees, a 16-year-old from Liverpool, was ashen-faced. 'But our captain's not like that?' he asked. 'He won't flog us, will he?'

'No, lad. He seems fair,' said Richard. 'Been no flogging on this voyage yet.'

Captain Kelly appeared from the companionway ladder. He looked at the men sitting together around the mast, catching the last part of the conversation. He stared them in the eye, then spoke deliberately. 'I know of this, lads. I had a report given to me by the ship's owners. Such madness will not be tolerated on my ship. Dwell on it not! Don't let it hinder our mission. Now look lively, wind's picking up. Chief Mate, a word.'

James McGowan came over to the captain and stood next to him.

'I want no bar of this story, Chief Mate. You know how superstitious these men get. No curses, no whispers that this is a death ship. I expect you to stamp it out. You were there, weren't you? You saw it?'

'I was, Captain. Me and Will Dodd. He spoke in court too, along with Ash. But we ain't saying nothin' about it to the men, I swear.'

'I expect you to keep my orders, especially after we arrive at Calabar. And be strict with the blacks. Keep them off my ship. No trading. And no women on board! That will be all, Chief Mate.'

'Aye, sir.'

The King of Bonny

It took 15 more days for the *Kingston* to arrive at their destination, Calabar River on the coastal delta of Guinea, by the end of April. For a time there seemed only the same monotony – the hot sun, the northern trade wind, the smells of the ship, the listless routine. Then Richard heard the cry from the crow's nest. 'Land ho.'

A sense of anticipation rose among the crew as they peered into the distance, to that fine line between the horizon and the sky. A slither of green wavered, like a mirage. They had arrived. One of the men started a jig on deck, clapping and hopping in an old shanty rhythm, while another yelled, 'Three cheers to the Captain!' There was a sudden feeling of optimism, after weeks of lethargy in the doldrums. For some, it had been the longest voyage of their lives.

Richard looked towards the shore, hazy above the sea. He saw the changing depths of water and a green layer of land, slowly becoming clearer. Beyond it was a veiled forest. It was Africa. He leaned against the bulwark next to a mate, Daniel Kerr, another Liverpool lad.

'Have you ever seen anythin' like this, Daniel? The green haze, the light of the sky. Can you smell it?'

'The dark continent. Full of blacks. Savages, if you ask me. Watch your back, Richard.'

They moored next to a hulk, a former British navy brig, now being used by a British trading agent, who lived aboard to avoid deadly diseases such as malaria and yellow fever. Alongside the brig were two long canoes, each over 15 yards long and covered by an umbrella of palm thatching, each with a number of natives sitting inside.

'See them, Richard,' Daniel said. 'They're war canoes, I reckon. Carved with axes and knives. I'd say there's a brace of arrows hidden inside as well. I'm not going anywhere wiv'out me knife.'

After they dropped anchor and furled sail, the crew were ordered to haul up the wood staves on deck for the cooper to assemble the casks in preparation to fill with palm oil. Over 100 casks had already been built on the voyage but more had to be coopered. It was exacting work and the men sweated in the heat. Fitting and clamping the curved staves onto cask heads, then pounding metal bands onto each curved section.

Meanwhile, the captain instructed the chief mate to select two stout men to prepare their jollyboat to row him across and meet the agent and to begin their trust trade, which was called a 'comey'. The formalities of agreement needed to be established, both with the agent and the village chiefs. The amount of palm oil, the cost per barrel, the labour, the tools of trade.

'Belsar, you go with John Butcher,' ordered McGowan. 'Look smart, take the captain to the hulk. And take your jack-knives in case, hidden in your breeches. Your duty is to protect the captain. Be sharp about it.'

'Aye aye, sir,' they said promptly.

As they lowered the jollyboat and began to row, Captain Kelly appeared to relax somewhat, now his ship had arrived safely, and he spoke about their mission, about the importance of palm oil. 'The trade is critical. Not just for our profit. Good oil greases the wheels of industry, lads,' he said. 'It's used everywhere in Britain. Soap, candles, street lighting, heating, factory machinery oil.'

'I hear railway engines use it at Liverpool, captain,' said Richard.

'They do indeed, Belsar. Now listen up, be on guard. I've been told two tribal kings are fighting hereabout for control of the oil trade. Follow my lead. Stay close by, watch my back.'

'Aye aye, sir.'

'There's a powerful broker here called William Dappa Pepple, the so-called King of Bonny. Looks like those are his canoes. War canoes, by the look of it. My orders are that we must trade directly with him.'

They climbed the rope ladder and boarded the hulk. The British agent, a jaundiced, sickly-looking man wearing an old navy jacket, met them and introduced himself as Captain Henry Smyth, Esquire. He welcomed them aboard and took them to his cabin where they saw a group of black men sitting on the floor, cross-legged, drinking wine.

Introductions were made. It was indeed William Dappa Pepple, King of Bonny, of the village settlement that manufactured and traded palm oil with British merchant ships. Dappa Pepple was tall – an intelligent-looking man with a broad forehead and cunning eyes.

He spoke English quite well. He extended his hand to the captain.

'Greetings, Master Kelly,' he said. He was quick to get to the business of trade. 'I have plenty good oil comin' in from the hills. How much you want?'

'Five hundred tons will fill our ship.'

'Ahee,' Dappa Pepple exclaimed. 'That will take time. Many weeks. You have muskets?'

'Aye, and power and iron. How many weeks?'

'Three, four. Maybe more.'

Henry Smith, the agent, spoke up. 'The king has been trading with our first British arrivals this season, so I have no hesitation in entrusting him with your requirements. If you wish, I'd be happy to mediate on your behalf with the comey. But first, join us for a meal and some wine. Let's do business and work out these details later. As host, I'm here to offer my services to you and your men. A sign of goodwill.'

Captain Kelly agreed. They sat around the large table, Englishmen on one side, Dappa Pepple and his men on the other. Plates of stewed goat, fried fish, and yams soaked with red palm oil and pepper were served by the steward. The British agent poured out cups of Madeira wine and made a toast, 'God save King William of England and King William of Bonny!' They all laughed and drank. Then the hard bargaining began.

British trading firms maintained separate agencies for the Bonny and New Calabar River trading stations, barely seven miles apart. It appears from published reports in the *British Newspaper Archives* that the *Kingston* used New Calabah for its 1836 voyage and Bonny for its 1837 voyage, the latter probably due to William Dappa Pepple's dominance after waging war against his rival, the Ann Pepple tribe.

Trade in palm oil was competitive and highly valuable for native Africans and British merchants alike. Trading agreements, or comeys, often used bars of iron, gunpowder, muskets, pieces of cloth, and iron pots and pans in exchange for quantities of palm oil. Five bars of iron purchased one ton of oil. Buyers had to check the oil for quality to ensure it was not adulterated with water, mud or palm fibre.

Prices for palm oil were high at Liverpool at the time, sometimes as much as £50 per ton, so profit, even after voyage expenses, could be considerable.

It was a long and tedious process, made worse by monsoon rain. Tribal chiefs used native workers, mostly slaves, to stamp and crush palm fruit nuts in factory pits, which were fermented and boiled to extract oil. The oil was ladled into calabash pots and kept in large cask houses, set aside by their king, to trade with predominantly Liverpool vessels. Trading houses used large war canoes, each of which could hold up to 2,000 gallons of palm oil in large calabash pots. Loading, carrying and lifting onto ships was slow and arduous, especially in the intense heat. Kroo people from the region emptied pots of oil into casks, then hauled them below for the crew to secure in the hold.

Calabah Village

Daniel Kerr and Richard had become close on the voyage. Both were of a similar age. They had grown up together in Liverpool, laboured at the same docks, lived in the same district. They trusted each other's skills, on deck or aloft, worked on the same watch, shared tobacco and drank their rum during rest periods. They shared stories of growing up in the city, running the streets, fighting gangs, even listening to the same sermons at the Catholic church.

'God awful work,' Daniel complained one morning, out of range from both the captain's ear and the first mate. 'Liftin' and pourin' this stinin' muck from gourdes. Waitin' for the next load.'

They were covered in oily sweat from head to toe, their backs burned by the fierce sun, lowering a barrel down the foredeck hatchway into the hold.

'Aye, but tomorrow's the Sabbath. Our day off.' Richard had a mind to leave the ship and go exploring on land. After seven weeks on board, he desperately wanted a change and walk on some dry land. To explore the place the canoes kept coming from, each day, back and forth with their calabashes of palm oil. 'Let's go to a village. Find some of their brew to drink. The Kroo boys can take us. What say you? Are you in for it?'

Daniel looked doubtful, worried about leaving the ship, thinking of how they could swing it with the chief mate. He knew they needed a good reason for shore liberty, something the chief mate could defend as being a work-related duty. 'Let's say we'll try and barter for more oil at the cask house. Get more Kroo boys workin'. Push them to get us a bigger canoe load. Think that'll work?'

'How do we do that?'

'Trade somethin', said Daniel. 'I got me medallion. We could trade that.'

'Daniel, you can't trade your Saint Christopher's. It's your protection.'

McGowan, the chief mate, agreed to released them on strict condition they returned before six bells in the evening. 'Don't foul up, lads,' he warned. 'One day only. Otherwise, there'll be hell to pay. You know the punishment.'

At sunrise the following day, they hailed a group of Kroo boys sleeping in a canoe, led by a boy named Warrahow, to come alongside and paddle them to the village at the river entrance on the outskirts of Bonny. The village, a mile or so away, was a jumble of thatched native huts set in a jungle of greenery. Broken pots and calabash gourdes lay scattered about. Nets dried on poles and the remnants of fish scales glistened in the sun.

They walked to the palm oil factory camp – a wide undercover thatched hut set on stilts next to a muddy mangrove swamp. The camp stretched for a hundred yards or so, with hundreds of tired workers milling about, hauling long branches of palm trees laden with fruit and stacking them onto mounds. Small groups of native men lay about, fanning themselves, eating from bowls, eyeing the two white men cautiously. Several women sat listlessly next to cooking fires, poking some kind of red fleshy meat with sticks. They saw lines of thin, emaciated sweating men in iron leg chains shredding palm nuts with their hands and others crushing mounds of kernels with heavy posts. Young men and boys, many just children, were tamping the kernels up and down in large pits in the ground, hitting and crushing the fibrous nuts, their feet torn and bloody. The primitive scene, one of mass servitude, was shocking.

Inside the palm oil hut, Richad saw several rows of fermenting pits and ceramic pots full of boiling water on fires to extract the red oil. Old women were ladling out hot, spitting oil, which they poured into the open neck of calabashes and then stacked in rows on the floor. A chief, or headman, wearing gaudy coloured cloth, ivory beads and a belt with an ostrich feather headdress, walked up and down the line with a switch stick, hitting people on their backs and arms. Many of the men and women were scarred and bleeding from cuts. The hut reeked horribly of rancid body sweat and oily smoke and shit.

When the chief saw them, standing there, he gave them a toothless grin and stared venomously with deep-set black eyes, like a malicious snake ready to strike. He started walking toward them with his stick raised, in alarm, warning them off.

'What is this devilry? Slaves, by God. They're all slaves,' Daniel said, scowling. 'Let's get out of here.'

They turned and fled.

Warrahow took them to the nearby village, a shanty settlement of straw huts, pig pens, mud and squalor. Crowds of curious children came out to see them, then ran away and hid as they approached.

'You want wine?' asked Warrahow.

'Aye, lad,' said Richard. 'Lead the way.'

The boy took them to a thatched hut and invited them to sit. After a few minutes, he brought out a calabash of palm wine. The sugary liquid tasted milky and sweet, yeasty, with unusual earthy flavours. It had a powerful punch. Richard poured some and drank from a cup. Then they sat and drank their fill. 'Not bad, matey. Here's to you and our men at sea!'

'Down the hatch and up yer mizzen!'

They drank, got drunk, and slept on the dirt in the shade. When they awoke, lethargic and stuporous, it was late afternoon, and the sun was getting low in the sky. They rose groggily, hungover and stumbling about in the dirt, laughing like teenagers, and jogged awkwardly back to their canoe where Warrahow was sitting patiently, waiting with the other Kroo boys.

'Be quick, lads,' yelled Richard, fearful they'd be late and get the lash. More than the chief mate, he feared the captain most, especially if they broke curfew. Thoughts of unleashed terror by Captain Kelly, like that of Captain Cain, were utmost in his mind. As they pushed off from the river bank, Richard yelled: 'A shilling each if you paddle hard. Heave boys! Put your back into it.'

They arrived as the sun was setting, in the nick of time. McGowan was waiting for them by the gunnel rail at the middle deck. His face flushed with anger. He looked furious. 'A few minutes more you'd 'ave been flogged. Now get on board and be about your duties, quiet like. And thank God the captain ain't about to see this. He's over with the agent. Otherwise, he'd lash us all. Did you get more oil?'

'No luck, Chief,' Richard said. 'The headman ran us off. But we saw the factory. Hundreds of them gourds, full o' oil, ready and waitin' to go.'

'That's somethin' at least. Now get below and clean up. You stink like pig shit.'

Tropical sickness began to creep aboard the *Kingston*. They were bedevilled by mosquitoes, which were everywhere, even offshore. Many of the crew started to get fevers, cold chills, headaches, backaches, stomach cramps. They complained of weakness and constant tiredness. Several worsened, looking jaundiced, and began to bleed and vomit up black bile. Yellow fever and malaria had struck, although they only knew it as marsh fever, or the flux, thought to be caused by exposure to malignant ground vapours.

Some could barely raise themselves from their bunks, sipping water, not eating, weakening fast in the fierce tropical heat. There was little anyone could do other than alleviate discomfort by rest and cold compresses.

Then they began to die.

The first was John Butcher, a 22-year-old seaman from Liverpool, who died on 12 May. The second was Josh Gilroy, aged 25 from Jersey, the following day. Lionel Samford, an American sailor from New York, succumbed on 20 May.

Fear started to take hold among the crew. Who would be next? Would the flux strike everyone? The weak took to their hummocks, the strong kept up their duties. There was nothing to do but pray and, for the healthy, keep loading oil.

When Daniel Kerr's seizures started, he asked Richard to sit with him and hold his hand. His hammock was stained with vomit and blood, which oozed from his anus. He asked Richard if he was going to die. He was weak, and the fever and pain racked his body.

'Hang in, Daniel. You'll pull through. You're strong. Pray to God.'

'Will you look after me, if I go?'

'I promise, if worse comes to worse. Here, hold your Saint Christopher's medallion, Daniel.'

'When you get back, go see me ma. Give 'er me wage an' me medallion. Tell 'er I love her,' Daniel wheezed feebly. He squeezed Richard's hand.

Later that night, he whispered his last frenzied words before slipping into a coma. 'Ma, mother, come hold me.'

Daniel Kerr died on 5 June.

The last death was Michael Behrents, a German seaman from Hanover, on 22 June. The ship's carpenter, Jacob Witt, was kept busy building coffins so the bodies could be rowed ashore by canoe and buried on solid ground, away from sharks.

For each burial, Captain Kelly read Christian rites from *The Book of Common Prayer*. 'Lord, we commit this body to the ground, earth to earth, ashes to ashes, dust to dust, in sure and certain hope of the Resurrection to eternal life.'

Like one and all, Richard said words of farewell to each of his dead shipmates, then prayed that his own life would be spared. After each seaman's death, whatever remained in their locker – clothes, shoes, scrimshaw, lockets, knives – was auctioned among the crew. Money raised would be collected and given to the man's family.

By September, the *Kingston* was fully loaded with 950 casks of palm oil. The final payment of cloth, cooking pots and gunpowder was made by the captain to William Dappa Pepple aboard the British agent's ship. The covey helped secure the King of Bonney's trading kingdom for another year. The *Kingston* was then made ready for its 4,500 nautical mile return voyage to Liverpool.

The captain sent men ashore to refill their water casks and to collect as much dried fish, rice, yams and plantains as they find. Then they weighed anchor, secured the cargo and set sail.

It was a slow journey, beating against a slight breeze in the windless equatorial zone. Heat from the sun bore down on them relentlessly, causing air to rise straight up rather than blow horizontally, sometimes becalming them for days on end.

The voyage took nearly three months to complete. But they had their prize, 500 tons of oil at a cost of five lives. The surviving crew looked forward to 10 months' wages and a small bonus for each, based on the ship's profit.

The *Kingston* arrived in Liverpool on 17 December and was cleared for unloading. The palm oil was hauled up from the ship's hold onto the docks. After clearing the ship, Captain Kelly thanked the crew for their service and bid them farewell. However, it was a sombre return as the men cleaned the deck and cabins for the last time, then shook hands before they left.

Richard and the remaining crew, relieved to have survived to ordeal, were discharged on New Year's Day 1838.

He'd survived the hellish hole of West Africa.

The *Kingston's* voyage and an account of each crew member, including those discharged or died, survives in the British National Archives.[2]

Exactly which ships Richard served on for the next 10 years is hidden from sight among dusty crew agreements held in the British National Archives or the National Maritime Museum. If you don't know the name of the vessel, port of registration, and the date or port of sailing, it's impossible to track a crew member down in this period, at least until the various archives

2 Registry of Shipping, Agreements and Crew List, Kingston, BT 98/346. Showing Richard Belsar's name, age, birthplace, Date of Joining Ship, Discharge Date.

are scanned, digitised and made searchable. Even then, many records have been lost or destroyed.

Rory O'More

The *Rory O'More*, a three-masted, 295-ton barque, was a fast ship. The owners, a syndicate of Quebec gold-seekers called the Argonauts, were chasing profits in the Californian gold rush. The ship's owners, James Dean and William Stevenson, two wealthy Quebec merchants, had appointed James Brennan as Captain.

Stevenson had called the captain to a meeting in his office shortly before departure. 'The essential thing is speed, Mr Brennan,' Stevenson said. 'You must set sail before the ice sets in. We can't take no more risks in Saint Lawrence Gulf. Winter is upon us. The weather here is worsening.'

Stevenson handed Captain Brennan an envelope containing the ship's papers: the title of ownership, inventory, passenger list and instructions for the sale of the cargo upon arrival at Frisco Bay. He issued his final order. 'After arrival you are then instructed to sell the ship and deposit funds with our banking agents.'

Captain Brennan looked up in surprise. He knew merchants were cold-hearted for their profit, but shipbuilders and owners took pride in their fleet, especially a fast ocean trader like *Rory O'More*.

'Why, sir? She's a splendid ship. British oak and better than new. She'll beat them Yankee clippers any day.'

'I've nothing against the ship, Mr Brennan,' explained Stevenson. 'But we are merchants. We run a business, you see. My business is here in Quebec. I can't run my ships from California. Stay on if you wish but sell *Rory O'More*. That is my order. Now, you will take your leave. God's speed, sir.'

James Brennan loved the *Rory O'More*. He knew her history, how she'd run aground two years before. He knew the hazards of navigating ice flows into the cities of Montreal and Quebec. He'd spent weeks in the shipyard overseeing her repair, talking to wainwrights, working with stevedores, selecting his chief officer and first mate.

He had read the *Rory O'More*'s log and letters penned by her previous captain. Launched in 1842, built at Kirkcudbright, Scotland, fast and sturdy, sailing the Montreal trade, to and from Liverpool. Ninety-nine feet in length, made of oak, copper fastened. Barque-rigged, one deck, square-sterned, sheathed in copper. The *Rory O'More* had been a profitable vessel but she'd suffered one stroke of bad luck in hazardous waters in the Gulf of St Lawrence – she hit a field of ice off the Magdalen Islands in May 1847. There was considerable damage. The exhausted crew kept the pumps constantly going for two days to save passengers and salvage what they could of her cargo. It was fortunate the wreck could be salvaged at all. Her new owners had refloated her and brought her to harbour in Quebec under sail after the tug that was towing her broke down.

Now, two years later, the *Rory O'More* was patched up and ready to face the rigours of Cape Horn. She would sail on a five-month voyage with a number of passengers, in addition to freight – provisions, canvas for tents, frames and wood to build 20 wooden houses, mining tools – to California. By October 1849, Captain Brennan had selected and readied his officers and crew who duly signed their articles of employment. The crew included one ordinary seaman – a man named Richard Belsar.

On 13 November 1849 the *Rory O'More* cast off her moorings and headed against a bitterly freezing easterly wind into the Gulf of St Lawrence. It was Richard Belsar's birthday – he turned 35 – but no one celebrated, least of all him. It was all hands to work. Ropes to pull, sheets to raise, ice to avoid.

The little barque ran as fast as the sea, tacking south down the North Atlantic coast. She was a mover, dancing on the waves. Sometimes, when struck by a squall, she dashed into a wave and sent spray masthead high. She skimmed along deep valleys, between lofty waves and then, brought to course again, rightened with ease, while the sea carved in mountains of white foam along her sides.

Richard loved ocean sailing and was happy leaving Quebec's bone-chilling weather – the freezing snow, the hard ice, the sub-zero blackness. He was broke again and needed another long voyage to save up a few more guineas. He'd lost what little he had drinking whiskey and gambling.

There was a woman he'd met – a young widow with a child – who had wanted him to stay with her in Quebec. He'd been sorely tempted, but his heart, like the weather, was unsympathetic and he left her one morning without even saying goodbye. He did the only thing he knew – found another ship, joined a crew, ran away to sea. It was the prospect of adventure, a new land, another port; warmer if he could find one.

Richard was content working as an ordinary seaman on the deck of the *Rory O'More*. He watched the wind, the speed under full sail, constantly adjusting lines to squeeze some more speed. Years of Atlantic runs had hardened him. He was a skilful seaman who others turned to without question. Younger, less experienced men looked to him for guidance as he yelled orders on deck.

The *Rory O'More* slowed as she entered the tropics and crossed the equator. Days became almost lackadaisical, which meant cleaning and scrubbing. The crew celebrated the line-crossing ceremony with the passengers with extra tots of rum and brandy all round, and sang shanties to the shellbacks, the old sailors, now trusted subjects of Neptune, the Roman god of water. Captain Brennan appeared from his cabin for the crossing ceremony, colourfully dressed as King Neptune, trident in hand, and anointed each passenger as his new subject.

There was a sense of excitement sailing in the Southern Hemisphere as a belt of prevailing westerlies drove the *Rory O'More* on and on. She overtook several Boston gold-seeker brigantines and another Canadian brig that had left Quebec a week earlier. Then, after two weeks off the South American coast, she headed to Buenos Aires for a resupply of fresh water.

Richard joined the boat crew as they went to shore, but it was only a two-day stopover before they were back aboard with no time of their own. There was an exchange of news with crew from the other ships, and an agreement by each captain to sail within sight of one another, as much as possible, as they rounded the Horn.

Cape Horn was seen as the ultimate achievement for every ocean-going sailor. No other stretch of water on this planet had cost so many brave seamen. Deck crew wore oil skins for protection against the bitter wind and rain, while passengers huddled below deck in misery.

Richard led the starboard watch with two young apprentices. They soon ran into bad weather but, instead of letting the watch huddle under the fo'c'sle head or under the break of the poop, he made them clean brightwork with sand and water. What made them feel the cold so much was the lack of sufficient hot food from the galley.

As the days grew short and the temperature lowered, the bad weather increased, and soon passengers and many of the crew were 'shipping it green' over the weather bulwarks. It was dangerous on deck and lifelines were rigged the length of the vessel.

Cape Horn was rounded in thick, snowy weather, the passage against the westerlies having occupied from the fiftieth parallel in the South Atlantic to the same latitude on the Pacific side. The weather was continually rough and bitterly cold.

Rory O'More's skylights were battened down and a small oil lamp shone feebly in the main cabin. Passengers remained seasick, cramped below the beams, sitting woefully on trunks, lashed to their berths, or lying on rough pine floorboards.

Richard worked hard on deck with the chief mate, exhausted after each eight-hour watch, but continued ever on, as it was worse being under deck. Captain Brennan knew he needed his best hands on deck at all times. Richard's head was spinning. He experienced a combination of huge, physical fatigue with adrenalin-fuelled exhilaration that came with having faced danger and survived. Then they rounded the Horn. After two weeks hard sailing, off Chile's rugged coast, they were clear. The Pacific blessed them with smooth waters.

He climbed below deck, into the dank steerage cabin and saw the passengers huddled together, lying weakly on bunks, squatting on the floor, retching into buckets, white-faced from sea-sickness.

'We did it,' he said. 'We're over the worst.'

'Praise God,' one said. 'Bless you and the captain and your men.'

A service was held on deck giving thanks to God for saving their souls.

Captain Brennan ordered his ship to stop at Valparaiso in Chile for a short rest and to replenish fresh supplies for food and water. It was a welcomed break for passengers and crew in a warm port, who brought their bedding and clothes on deck to dry. Two other ships, the barque *Daniel Webster* from Boston, and the barque *Roger Sherman* from New York, were also moored in port, and the three ship captains agreed to continue the onward voyage together.

Later in April, the *Rory O'More's* foretopgallant mast was carried away in a white squall that lasted only minutes, and a new one was set up by Richard, now an experienced carpenter. But by then, there was an overflowing feeling of optimism in the ship. They had survived crossing the Horn, with no deaths or injuries, and they were nearing their destination. By now Captain Brennan knew he would safely deliver his ship, passengers, and his cargo, and reach California. Two weeks later, in early May, the barque *Rory O'More* entered Frisco Bay after a passage of 159 days. The crew edged her into the harbour, then gathered on deck and sang loudly:

Have another drink, boys. Well, have one with me.

We're home from the sea. Yes, we're back on the shore;

And if you get too drunk, boys, in this company,

You'll roar 'round Cape Horn on the Rory O' More.

We can't be absolutely certain Richard sailed on the *Rory O'More* to San Franciso. As yet, no official crew record has been found. In established ports, crew lists and articles of agreement were provided to the harbour master at the end of a voyage, but here there's no documentary evidence for this particular port.

The National Archives at San Francisco has no record of the *Rory O'More's* arrival; their collection only dates back to 1851. The customs office opened in 1850 and it took some time before it collected crew documentation (the vast number of ships that arrived for the gold rush didn't help). Sometimes, contracts with crew lists spanned more than one voyage. However, it's likely Richard was aboard this voyage, as another crew list document found in Tasmanian records his name on the *Rory O'More* on its next voyage three weeks later.

It was a voyage across the Pacific Ocean to the colony of Van Diemen's Land.

Pacific

Frisco Bay was filled with hundreds of ships, many abandoned, its wharf a forest of masts. Most seamen who arrived skipped for the California diggings, being discharged or deserting their ships, which were left empty and stranded.

San Francisco was booming, with gold-seekers arriving in their thousands each week, filling makeshift tent houses, hotels, warehouses, saloons, gambling halls and wood shanties before they walked or rode to the goldfields to try their luck.

After *Rory O'More* discharged its passengers and unloaded its cargo of mining equipment, house frames, doors, windows and shingles, the crew gathered on deck, standing to attention before Captain Brennan. While pleased to have achieved his mission – to arrive safely and return a tidy profit to the ship's owners – his next task was a challenging one. He had to convince the crew to remain for their next journey – to cross the Pacific Ocean and sail to Van Diemen's Land with a cargo of timber and a number of new passengers. The new Californian owners, Messrs Thompson, McKenzie,

Co., had purchased *Rory O'More* for the bargain sum of $6,700 and were keen to deliver merchandise to a British settlement called Launceston.

'I know many of you are sorely tempted to jump ship,' Brennan said. 'The lure of gold is strong. But beware, 'tis a fool's gold. Few are fortunate, most fail, many die.' Brennan looked deep into the eyes of the men.

Richard knew many would skip; on the voyage they had talked endlessly of gold, starting a new life, dreams of riches. There were 30 crewmen; at least half needed to stay or Brennan would have to find new ones; a next-to-impossible task.

'All I can say is, you're seafarers, lads. Better to feel the wind on a good ship than die in a dirt hole underground, or risk death by savages.' The captain held his arms wide in an embrace. 'Join me again on the *Rory O'More*! Let's cross the Pacific to a new British land!'

Men looked nervously at each other. Richard knew many had already made up their minds to leave, including the chief officer, Archibald McIntyre. Richard, still uncertain, wanted to remain with the captain, whom he admired and regarded as a fair and decent leader. What should he do? Stay on board or stick with some of with his mates and leave?

Brennan had one more ace up his sleeve, leaving it to last. 'I'll offer double rates of pay. Come on. What say you?'

In the end, it was enough. Sixteen crew re-signed their articles of agreement, as did Richard, this time as first mate. He would cross the Pacific, the peaceful sea – every sailor's dream.

Rory O'More warped out of San Francisco harbour on 6 June 1850, and the captain set a course due west. She headed to Otahiti for their stopover and made good time, arriving four weeks later, on 10 July. The little barque furled her sails and dropped anchor at Papeete; a perfect harbour protected by a barrier reef of coral.

As they anchored, Richard gazed in wonder at the magnificent sight before them, an island paradise, alluring like a vision from heaven. A number of whaling ships and trading schooners lay moored nearby. The setting was hypnotic – tropical warmth scented with fragrance; high, lush, verdant mountains; clear turquoise waters; brown-skinned people arriving in canoes with woven bowls of fruit and mother-of-pearl carving to trade.

'How long, captain?' Richard asked hopefully. He'd heard of these islands before. Word travelled widely among seamen about which places to seek out and which ports to avoid. Otahiti had been a sailor's dream ever since the arrival of Wallis, Cook and Bougainville. The lure of the Society Islands had captivated the minds of sailors around the world for decades.

'Two days to replenish our water and supplies. Then two days' shore leave. I only need two men to remain with me on board,' Brennan replied, smiling.

Richard understood. This was to be the captain's additional reward for those who stayed with the ship. 'Which men, captain?'

'It's alright, Belsar. I'll just keep the two old ones. Bradley and Marks will do. You may have leave after your duties.'

Richard rowed ashore in the longboat with four of the crew and moored at the bustling wharf, crowded with American seamen loading barrels of copra and coconut oil. The wharves surged and clamoured with the usual lumpers, hucksters, beggars, costermongers and women selling their flesh. The taverns and inns were lined with men drinking and carousing, and with gamblers and bunters, even here, in the place they called paradise.

He found the commissaire's office and arranged their resupply of fresh food and water to be collected the following day. There was a plentiful supply of fruit and vegetables: breadfruit, coconuts, plantains, bananas, yams. Then he walked past the dock and market and headed inland, leaving the throng of noisy labourers and his mates to get their tattoos or trade for souvenirs and drink liquor until they passed out. He left the stink of rotting fish, the strict policing by French officials, the brawling between ship's crews. He needed to stretch his sea legs, explore the island and admire this handsome-looking race of people.

The further he walked, the quieter and more peaceful it became. He was bewitched by this strange land: its exotic beauty, the lush tropical greenery, the clear waterfalls, all set beneath a range of magnificent, imposing mountains. He noticed a nest of thatched huts, men and women walking slowly around, children playing, young boys running. They were bronzed and healthy with black eyes, white teeth, jet-black hair, and rounded limbs. They wore bark-like dresses and lived in elegant huts with woven roofs made of palm leaves.

A man waved at Richard, smiling, signalling for him to come closer.

'Maeva,' he said. 'Ma'a?' He pointed his fingers at his mouth.

Richard didn't understand but the man was insistent, handing him a bowl of cooked meat mixed with a vegetable.

He sat down and tasted the food. It had a mild, sweet potato-like flavour. The man smiled. 'Good, good!' he said. 'Vahine.'

An older woman appeared at the door of the hut – the man's wife. She was bare-breasted, unabashed by her nakedness, showing a full set of smiling white teeth.

'Thank you,' Richard said, pointing at the bowl. 'The food is delicious. Good.'

The woman ducked inside the hut and returned with more plates of food, which she placed at Richard's feet. 'Amu, amu,' she said.

He accepted it gladly. It was roast pig, he realised, with taro root and what looked like banana and copra. He ate heartily, all the while saying, 'Good food. Thank you, thank you.'

He spent the day with the Tahitian couple. He met their two children and, after overcoming their wariness of the tall, bearded, white-skinned, blue-eyed stranger, they played chasing games with him, touched his hands and poked at his beard. They seemed fascinated by his skin and eyes. He drank a bowl of milky liquid from a coconut cup that tasted of the earth. 'What is this? he asked.

'Kava,' the man said.

In the evening, Richard bade them farewell and gave the man the only thing of value he had – his small jack-knife. *I can trade for another one*, he thought. He wandered down to the beach and lay on its white sand, falling asleep under the stars.

Two days were not nearly enough. Not in this paradise. He could spend months here and not tire of it. The island was captivating, the women alluring. *Perhaps I could find a wife*? he thought. The women wore their hair in plaits, with flowing skirts, some showing a large pearl in their ears, which they valued highly. They wore flowers and a band of feathers on their arm. Could he dare hope of such a dream?

He walked in a desultory mood back to the docks, back to his reality – his drunken shipmates, their sunburned mottled skin, reddened faces and missing teeth, their nasty cursing and foul breath. He saw their bloodshot eyes, their pox-marked faces. *What am I doing*? he thought. *Why don't I stay*?

But there was no chance of escape. Where could he hide, anyway? He knew he'd be caught eventually. He knew the penalty for desertion. Loss of wage, heavy fine, imprisonment for six months. Worse if he'd been a navy man; they could hang you. Even doing a bunk for a few days was enough to be charged as a deserter. Reluctantly, he rounded up his drunken mates and they returned to their ship before curfew.

Rory O'More departed Tahiti on 13 July and continued sailing west in perfect weather. She crossed the South Pacific and arrived in the town of Launceston on the northern coast of Van Diemen's Land, on 17 August, a passage of 34 days. *The Launceston Examiner* published a small line announcing her arrival in its shipping news:

> *Arrived 17 August 1850, Launceston, Rory O'More, from San Francisco.*

After being discharged and collecting his wage, Richard bade farewell to his master, Captain James Brennan, who planned to continue sailing north to Sydney, then on a return voyage to San Francisco with more passengers and new cargo. He'd already told Captain Brennan he was leaving the ship and had received his discharge and pay.

As he was about to step ashore, Captain Brennan took him by the hand. 'My thanks to you, Belsar. You've served me well. Farewell, lad. May the seas lie smooth before you.'

Half of the crew took their wage and remained at Launceston. Half decided to continue with the ship.

Richard was again a stranger in a new land.

Whaling on the *Launceston*

Richard's money ran out. After eight months renting rooms in Launceston, spending his meagre savings on food, a new set of clothes, plenty of grog, and with women in bawdy houses, he needed to find work. Another ship.

He scanned notice boards for employment and asked about the docks. An American whaler had arrived and was being re-fitted for its next journey to the Southern Seas. He knew about whalers from Quebec – stinking ships reeking of oil and blood, with crews paid by a share of the catch, generous or poor, depending on the number of whales caught.

He saw the chief mate and asked for permission to board, who questioned him directly at the gunwale. 'Tough seaman are you? How long?'

'Going on 15 years,' he replied. 'Atlantic traders, mostly. Barque from Quebec to San Francisco, rounded the Horn, crossed the Pacific.'

'Come aboard then, see the ship's master, Captain Thomas Cook.'

Richard jumped aboard and walked over to the master, inspecting several men sharpening and storing their tools of trade: staves for barrels, harpoons, flensing knives, gaffs, pikes and boat spades. 'Excuse me, sir. Needing crew?'

The master turned and looked him over without saying a word. That's the way it was with old seamen. They looked at men's faces, at their eyes and expressions, the scars on their hands, and made quick judgments. A layabout or leader. Deckhand or boatman. Strong man or weak.

After a short discussion, mostly to determine if Richard was literate and free, and not one of Van Diemen's Land's poorly regarded convict lags, he agreed to take him on. He instructed Richard to report to his agent, George Fisher, to sign his articles and get his first month's advance wage.

The shipping agent's office, located nearby on William Street, was a dingy room full of musty papers, admiralty maps and chandlery equipment for sale. Outside, a group of sailors sat grumbling about measly wages, poor conditions and cursed ships, like they did at every port. Richard pushed inside to see Fisher about signing on to the *Launceston*. He said he'd met the captain and had been cleared to sign on.

'Whaling experience?' Fisher asked.

Richard said none.

'Then you'll be appointed either as shipman, oarsman, steersman or cutter.'

'What pays most?'

'Headsman. The harpooner, man! But know this, the ship's prize depends on him. Fail in that and you're a dead man walking, if you take my meanin'. And all muck in for the cuttin' work.'

'I can steer and pull an oar better than any. Steersman then.'

Fisher pulled out the articles and explained the conditions of the voyage. It was a long paper with many legal words, but Richard was familiar with most seaman's agreements. The old man read through it slowly to clarify the terms.

'Your lay shall be a fifty-fifth's share of the catch, based on sperm oil taken, less ship costs,' Fisher explained, pointing at each article. 'Each seaman to receive a weekly supply: 12 pounds of beef or mutton, 12 pounds of flour, half a pound of sugar, a quarter pound of tea.

'You are charged to go anywhere in the Southern Seas to chase and kill whales, faithfully do your duty, follow orders and remain with the vessel. If you're absent for more than 12 hours without a lawful excuse, you're a deserter. You'll forfeit your payment. Know this, boyo.' Fisher looked up at him sternly, his eyes narrowing like slits. 'I just charged a fool, James Smith, for being absent without leave after he signed his articles and got his advance. Town constables nabbed him. Sixty days hard labour. Ha! And there's warrants out for two more.'

'I'll do no bunk,' Richard said. 'Just tell me the rates for the prize.'

'The lay for oil or whalebone is set at a rate of £70 for every ton of sperm oil, and £40 for every ton of clean whalebone, in lieu of wages.' He pushed the agreement toward Richard. 'Make your mark, swabby.'

'I can sign my own name.' He took the pen, dipped it in ink and scrawled his name.

The ship's register of 24 crewmen, now digitised, can be found in Tasmania's State Archives, and includes the name:

Richard Belser.

Rank: Seaman.

Status: Free.

Ship to Colony: Rory O'More.

Bound to: South Seas.

The 328-ton barque *Launceston* departed Launceston on 13 May 1851, her hold stowed with barrel staves, iron hoops and whale-killing equipment. After the harbour pilot steered the barque up the forty-three-mile length of the Tamar River, she was cleared by the harbour master, and sailed north into Bass Strait, then veered west to the Southern Ocean. The *Launceston* headed to what was called the Western Hunting Grounds of the Great Australian Bight, which reached as far west as Cape Leeuwin on the tip of Western Australia's southern coast. Launceston Town's *Cornwall Chronicle* newspaper gave a brief mention in its shipping intelligence:

Ship: Launceston, departed Launceston 31 May, 1851. Barque. Cook commander. G. Fisher agent. Sailed on a whaling voyage.

In July, winter's cold southerlies hit the barque and she rolled in the great ocean swells being pushed up from Antarctica. The *Launceston* was fast and made good time, overtaking several other whalers that had come from Hobart Town. By the time the *Launceston* arrived at its hunting grounds, William Green, the first mate, had allocated his teams into either boatmen, blubber cutters or boilermen, and the men were well-practised in their duties.

They hunted Southern Right whales. Easy prey, they swam slow, right for killing. Richard was the steersman in one of three whaleboats, watching another man called William Culpitt, his headsman, standing at the stern, ready to direct four oarsmen to position their boat close enough to throw his harpoon. They were anxious to get started and ready to test their skills. They didn't need to wait long.

'She blows!' cried the lookout.

'Where away?' Green shouted back. 'Two points on weather bow. Half a mile away.'

The *Launceston* hove to and the three whaleboats were lowered to the sea, and then pulled away, oarsmen straining hard to make the distance. Pulling hands rowed at speed and Richard guided his longboat near to where the whale might breach the surface for air. Then more blows were seen all around them. Pods of them!

One huge creature rose by Richard's boat and all that Culpitt had to do was plunge his cold irons, two hard, fast throws, secured to the boat's tow line, into the beast. Their boat spun as it dived, pulling the crew one way and another, then laid still for half an hour, before the whale rose. Culpitt quickly finished it off with his lance, then it rolled over on its back and died, blood gushing from its spout and mouth. They fastened a rope around its fluke and rowed it hard back alongside the ship, straining by the drag. 'Cut it in boys,' yelled Culpitt. 'Be quick about it.' Then they rowed back for more.

Men proceeded to reeve huge strips of blubber, hauling it on deck. Fletchers cut blubber into blocks and lowered them into the ship's blubber room. Some men pitched it on deck, others forked remains over the side. One of the mates worked coal fires for the three iron cauldrons, another bailed the boiling oil into copper tanks. The cooper was busy building his barrels to store the oil. The yield of one Southern Right whale, giving perhaps 30 to 40 barrels of oil.

That's how it went, killing the whales, cutting the junk, boiling it down, cooling the oil in tanks, filling their barrels. Three months of stench, black smoke and oil. Whale blood spilling on deck, blubber oil permeating clothes, sticky fat on skin, in hair and beards. They couldn't get clean in the sea because of the sharks, and they couldn't swim anyway. They pulled oars and killed whales, then worked in the hold to secure barrels. They sailed further on and started killing over again.

Richard was sick of the stench covering his skin, stuck to his clothes, filling his lungs. Like Culpitt and the other seamen, all he could think of was his share of the lay. Men tried to calculate the ship's prize, but no one knew the owner's costs.

By October, they left Cape Leeuwin and moored back at King George's Sound, a safe harbour and coaling station for passing steamers. Master Cook rotated the crew with shore leave. Richard rowed to the beach with his boat crew and they scrubbed their skin raw on white sand, cleaning away months of whale grime and blood in the shallow waters.

He lay on the wet beach sand, and looked about, taken in by King George Sound's magnificent surroundings: its vast natural harbour, several desolate islands poking up from the sea, huge granite boulders, turquoise waters, long stretches of dunes and sand. Everything about the Southern Hemisphere amazed him – the bright light, the strange animals, the desolate cliffs, the size of this land of Australia.

After taking on fresh water and supplies at King George's Sound, some of the men were given shore leave and they planned to get roaring drunk at one of the public houses, the Ship Inn. The mood was high; it had been a good season for them. The Master, Captain Thomas Cook, was pleased with the catch so far: 138 barrels and oil, 40 baleens, and dressed whalebone filled much of the barque's hold. *The South Australian Register* reported their catch on 20 November 1851:

> *The whaling barque Launceston, of Launceston, arrived at King George's Sound on the 30th October, with 20 tuns oil.*

Richard and Culpitt's boat crew planned to get drunk, as did most of the lads. His team had won a bonus for the highest catch so far and they wanted to celebrate – a week drinking at the Ship Inn, a public hotel owned by John Bruce and his wife on the waterfront jetty, the best establishment in Albany Town. Captain Thomas Cook and several men remained on board to watch over their prize and keep the ship safe from changing weather or absconders trying to board. The first mate, William Green, was in charge of getting the men back aboard. They were reminded of the consequences of remaining ashore. 'Be late, lose your lay.'

In 1851, Albany was a forgotten town of drifters, whalers, deserters, thieves and escapees. One man, John Sales, on hearing the *Launceston*, an American-owned whaler, was at anchor, tried to get on board and seek passage. But Captain Cook was a good judge of what he was up to. Sales claimed he belonged to the government survey department and was trying to return to his party, who'd left without him, then became lost. Could he return with the ship? Cook and two mates escorted Sales back to town and handed him over to the district constable.

On shore, however, there was growing enmity between some local whalers from Western Australian and American whaling ships, now harvesting in their waters. It didn't take much for a spark to ignite a bonfire, and the *Launceston's* crew got in the thick of it. A bloody fight broke out between men from the *Launceston* and men from another ship, *Amicus*, recently arrived at Albany from the Swan River settlement, near Perth.

Bad blood had been brewing for days. Each kept their distance at the Ship Inn, but the crew from *Amicus* constantly cursed and complained about foreign vessels in their waters. *Amicus* had had a bad run. It hadn't caught many whales and now it was getting late in the hunting season. The spark lit when a drunk sailor from *Amicus* called out an insult, which everyone heard: 'Cock-sucking American ship sodomites, come over, stealing our whales!'

William Culpitt exploded and launched himself across the tables at the accuser and struck him hard on his face with a blow that knocked him clean to the floor, unconscious. Then he pulled out his blade, bent down, and cut off the man's ear. Richard, pumped up by grog and adrenalin then yelled out, 'Come on, boys. We don't take that shit.'

Punches flew and heads cracked. There were knife cuts, on arms and hands and faces, as seamen always carried pocket blades, but fortunately, no fatal stabbings. The fight, vicious and brutal as it was, was over in minutes.

By the time the hotel owner rallied for assistance to break up the brawl, most of the seaman had run, knowing full well that if caught by police, they would lose their pay and be sent to gaol. The men scattered, first to their longboats, then to their ships, trying to staunch their wounds while boasting of victory. The publican, John Bruce, didn't press charges for fear of losing his licence. The mess was quickly cleaned up and an order of silence given.

After their two-week layover in Albany, the *Launceston* was ready to sail again and made ready to keep hunting whales. The seamen, hungover, swearing and complaining, returned to their duties. They weighed anchor, set sails to catch the southeasterly trade winds, and left King George Sound, while the boatmen sharpened their killing tools.

Richard spotted a Leviathan one week out. A huge creature – a sperm whale – swimming alone. As the *Launceston* reefed its sails and heaved to, the oarsmen prepared their boats and irons. Then it was on, the boat crew heaving and sweating to pick up speed. This time Richard took over as lead harpooneer, with William Green, the first mate, spotter and steersman.

Approaching the sperm whale, twice the size of their boat with an enormous fist-shaped head, was one of the most exhilarating and terrifying moments of Richard's life.

'Give it to him!' yelled Green, and Richard heaved the iron, aiming for the heart. The line was paid out and he snubbed it to the loggerhead, dousing it with water to keep it from burning. Their boat raced across the sea, tugged behind the whale, as it tried to escape, sounding into depth, before it rose again several minutes later, mortally wounded.

Richard threw a killing iron, a three-foot lance with a leaf-shaped blade. The leviathan convulsed, beating the sea into a foam with its tail fluke, and slowly it died. They tied their ropes around its tail and towed it back to the ship, then stripped the blubber into blankets, ready to boil and store in barrels, working late into the night, like they always did.

It took three days to strip the beast. The sharks did the rest, leaving a bony carcass.

The ship eventually returned to Launceston town after three months at sea. There was barely a mention of its arrival in the newspaper or harbour master's log book. No report of their total catch. No record of the sale of the oil. No names of the crew. *The Examiner* reported a few words on 24 January 1852.

Shipping Intelligence. Arrivals January 21. Barque Launceston, 328 tons, Thomas Cook master, from a whaling journey.

The whale oil was sold in Launceston and possibly Melbourne, as was the ship itself, which went up for sale. In February, the *Examiner* advertised the barque for sale, as freight or charter through the shipping agent, George Fisher.

By 1852, Richard Belsar was a hardened, experienced sailor and ship carpenter. He'd circumnavigated most the world's oceans, almost completely. He'd crossed the Atlantic and Pacific, survived the tropical hell of West Africa, rounded Cape Horn, and traversed Australia's Southern Ocean. He knew toil, violence and debauchery, but not fear. He might have been an illiterate seaman, but he'd faced and overcome death and hardship that would break most landsmen.

Schooner *Pearl*

As Richard waited for his lay and bonus wage by the *Launceston's* captain, he took a room at a boarding house on William Street, close to Launceston Town dockyard. Most of the crew were drunk, bedding whores and spending their wages on gambling and carousing. Some said they were heading across Bass Strait to Melbourne or south to Hobart Town by coach. Even William Cutlpitt, his friend, said he was going to south to find a woman and shack up for a few weeks.

What next? he thought. *Here I am, half-way round the world. Will I ever see home again, old Liverpool?* He knew he was a wanderer, an itinerant soul, and this thought alone kept him going. Here he was a stranger in a strange land. This Southern Land and the new colony of Van Diemen's Land seemed extraordinary. Unburdened by the harsh discipline of ships, he was a free man with a fat wallet. He could go anywhere.

He began to walk. To stretch his legs away from the cramped confines of a ship and the close-packed huddle of men. For walked for miles on his own, following rutted tracks over hills, passing small farms and settlements along the Midland Road, seeing strange hopping animals, listening to the cries of large white birds. He slept at small inns where he could, but didn't drink. He kept to himself, mostly. Not trying to mix or make friends. The land healed and refreshed him. Just the openness of the southern sky, the tussock grass, the fresh, minty smell of eucalypt gum trees. He climbed rocky outcrops just for the view and hiked across the windswept midland plains where sheep grazed. After a week of constant walking, thinking about his life, he turned around. Back to Launceston.

Richard had recently turned 37 and was thinking about what he would do next. He was tired of long voyages at sea, poor food and constant hardship. He never wanted to see another stinking whaler again. Would he ever know the sweetness of affections or the refuge of a house? Would he ever stop voyaging? He knew his youthful adventures were coming to an end. But what else could he do?

The lay payment had been generous. He had £145 in his pocket – more than he'd made as an ordinary seaman from his Atlantic or Pacific voyages, where he only earned £3 a month. He thought about putting his cash notes into the Launceston Town Saving Bank to keep it safe but didn't know how to go about it. He didn't understand or trust banks. Like always, he had rolled the notes tightly and squeezed them inside a long, carved, hollow whalebone, which he kept tied to a leather string around his neck. Hidden safe under his shirt. They'd have to kill him first for anyone to steal it.

In Launceston, news was spreading about a new gold rush happening across Bass Strait in the colony of Victoria. He'd seen it all before in San Francisco, of course, where people deserted cities in their thousands for the rush to the goldfields. Harbours filled with empty vessels without crew, who deserted and jumped ship to try their luck. *Perhaps I should go?* he thought. *Try my luck on land.* But he dismissed the idea as fanciful. *What do know of mining?*

One evening, sitting in town leisurely smoking his pipe, he saw William Green, his former first mate, walking down Canning Street, sober, looking excited and happy for some company.

'Ahoy, William! You stayed!'

'Aye. I'm making other plans.'

They agreed to have an ale and a meal of battered kangaroo brains, called Slippery Bob, at the nearby Tam O'Shanter Inn.

'Where to now, William?' Richard asked. He knew Green held hopes of being master of his own vessel one day and had the skills to do it. He was a man of sober temperament, could read and write, and knew mathematics and astronomy well enough to navigate.

'I'm off to the goldfields, Belsar,' replied Green in a low voice, then whispered, 'They say you can pick up nuggets as big as your finger.' He pulled several folded newspapers from his coat pocket, laid them on the table and showed Richard. 'There, look at this in the *Geelong Advertiser*: "Gold bonanza in the Victorian diggings". Here, and another here, see this article: "Parties bring back large quantities to Melbourne, 50 ounces after one day's labour". He stabbed each article with his finger. 'Gold found in Ballarat and a place called

Mount Alexander. It's a four-day walk from Port Phillip. The rush is still new. There are early whispers of gold found at a place called Bendigo Creek. It all happened while we were whaling.'

'I can't read quick like you, William.'

'Let me tell you, Belsar. I've been doin' a lot of readin' this week, catchin' up since we got back, and they say it's everywhere. Bigger than California. Goldfield's bein' found all over.' His expression was eager, filled with hope and dreams. 'Come on, Belsar, what do say, man? Come with me. We can partner up. Stake our claim. You're an old sea dog. I seen handle yourself in a scrap.'

But risk a gold rush? He'd heard it before. Usually, the gold was gone by the time most arrived and then it was all fighting and disappointment. He sat silently, weighing up his choices.

'I'm not sure. What do we know of diggin' and livin' on the land? In the bush. We're sailors, me and you.'

William gave him a knowing look. 'Surely not worse than killin' whales.'

'I grant you that.'

Green took that as acceptance and held out his hand. 'Well then, it's settled. Come with me. We'll make our fortune, return to England as rich toffs. Marry and buy property. Here, as toast to our future. Drink up.'

They talked for hours; at least, William did, making plans about what they'd need: canvas tents, ropes, digging equipment, spades, barrows, pans, a machine called a cradle, swags and pots. And weapons – they needed two good revolvers. They'd hire or buy a wagon or bullock cart.

By midnight, Richard, unusually sober, was full of William Green's unbridled enthusiasm, excited by the prospect of a new adventure. Still, there was something niggling at the back of his mind and it made him tense. Leaving the sea behind. No more a Jack Tar. Becoming a landsman. He wasn't sure if he felt regret at leaving the ocean world or if it was a premonition that he was going on a fool's errand.

Their names are recorded in the shipping register found in the Tasmanian Archives: Richard Bulser (not spelt Belsar) and William Green, paid seamen on the three-master schooner *Pearl*, which departed Launceston on 5 February 1852, bound for Melbourne. Not listed as passengers but as crew. The *Pearl* arrived in Melbourne two days later and they eventually joined the vast crowds of new emigrants, gold seekers, ex-convicts, ship deserters, all making their way to the Victorian goldfields.

Then the trail of Richard and William goes cold. The are few official records of diggers moving to and from the Victorian goldfields. Did they make it to one of the goldfields near Ballarat, Forest Creek or Sandhurst? Possibly. We'll never know. Public records in this new, hectic colony were few and far between.

We know nothing more of William Green. What we do know is the partnership must have dissolved at some point.

The next time we come across Richard Belsar is four years later, when he finds love.

Elizabeth Carter

The year is 1854 and Elizabeth Carter was travelling by Cobb and Co. coach from Melbourne to Sandhurst where she had arranged employment as a domestic servant. She had left Van Dieman's Land and had taken a steamer across Bass Strait, a voyage that pitched and rolled in the swells and had left her feeling seasick. By the time she arrived by coach to the city, she was exhausted and, after finding a room at a boarding house, went straight to bed. The next morning, however, she woke up bright and alert, excited to be making her way to the goldfields.

Melbourne was startling, the most remarkable sight Elizabeth had seen. Crowds of people all together, jostling in the wide, dusty city. Slow walking pedestrians and noisy urchins dodging horse carts and carriages as they crossed the roads. Shops and buildings of all kinds. Dress shops, hardware suppliers, timber yards, coffee stalls and saveloy stands, all mixed up together. So many crowds of people in the rough and tumble melee. Roughly dressed miners, grand gentlemen with tall hats, ladies in beautiful crinolines, some with parasols, one carrying a dog. The ladies seemed to glide, while the gentlemen strode. Something fantastical about it all.

Her mother had warned her before she left to be careful, not to talk to strangers, not to smile or make conversation. 'You never know what might happen to you. All manner of things men and women get up to.'

'What things, mother?'

'Never you mind. Just keep to yourself and don't smile. You may give the wrong impression.'

But Elizabeth couldn't help smiling. She knew how well she looked in her bonnet and her best skirt, the one she'd bought herself. Why shouldn't she smile? For a while she stood on a pavement, next to the Cobb and Co. station, uncertain but smiling, among the milling people, until one of the coach attendants took her case and stowed it on the rack and showed her where to sit. The interior was hardly luxurious – bench seats of plain wood on each side – but she was happy to take a seat next to the door, so she could look outside. Other passengers entered, men helping women up, skirts crushed, strangers edging past, nodding and apologising. A young man sat beside her. There were four to a bench and he was pressed against her, there legs touching.

'So sorry, miss,' he said, smiling.

He was good looking, so she smiled back, just as her mother had warned her not to do. 'That's quite all right.'

Suddenly, the coach driver yelled out, 'Ho to!' and the coach jolted to a start. They were away, bumping and swaying together.

Should she acknowledge him, she wondered. Strike up a conversation with other passengers. He seemed decent enough. Cleanly dressed, an open, honest face. Was it possible, she thought, to tell a man's character from his face? There she sat, next to a total stranger, pressing thigh against thigh, looking at other strangers on the opposite bench, and she had no idea of their thoughts towards her. Were they watching her? Maybe she should start a conversation? Perhaps it was better to take heed of her mother's advice.

In any event, the question was soon answered.

'Going to the goldfields, are you?' the man asked. The question startled her. Did he have the right to ask that? Did she have any obligation to answer? She didn't understand the proper code of behaviour in the confines of a coach.

'Yes. I am.'

'Which one?'

Should she say? She blushed, as though she was to blame for breaking the silence inside the cabin. Several passengers looked at her, curious, waiting for her answer, to say something.

'Sandhurst,' she said. 'I have employment there.'

'Ah, the Bendigo Creek fields. Busy settlement there, miss. I'm heading there myself.'

Was it a thrill? Bouncing inside a coach, leg against leg, passing groups of people walking along the road to the goldfields. Her imagination let loose. Maybe this would be one of those moments she had heard of, a moment when your life changes.

'Bit awkward to be squashed up like this with strangers, isn't it?, he said. 'But all in all, rather peasant,' he said, better than the poor souls out there. Walking and carrying their load.'

'I think it rather unpleasant. So much dust.'

He laughed. 'It's going to be a lot dustier where we're heading. Especially over summer. But I've been remiss. I should introduce myself. One should not talk to a lady without an introduction. Allow me to introduce myself – Reginald Smyth.' He put out a hand to be shaken. But she kept hers firmly together. 'Ah, quite so,' he said. Several passengers looked on suspiciously, but didn't say anything.

'Miss Elizabeth Carter,' she said. Not wanting to offend him.

'And may I be so bold as to enquire what Miss Carter will be doing on arrival? Perhaps joining her family there?'

'I am taking a position at a guest house.'

'Ah, you're in the service then.'

At which she took some offence. She moved away from him, as much as she could on the seat and remained silent for a time, thinking about her circumstances. She knew her choices were limited. She was not well educated. Born in Hobart Town, she had little schooling. She could barely read or write. However, she could sew, prepare meals, churn milk, wash clothing, butcher meat and all manner of household duties she'd been taught to do by her mother. She knew she could look after herself.

After a short stop at Gisborne to change horses and allow passengers to stretch their legs and take refreshments, they got underway again. There were a couple of new faces. Reginald Smyth again sat next to her. To break the silence, and not appear so impolite, she asked, 'And you, Mr Smyth. What is your occupation?'

'I'm a clerk. One my way for a position at a bank at Sandhurst. I have great expectations.'

Which sounded rather boastful, she thought. Then, perhaps he was educated. Far better than her. Should she get to know him more? They were traveling to the same destination and, despite his manner, he was rather good looking. A thin moustache, a pale complexion and long sideburns. She sat, uncertain about continuing the conversation. At the back of her mind, she heard her mother's warning.

There was a sudden jolt, and the coach swerved hard, almost going over on two wheels before it righted itself. Elizabeth gave a little shriek. 'You'll be all right, my dear,' Smyth said. As though to reassure her, he took her hand, actually took hold of her hand. And then he released it. 'Nothing to be afraid of.'

He leaned across and whispered, 'I'm sure you'd feel safer knowing someone in Sandhurst was there look after you. I'd be happy to see you sometime, if you like. Look out for you, if you need a friend.' He sat back and folded his arms, not expecting her to reply.

She remained silent and adopted a look of cool indifference. Generally, Elizabeth was unimpressed by men's flirtatious teasing. She had seen, all too often, women of her station fall into seductive predation with dreadful consequences and Reginald Smyth could be just another sweet talker. She had to be careful. Soon she nodded off, the rhythmic motion of the coach and the previous days travel making her feel sleepy.

When they arrived late afternoon in Sandhurst, Elizabeth decided to stay at the Exchange Hotel, next to the coach staging post, rather than continue to the boarding house. It had been a long and tiring day. Reginald Smyth, despite his early interest, seemed to have taken the hint and had remained silent for the rest of the journey. As the coach pulled in, he turned and politely wished her to have a pleasant stay. But there was a glint of determination in his eye.

'Perhaps Miss Carter, could you let me have your address? I'm in much need of a restectable boarding house myself and you mentioned you are going to one? I would be ever so grateful. Of course, if it seems improper, I will understand completely. I don't wish to offend.'

What to do? Should she tell him? He stood tall, and looked handsome, in his way. He did appear to have good prospects. Perhaps they could become friends after all. She knew there would be a division of class and power at the boarding house. She, a domestic servant. He, a paying guest. In the end, she relinquished. She told him the name of the boarding house.

'Jackson's boarding house in Bridge Street.'

He took out a fountain pen and card from his pocket and wrote it down. 'Then perhaps I will see you again sometime, Miss Carter. It's been a pleasure traveling with you. Good evening and God bless.'

With that, he bowed his head and left to collect his case, and she watched him melt away down the street. Although he left abruptly, she had no doubt that she would be seeing him again.

As Elizabeth stepped off the coach rail with her small suitcase, she was overcome by the foreign landscape: dusty roads, sweeping hills of mullock and dirt, scattered shanty huts, and masses of canvas tents. She walked into the Exchange Hotel and asked for a room for the night.

'Is this the main town?' she asked the hotel manager.

'It is, miss. What were you expecting?'

'I'm not sure. It's just … so much dirt and dust.'

'It's the diggin's, miss. Here, we eat dirt, drink dirt, sleep in dirt. All for gold.'

She walked along the main street to stretch her legs and get a feel for the town. Everywhere, she saw roughly dressed men carrying packs on their backs, pushing carts and wheelbarrows, driving oxen and wagons, riding horses. Signs pointed to strange and wonderous places: Kangaroo Flat, Golden Square, California Gully, Matilda Battery, Long Gully, Dead Horse Gully.

Women passed by wearing colourful blue crinoline dresses with ribbons and rosettes, carrying parasols. Beside them, men in blue flannel shirts, moleskin trousers and leather boots.

There was a square-shaped town common with dry, parched gum trees and a muddy creek, beside it a row of slab huts with furtive women and shoeless children playing in mud. There were foreign-looking men walking about: Chinese men in broad, flat hats carrying bags slung at each end of sticks, balanced on their shoulders; American sailors in navy jackets drinking in noisy saloons; Germans, unloading their wagons, arguing in rough, throaty, guttural voices.

The town had a wildness to it, a gaudiness, loud and brash. Hard, sunburned, bearded men moved in masses, travelling nomads, some with large-bodied wives and small bare-footed children. Some people called this place Bendigo.

It appeared wealthy in parts with newly built red-brick two-story houses. There were several impressive stone halls, a theatre, hotels with balconies, merchant shops, even a park where couples promenaded. But it was nothing like Hobart, where she had grown up, with its elegant Georgian stone buildings, green gardens and flower beds, and a sparkling harbour. The gentry there seemed refined by any comparison.

Sandhurst was rowdy and riotous and garish, hammering construction everywhere. It was bewildering and disconcerting.

Have I done the right thing, leaving my home? thought Elizabeth. She felt as though she had rushed headfirst into an abyss of uncertainty.

She was almost swept off her feet when a horse carriage rushed by, swerving wildly down the street, driven by two men wearing top hats and fancy vests, each drinking from a bottle of champagne and throwing handfuls of coins high into the air. 'Watch out, my lovely! Here, catch this!' One threw her a gold coin, which landed at her feet. 'Take this, girlie! A sovereign! My oath, we struck it rich!'

Then they were gone, their carriage continuing on its mad journey. Elizabeth stared on in shock. She bent to pick up the coin, a gold sovereign worth almost two weeks' wages, then she hurried back to her hotel room.

After a restless night locked safely away from a rowdy crowd of diggers drinking at the bar, she was met early next morning by her new employer, a middle-aged woman named Mrs Jackson, who owned the boarding house in Bridge Street. The town was strangely quiet, as if it was resting from the previous night's revelries.

They sat in the hotel lounge and ordered a pot of tea. Mrs Jackson poured when it came. She was a no-nonsense woman and gave Elizabeth a severe look.

'Now then, love, I read your reference. Mr Jackson and I run a respectable house. You're not bringing followers, are you?'

Elizabeth wasn't exactly sure what she meant. 'Followers?'

'Yes, single men or children. You're not attached, are you?'

'No,' Elizabeth assured her, feeling a little shocked. Would she have come all this way if she were attached? 'No followers.'

Mrs Jackson nodded with satisfaction. 'Good. We don't abide women of easy virtue. Or hire single mothers. They bolt with the first wink and a nudge. Like our last girl.'

Elizabeth sat up straight in her chair and looked the woman in her eye, like she'd been told to by her father. It was time to set the record straight. 'You can be assured Mrs Jackson, I have no such intentions. I'm a good worker. I understand my position.'

The woman's eyes shifted a little. 'And coming from Van Diemen's Land. No ... history?'

There was no doubt what she was referring to. Was she a convict? Were her folk? 'My family arrived free, Mrs Jackson. My record is clean.'

The contract was agreed to, the household duties outlined. Cleaning the floors and guest rooms, washing clothes and linen, ironing clothes, preparing meals, washing up dishes, lighting ovens, collecting water from a well. No fraternising, no drinking liquor, no being idle. Sundays off, 20 shillings wage a week plus food and lodgings.

Elizabeth collected her luggage and took a coach cab with Mrs Jackson to the boarding house at Bridge Street. Her new life at Sandhurst began.

John's Letter

Richard had worked as a labourer on a farm at Dunolly for two years now. He was down and out, most of his savings gone. The gold riches that he and William Green had chased had eluded them. They'd been driven off their worthless claims. Exhausted from constant digging, cradling and panning dirt in gullies and creek beds with little reward. Only a dozen small nuggets and a handful of gold flakes, hardly enough to pay for food. They couldn't afford to keep paying their licence fees; prospects were getting grim. They had worked like dogs for twelve months, digging with picks and shovels up and down the gullies, panning in mud, sleeping in a hovel of a tent, freezing in winter, sweltering in the summer heat, fighting with other diggers, cowering from the goldfields police, the hated traps. Their miners licence cost thirty shillings a month, which ate through their depleted savings. By the end, their money and luck had gone and so had their friendship. They abandoned their claim, sold most of their mining equipment, and walked away with a handshake.

They bid each other farewell.

'Where to now, William?'

'Back to sea. Another ship, I reckon. And you?'

'Dunno. Go where the wind takes me, I suppose. Fare thee well, mate.'

Where to now? Richard thought. *Not back to sea. I've had enough.* He wandered aimlessly at first, following rough tracks in his horse and cart, only few belongings, mostly carpentry tools – a handsaw, hammer, adze, broadaxe, auger, chisels and a pickaxe – camping at night, watching the stars, looking for a sign. He followed Sirius, the star of the east in the southern sky, then turned north and ended up at Dunolly, 17 miles west of Sandhurst. *Another goldfield, another chance.*

Drink and a public house had stopped him. Liquor on hand at a bar, a crowded room and better food. He found a place to sleep and got work as a bush carpenter. Casual labour at a property known as Halfway House and Hotel on the road, halfway between Kingower and Dunolly, owned by a man called William Tyler. It was a popular resting place for diggers and a staging post for Cobb and Co. coaches.

He worked on Tyler's property doing all kinds of jobs – building fences, raising a stable, adding a veranda to the front of the hotel. By day he laboured in the hot sun, six days a week from dawn till dusk, doing what he did best, working with wood. At night he drank his wages away in whiskey, beer and rum. He lived in a lean-to cabin next to the stable, sleeping in a bunk he made himself with ropes stretched across it. At night, he became a drunk, but Tyler didn't care as long he was sober each day. As long as he got the job done. Richard led quiet, solitary life, and didn't cause a problem with the guests; he was taciturn by nature anyway.

One afternoon in October Richard was sawing timber in the yard, bare-chested and sweaty, when William Tyler walked over with some news.

'Belsar,' Tyler called out. 'Take a smoko break,' and handed him a rolled cigarette while he sat on a post rail. 'I just returned from Sandhurst,' Tyler said. 'There's a notice at the postal office. A list of unclaimed and dead letters is nailed on the postmaster's wall, published in the *Government Gazette*. It says, "Richard Belsar, Colony of Victoria, number 316". Must be yours, hey?'

'Me, a letter?' replied Richard. For a moment he looked puzzled. If true, if this letter was for him, it might be from home. It was years since he'd sent a letter to his ma – a few short words to let her know he was in Port Phillip. After years at sea, he wanted to let her know he was alive, comfort her poor heart, and reach across the vast ocean to put her mind at rest before she became too old.

Perhaps it was news from Liverpool. She would be what, 54 or 55 in age now? He had penned his brief note, poorly written in a shaky hand, and had given it to a ship returning to Liverpool over two years ago.

Dear Mother, I hope God is watching over you, my brothers and sisters, and you and Pa are in good health. I am no longer a sailor. I am in the Colony of Victoria, to seek my fortune, near a town called Sandhurst. Blessed wishes. Your loving son, Richard.'

He looked at Tyler, wiping the sweat from his brow with his handkerchief. 'What do I do? How do I get this letter?'

'Ride to Sandhurst and see the postmaster. Give him your name and the number. Or you can give a signed note to Smithy's next coach run. He can collect it for you.'

Richard pondered his choices. Lose a few days' pay or wait for next week's mail run. 'I'll talk to Smithy. I can write my name and number.'

Richard waited nervously for the letter to arrive the following week, anxious it might only bring bad news. He thought of home, of Liverpool and its filthy docks. His brothers and sisters, some dead and gone. The bustling old city of squalor. His tough old pa who sometimes hit him yet had taught him so much about hard work and ships. His adventures as a boy exploring the banks of the Mersey. Freezing, overcast days in winter. The green of spring. But mostly he thought of his mother.

When the coach eventually arrived, he left work to wait by the hotel's staging rail. Smithy's six-horse coach pulled to a stop in a cloud of dust, laden with passengers and goods. After helping to unload the cases and supplies, Richard lifted the locked mailbox out and took it inside. Tyler was waiting by the bar. 'Give it here. Let's see what we've got,' Tyler said.

He unlocked it and rummaged through the packages and letters, removing those addressed to Dunolly diggers. 'Here you go, Belsar. Here's yours.'

The letter was thick, sealed in wax paper, looking battered and beaten, with his name faded from months at sea.

He gently cut open the wax envelope with his pocket-knife, careful not to damage what was inside. He sat and unfolded the letter to read. What he saw in the opening line surprised him. The letter was from John, his brother! There were two pages of neat handwritten words, in copperplate, with flourishes and swirls, too difficult and too long for Richard to read easily.

He looked at Tyler. 'Can you help me? I can't properly read all of this.' Tyler sat down, put on his glasses and read it to him.

22 February 1853

Salt Lake City

Dear Brother

I truly hope this letter finds you, wherever you are. If it does, then God has smiled on me, for I am a pilgrim in his Light. My missive will have travelled the world for I am now living in the United States of America. I had news from our family in Liverpool, before I left on my journey on the Overland Trial, and they said you are living in the Goldfields in the new Colony of Port Phillip, somewhere in Australia. May you be blessed and hopefully remain in good health. First, news from our home. Our Father has died, leaving this Earth and our dear Mother in 1851. Our young brother James was convicted and transported for seven years, departing Liverpool with other convicts in July 1847 to a place called Moreton Bay, also in Australia. Do you know of it? Perhaps someday your paths may cross. Lewis and Edward remain seamen on the high seas. Fred works as a port labourer and lives with our sister Ellen, who has taken up with a man called Smith. She has a child by him. They live in Kitchen Steet. Remember us running up and down there?

I am married. My life as a sailor is over after ten years. I have embraced the Gospel and Church of Jesus Latter Day Saints and have found my true calling. After I arrived at St Louis in Kansas, a place of wonderment, I married a widow, her name being Emma Evens, another Saint. She is a good, Godly woman. We were joined in matrimony in March 1846 and were blessed with two children, who both sadly passed at St Louis, as being God's will.

We travelled overland in a long trek to Zion in the year 1852 to the Great Basin, a place called Salt Lake, suffering much hardship over many months. I left St Louis on the wagon train with my Emma, her mother Mary Stand Evans, a friend John Carpenter, his wife and children, and another 220 souls. Our company took many months, with 33 wagons, cattle and horses, across great rivers and over rugged mountains. We suffered much sorrow and hardship, but now live with our brethren, building our lives with thousands of other Saints. Ground has been broken for farming, irrigation ditches made, buildings erected, potatoes grown. We are a beacon of light in Salt Lake and settlers keep arriving to build our city.

I recall sometimes, Richard, the times we played together. How I looked up to you! You protected me in the street, helped feed me, took me aboard ships at dock. Helped get my apprenticeship on the ship Wilberforce. I will pray for you. I trust this missive finds you in good health. I would dearly like to hear from you.

Your Brother and fellow servant in the Kingdom of God.

John Belsar, Esq.

Tyler looked up and took off his glasses. 'Well, I bet that's a jolt. Mormons! I guess you need to think things over. Take your time, mate. No rush.' Tyler could be good like that; he was a decent boss. While Tyler employed Richard at his station, he allowed him to work with other landowners in the district. He handed Richard back the letter and walked away, shaking his head, telling his men to pack the crates of liquor in his storeroom.

Richard's head was spinning as he sat pondering the news in his brother's letter. It had taken two years to arrive, and it was a stroke of luck that Tyler had noticed it. He knew that John had always been religious – the serious one, taking after ma in that way – but what was this strange Mormon church he wrote of? The family had grown up Catholic. That he could understand. But who and what were these Saints? And where was this place he called Zion?

The news about the old man shocked him the most. Tough as nails and strong as an ox. Gone! He felt overwhelmed, more alone than he'd felt before. Then there was James, a convict, living somewhere in the colony of New South Wales, sent to a place called Moreton Bay. He needed a map to find out where it was.

For the first time in his life, Richard was overcome with homesickness. He was well and truly on his own, disconnected in a family spread around the world. He knew he would never to see any of them again.

You can find John Belsar (his surname is spelt as Balser) and his wife Emma Sarah Evans in the Church of Latter-Day Saints' extensive family history records. They were pioneers on the Overland Trail of America, crossing in a wagon train from east to west. He and Emma had 10 children, including two sets of twins, many who died young.

John lived in Salt Lake City with his family for the rest of his life and became a Sunday school teacher, carpenter and manufacturer of tents and awnings. He died in 1899 aged 75. His obituary and picture are in the Mormon's book, digitised online: *Pioneers and Prominent Men of Utah: Comprising Photographs, Genealogies, Biographies.*

Sandhurst

Tyler's Halfway House had expanded and business was profitable. It was in a perfect location on the track midway between two rich goldfields, Dunolly and Kingower. Hundreds of weary diggers, many with wives and children, travelling on foot or by dray, stopped for a meal of roast mutton and a drink of ale and tea or ginger beer at the hotel.

Tyler was pleased with Richard's work around the property. He became a foreman of sorts and often suggested improvements before Tyler could think of them himself. In winter, Richard dug a well by the creek and lined it with stone to keep it clear and fresh. He built yards for the dairy cows and pens to hold them for milking. He covered the stable with shingles and put an enclosed roof on the veranda to shade the house. He enjoyed the physical labour, working with his hands. There was a natural rhythm to it. Each task calculated and planned, first in his mind: the depth of the well for water, the angles to saw trusses on the stable roof, the lengths of posts and rails for the veranda. Sometimes he sketched the designs on paper. Mostly, he solved joinery problems in his mind. He knew the carpenter's adage: measure twice, cut once. He even helped teach some of the boys from time to time, the stable hands and grooms from the coaching station, who took an interest in learning carpentry.

Occasionally, Richard fossicked in the nearby common field, one that had been worked over, but only scratched out small flakes of gold here and there, enough to pay for a glass or two of whiskey at Tyler's bar. Nothing to get excited about; he didn't want to become a serious miner. Not since he'd lost most of his savings with William Green on their ill-fated journey to Forest Creek. If he got lucky and found a small nugget or two, he'd ride to Sandhurst with Smithy on the Cobb coach mail run, 35 miles away, and get it assayed at the gold office. A few extra pounds in his pocket. Enough for a night out at the Shamrock Hotel, or some new boots. The money was spent as quickly as it was earned.

There'd been talk in Sandhurst recently about a rowdy performance at the Theatre Royal where a visiting performer, a woman dancer called Lola Montez, kicked up her skirts and showed off her bare legs. They'd been an enormous fracas during the show when she performed her spider dance.

'Sandhurst city officials are up in arms about it,' one of the miners told him, in between bites of his meal. 'But I thought it was pretty good myself. We tossed nuggets on the stage floor, would you believe!' Richard saw a gleam in his eye that made it pretty clear what had appealed to him.

Hm, might be worth a look, he thought, *next time I'm in Sandhurst.* The idea sat with him, fermenting in his subconscious, until he decided to do something about it. A week later he asked Tyler. 'Mind if I make the next resupply trip to Sandhurst?'

Tyler nodded from behind the bar, where he was busy cleaning glasses. 'Aye. We could do with more liquor. Beer and rum kegs are low. Been a busy month. Go see my missus. She'll write a list for such things. A flitch of bacon, extra bags of flour and vegetables, and other stuff. And she'll give you a cash advance.'

Tyler ordered his supplies from a general store in Sandhurst: bags of flour and sugar, crates of brandy, rum and whiskey, casks of salt, barrels of tobacco, sacks of vegetables, and bacon if they were lucky. Usually, he or Richard took turns to drive their wagon, harnessing the horses early so they could get there in a day, in the daylight. Night travel was always dangerous on the roads with bushrangers and thieves about. They would return the following day. If they couldn't make the journey before nightfall, due to wet weather, or breakdown or delay of any kind, they stayed in Sandhurst or stopped at one of the farms along the Sandhurst road. They never camped out alone.

Richard left at dawn and made good time. He arrived at Sandhurst by mid-afternoon.

The general store owner on Bridge Street, an elderly Englishman named Morgan Burgess, was obliging, and helped Richard with his order, loading the dray, tied up and ready for Richard's departure the following morning.

'You can lock it down here and stable your horses, if you wish,' Burgess said. 'I unlock the stable gate early each day.'

His horses were watered and fed and secured in the grocer's rear yard overnight.

'Can you suggest a place nearby to stay?' Richard asked. 'Nothin' fancy.'

'Best place close by is down the street,' said Burgess. 'Mr Jackson's boarding house. Clean rooms, good rates.'

'And meals?'

'Food is good, I hear. No complaints in that aspect. There's a bath a well.'

Richard walked down the street and saw Jackson's name on a small wooden sign by the front door.

Boarding House, Only Respectable Customers Apply, Overnight Accommodation, Separate Rooms, Moderate Rates, Abstinence Society Pledge Book to be Signed.

Richard rang the bell and waited for the front door to open, thinking there would be no drinking at the Shamrock Hotel if he decided to stay there.

He turned to leave as a small, elderly man opened the door. 'Can I help you, sir?' He looked up at Richard staring blankly, waiting for a reply. 'Cat got your tongue?'

'Well, I'm looking for a room. Just overnight. And a bath. Mr Burgess up the road told me of you. But if you're full ...'

'Sir, we have overnight lodging. Separate bed, five shillings overnight. One shilling for the evening meal, another shilling for a bath.' The elderly man was bald with a hooked nose had a crooked smile, showing several missing front teeth. He extended his hand. 'Mr William Jackson, proprietor.'

They shook hands. 'Richard Belsar. Pleased to meet you.'

He walked inside. A long hallway painted in rich maroon extended to a rear kitchen, with an impressive staircase leading to the second level. On the sides of each wall were large framed Georgian portraits of individuals in formal attire and English landscapes. A massive picture of Queen Victoria sat above the sitting room door.

'A new lodger, Mrs Jackson,' the old man announced, as they walked down the hallway. 'A Mr Belsar, ready to sign in. One night.'

Mrs Jackson appeared from the parlour room, looking somewhat flustered, wearing an apron covered in flour. A stern-faced woman of equal temperament. 'Well, sort him out, Mr Jackson. Can't you see I'm busy with bread? Extra seat for dinner I expect?' she asked brusquely.

'Er, yes, that would be appreciated,' said Richard. 'If it's no bother.'

'Seven sharp,' she said. 'And be clean and tidy, if you don't mind.' With that she turned on her heel and left, leaving Richard with her husband to pay and sign his pledge not to drink alcohol.

The hot bath was luxurious; a rare treat compared to a splash bowl and damp cloth he used each evening to wipe off the dirt and grime after a day's labour. Richard lay with his knees up until the water was almost cold. He scrubbed his skin with a sponge, washed his hair with soap, soaked and hung out his used clothes, then shaved. He put on fresh clothes and felt refreshed.

It was ten minutes past seven o'clock.

The dining room had three other guests, all seated and waiting to be served. They looked like city workers wearing crisp linen shirts, collars, and ties. Bank jockeys or shop assistants, perhaps. Not the kind of men Richard was used to. One had Macassar-oiled hair and a waxed moustache pointing up either side of his cheeks.

'Our new guest,' the man said extending his arm. 'A miner, I presume. Take a seat quickly before Mrs Jackson scolds you for being late,' he said. 'Reginald Smyth. How do you do, sir?'

Richard took a seat. 'Richard Belsar from Kingower.'

'Told you so. Another miner in from the bush. And these two chaps are Simon Curruthers and Peter–'

Before he could finish, Mrs Jackson swept in with a pot of hot stew, placing it on the table, with a stern look at Richard. 'Oh, you're here now, Mr Belsar. Well, in this establishment, we run on time if you don't mind. Punctuality is good manners, I say.'

'I'm sorry, missus,' said Richard. 'The quality of your house, the warmth of your bath and the smell of your cooking simply swept me away.' He sat back and stared directly into her eyes, challenging her moodiness with a slow smile.

'Well then,' she replied, her eyes softening. 'No matter. Enjoy your dinner. Mutton stew and potatoes. Serve yourselves.' She turned abruptly and left.

'You charmer,' whispered Smyth. 'Stood up well to the old girl. Here, pass your plates. I'll serve now she's left.'

They tucked into their meal, ladled a second serve, and waited for their empty plates to be taken from the table.

Instead of Mrs Jackson returning, another woman entered the room. Younger, brighter, better looking.

'This is Miss Carter, our delightful housemaid. The one reason we remain at this boarding house,' Smyth said to Richard, by way of introduction. 'Eliza, meet our new guest, Mr Belsar.'

There was a moment's embarrassed formality. Elizabeth Carter seemed a little distracted for a second as their eyes met. Then she gathered herself, even bobbed a small curtsey. 'Pleased to meet you,' then she collected their empty plates and left.

Richard stared, momentarily frozen. The room seemed silent ... or was it his head?

It took Smyth's voice to bring him back to the table. 'Like I said, old boy. Lovely girl. Quiet, but delightful. Kept on a tight rein by Mrs Jackson. We've all tried to chat her up. I met her in a coach on our way to Sandhurst. I've asked her out several times. Even invited her to a picnic at the park on a Sunday. No such luck.' Then he leaned over, with a sly leer in his eye, and whispered, 'But I'll have her one day soon. Mark my words.'

Richard stood up, stretching his legs. He was in no mood for the company of these men, particularly the lascivious Smyth. 'Well, gentlemen, if you'll excuse me, I plan to take a short stroll before bed. I need to check my horses and gear. And it's an early start in the morning. Nice to meet you. Goodnight.'

'Don't be late, Belsar,' said Smyth. 'Doors closed tight at nine o'clock, sharp. If Mrs Jackson smells a whiff of liquor on your breath, you'll be locked out.'

He walked up the street, all the while thinking of Eliza. There was something about her stare. Her dark eyes were quick and sharp. The look she'd given him, taking in his measure, confident yet reserved. Had there been a shy smile?

In the dimness, he passed the grocer's shop and entered the side yard. He saw his horses in the stable, then suddenly felt the hairs on the back of his neck rise. The horses looked skittish, tossing their heads, struggling to move in their hobbles. Something was wrong. Someone was out there, moving in the shadows behind the dray.

Richard crouched down, approached slowly, step by step, then yelled, 'Who's there? Show yourself!' He was about to leap around the dray, fists ready, blood up, prepared for a fight, but was hit hard by something on the back of his head, sending a bolt of pain through his brain. Then everything went black.

He woke sometime later, lying on the ground, his head throbbing, eyes blurry and spinning. He felt a lump on the back of his head and his fingers came away wet with blood. He struggled to his feet and walked to the dray, now empty. At least the horses had settled. The lights were off in the store. He had no idea of the time. Cursing his bad luck, he walked slowly back to the boarding house, there being little he could do tonight, whatever time it was. Perhaps he'd report the theft to the police in the morning.

He was about the ring the bell, then saw a light in a window by the side of the house, near the kitchen. Better to wake one of the men, rather than wake the household.

He knocked on the window, 'Smyth, is that you? Or Curruthers.' What was the other man's name? He couldn't recall. 'It's Belsar. I've been mugged. I can't get back in. Can you help?' No sound, then he heard the sound of soft footsteps, coming to the window.

'Who's there?' A woman's voice. For a moment he was unsure if it was Mrs Jackson. It sounded too young. 'It's me, Richard Belsar. I'm sorry to disturb you but I've been attacked. Can you let me in?'

The window opened slightly, enough for a pair of eyes to see for herself. 'Wait,' said Elizabeth. 'Be quiet or Mr or Mrs Jackson will hear. Come to the front door, I'll let you in. Not a sound. Go.'

Richard walked back to the door and waited. He heard a key turn at the lock, then the handle turned and the door opened. Inside was Elizabeth Carter, in a nightgown, holding a candle. 'Come in quickly. Quiet! Do you know the hour?' she whispered.

As Richard walked past her, she gasped. 'You're hurt. Are you drunk?'

'No, I was checking my horses and supplies before bed and was attacked. The curs stole my supplies. A coward's strike from behind.'

'Quiet. Go through to the kitchen. Everyone's asleep upstairs. It's one in the morning.'

They walked carefully to the kitchen and Elizabeth placed the candle on the bench.

'Here, sit down. Let me see,' she said. She took his head in her hand and parted his hair. Richard leaned over so she could inspect the wound. 'Lump the size of a goose egg, and bleeding still. Hold there while I clean it.'

She took a clean cloth, wet it with water and soap, then washed the wound and removed as much sticky blood as she could. She went to a cabinet and took a small bottle of ointment and applied it to the cut, then pressed another folded pad of linen on his head. 'Hold that while I bind it.' She wrapped a roll of ribbon around his head to hold the cloth.

'Now, at least you won't stain your pillow. It may not look serious, but that lump is enormous. Knocked out, were you? You'll have a concussion. That can be serious, might cause bleeding inside the brain.'

'I'll survive. I've had worse.'

'No doubt. But you need to rest. But remain awake for half an hour. Then tap three times on the floor so I know you're well. If you get sick, or vomit or have blurry vision, bang on the floor. I'll hear it. Your room is above mine. I'll get the doctor. Now get to bed.' She pushed him away and started to clean up the kitchen.

'Thank you, Elizabeth,' he said. 'I believe you've saved me.' He took hold of her hand and kissed it before walking back to his room.

The following morning, Richard woke with a splitting headache. He did what she had asked, lying restlessly for half an hour, tapping three times, thinking of her downstairs.

He slept in late and took his time packing up. He removed the binding and combed back his hair, tying it in a pigtail to conceal the wound, then washed his face and drank a glass of water, before walking downstairs to the dining room. There was tea, coffee, milk and porridge still on the servery table, even at this late hour of 9:30 by the wall clock. He sat and poured himself a large cup of coffee when Elizabeth walked in.

'How are you this morning, Mr Belsar?' she asked.

'It's Richard, please. All the better for seeing you. Again, thank you for your help last–'

'Mr Belsar!' All of a sudden Mrs Jackson appeared from the kitchen. 'Late again, I see. You're lucky we are such good Christian folk and look after our guests, even indolent ones. I trust you slept well?'

'I am in your debt, Mrs Jackson. Your house is a haven of charity for the humble worker.'

She stared at him, unsure whether he was being genuine or not. 'Well, I expect you'll be on your way now, Mr Belsar. Safe travels in the bush. I hope we see you again one day.'

'You can be sure of that, Mrs Jackson.'

Richard looked once more at Elizabeth, and quietly passed the cloth and ribbon to her, holding her hand for a moment. A light touch. She smiled at him – a genuine smile, wide and friendly.

He picked up his bag and put his hand on her shoulder, a simple gesture, not assertive or impolite, and looked into her eyes. 'May I see you again next week, when I return?'

'I'll be here,' she said.

Standing there, holding his stained cloth and ribbon, she watched him leave.

Kingower

The loss of Tyler's supplies was duly reported to the police but as expected, nothing happened. Richard made a statement before he left, a constable writing down the charge on paper for him to sign.

The store grocer, Morgan Burgess, hadn't seen or heard anything. While apologetic, he said he couldn't take responsibility for the theft. He did, however, agree to resupply most of the stolen goods at a reduced rate for Richard to take back to Tyler's hotel.

When he returned late that day, William Tyler was furious, more so about losing his money than in Richard's assault. 'Why leave the packed dray in the yard? Surely you could have stowed it in the morning?' he yelled.

'I planned to head off at first light. Burgess said it was safe in the yard.'

'What were you thinking, man?'

'You can dock my wage,' said Richard, knowing it was worth two weeks of his labour.

'Don't be a fool, man,' he said, shaking his head and walking away to unload the dray. 'What's done is done. The gold fields are full of thieves and blackguards – weekly robberies on roads in plain daylight. Yesterday, another stabbing at McKenzie Creek!'

Richard wandered back to his room. His head hurt and he took a swig of whiskey from a bottle he kept by his bed to dull the pain, all the time thinking he needed to somehow make a quid, knowing he'd eventually have to return to the diggings. Labouring and carpentry, where did that get him? Low wages and no savings.

The diggers passing through kept saying Kingower had a new gold field. They claimed it was large and rich. Hundreds of miners kept arriving. There were camps all over the creeks, with a big quartz crushing machine, a gold commissioner, and general stores, butchers, blacksmiths, even a public house. The yield, some claimed, was the best ever!

But they always said that. Gold fever had set in again. Richard was distrustful of diggers; he knew their boast and garrulous exaggeration, their intense excitement and greed. He knew the odds – few winners, mostly losers. He knew the physical hardship of the camps, the fights that broke out between Germans and Irish, the racial hatred of the Chinese.

Despite all this, he looked at his future, not in years, but months. He was 39. He'd saved little. He owned a cart, a swag and tent, his carpentry tools. What choice did he have? Buckley's or none. He had to go back to the diggings.

By late afternoon, he'd packed his kit and was ready to leave. He walked to the hotel to see Tyler, who was serving drinks at the bar, now filled with weary men looking for a hot meal before they set off for camp by the creek.

Tyler watched him as he came over. 'Saw you packing up Belsar. Heading off, are you?'

'Heading to Kingower fields. Try my luck again.'

'Well, good fortune to you, Belsar. Let bygones be. You've been a good worker and a mate. Hope you strike some nuggets. Come back here if you do and spend your fortune.'

'Thanks, William, I'll see you around.'

'Wait,' said Tyler. He turned and walked to the cash box, taking some notes and stuffed them in an envelope. 'Here, take this. Help get you started. Let me know how you go.'

By the time Richard arrived at Kingower diggings, he saw a sprawling camp that looked like any other. Barren, treeless and dusty, tents and bark huts, mounds of rocky soil and mullock heaps. Crude shanties and timber windlasses hauling dirt up from pits. Miners scattered everywhere. A butcher shop with fly-ridden meat hanging from hooks. Hawkers in coffee tents selling sly grog. Shoeless children and mangy dogs running about. A general store selling wheelbarrows, picks and spades.

He passed rough, bearded men winching crushed rock, and puddling clay in circular troughs. Hard men, yelling in foreign languages - German, French, Irish, even Italian - all hustling, running, appearing from holes in the ground, digging, always digging. The creek panners had mostly moved on, the easy alluvial gold had gone.

Now it was deep pits. A mining company had moved in, chasing a lucrative quartz reefs. Men with capital, shareholders and investors, crushing machines, employing labourers.

Richard camped at the outskirts, then the next morning sought out the warden to get his mining licence. He asked a digger sitting idly outside his tent next to his claim. 'Morning, friend. Where can I find the warden?'

The digger eyed him over. 'New chum, are you? Official business or what?'

"I'm looking for a miners right and place a claim,' said Richard. 'How's your luck? Any unworked ground left?'

'Ha,' the digger chortled. 'Most ground around here is already taken, mate. Only ground left is at Long Gully, a mile or so south. A few diggers tried it, sunk a few shafts, came back empty. Don't reckon it's any good myself. Bad dirt, and no leads. Licence day is next Wednesday when the warden's back. At the police hut with the flag.'

Richard knew the miner's right had replaced the gold license in May 1855 and cost one pound per annum. A digger holding a miner's right could dig for gold and had the right to take a parcel of land, even erect a cottage on it with a garden. It also gave him the right to graze animals on the goldfield's commons and vacant Crown land. He planned to take several 12-foot square claims with an alluvial lease, perhaps with a partner. If he failed, he could find wage work with the mining company. He'd heard some paid wages of six pounds a week – good money – just to keep miners from leaving. More than twice what he'd earned with Tyler.

Crossing the spurs and gullies was rough going with his cart. He passed groups of men working shafts, trying to wash dirt to get to the richer bottom, where gold might be hiding. He greeted them, but they mostly remained silent, looking on suspiciously, not wanting strangers to know about their find or jump their claim.

After several hours of struggle, he stopped at a plain where the gully widened, surrounded by high rocky outcrops. There were a few abandoned pits and some fresh water in the creek from recent spring rain.

Perhaps this is Long Gully, he thought. He studied the lay of the land, the direction of run-off and type of rock. He assessed the potential, a conjunction of two gullies, which always helped. Downstream was a plain of gravel and finer dirt, chunks of scattered quartz, pools of water. *You must have water.*

Fifty yards ahead he noticed a man working half-underground, singing while shovelling dirt with a spade. He looked old, rangy, and grey-haired with a wrinkled face. He was wearing dirty clothes, his boots thick with mud, and was singing to himself.

'G'day, mate. How goes it?' said Richard.

The old man stopped singing and looked up. 'Ho, old China. A few nuggety specimens here and about. You here for a claim?'

'Hope to if none's taken. Ground here looks promising.'

'Plenty to go around now you're away from Mckintyre's camp. A group of fools walked off here last week. Kept following a lead higher up, found nothin'. Watched them, I did, chasing fool's gold.' The old man lifted his arm, a bony finger pointing. 'They were digging in the wrong spot.'

'That so?' said Richard. 'Seems you got the right idea. Digging here near water, sieving and washing. Not cracking quartz.'

'You're right there.' Then he started spading, singing again, 'Hm, a nugget is found, then they rush the ground, but most look sad and melancholy ...'

Richard smiled at the old man. 'I'll head down there a bit if it's all right with you.' He began to lead his cart before turning to ask, 'What's your name?'

'Sampson Fish.'

'Well, pleased to meet you, Sampson Fish. Mine's Richard Belsar. Maybe we can share a billy, some damper and a tot of rum tonight.'

'Good-o. Love me rum, tum-tum-a-tum. Fare thee well, Mr Belsar.'

After Richard had unpacked and pitched his tent – canvas thrown over a timber frame and pegged to the ground – he pegged his claim, three 12-foot square areas, and got to work. As they were isolated, he thought he'd dig shallow exploratory holes with a pick and shovel, wetting the dirt from wood buckets as he worked, searching for nuggets. He had supplies of tea, sugar, flour, salted mutton, oats and rum to last two weeks.

It was hard going. Made worse by the heat of summer. The top wash soil was dry and rocky, jarring his arms, but he broke the ground quickly, his strong back and hands moving rhythmically, conditioned by years of hard labour. He looked carefully at each shovel load for a glint of colour, then threw the dirt and clay onto his cart to wheel to the creek. He threw buckets of water into the hole. A few tiny specks of gold appeared, giving him hope he'd found the right area.

Richard laboured for days, digging, washing, panning, picking specks out of his ever-growing pile of dirt. It was backbreaking work, surfacing and roving the topsoil. He dug and hauled his cart, washed and puddled the dirt, cut his hands and arms, his boots and feet soaked in mud. At night, he sat by the fire with Sampson Fish, eating the same monotonous food, drinking rum, then collapsed and fell asleep, sometimes drunk, always exhausted.

Fish showed Richard his haul of small nuggets, perhaps 10 ounces. He talked about what he'd do once he'd had enough of digging. 'A little cottage at Saint Arnaud. I'll bring up Mrs Fish, then put me feet up. Sit and smoke me pipe.'

'You married, then?' Richard asked.

'Have been 10 years now. Diggin's ain't a place for a woman. I'm gettin' too old for this life,' Fish said. 'It's me last shot.' He stared at the embers and scratched his beard. 'Diggin's for dreamers. Few make it, most don't. Get out while you can. Or you'll die from dysentery, fever or snakebite. Want some advice? Find a good woman. Settle down.'

He smoked his pipe, stared at the stars, hummed, then in a low voice, sang, 'Mothers mourn their manly dears, wives they miss their men, women mourn their sweethearts true, Lord, I'm coming home to you ...'

That night was empty and desolate. Richard never felt more alone or forlorn, the old man's song ringing in his ear. He had no one. No sweetheart to share his life, no prospects for a family of his own.

The next day, sweating in the hot sun, he thought about what Sampson Fish had said. Working his claim, heaving and digging, thinking of his childhood at Liverpool, his years at sea, his failure mining with William Green. Still a single man. *What have I achieved?*

His thoughts turned to Elizabeth Carter, who'd helped him at the boarding house, her dark eyes, her confident hands holding his head. Could he ever hope – a rough labourer, a poor carpenter, owner of no property?

He picked, he dug, he washed. He felt unwell, his stomach beginning to cramp.

Two more days, digging deeper, another hole. Nothing of any note – only specks, teasing and frustrating. He coughed, spitting phlegm, cursing the ground, and was about to stop for a rest and get something to eat when he struck a small rock and saw a flash of colour. He threw water onto it and more colour appeared. It was gold about the size of his little finger.

He pulled it out and kept digging. Another piece, then another. Some round, some flat, the size of shillings. Some chunks attached to quartz. His heart raced, blood pumping through his veins. He dug faster, sprinkled water over the dirt, found more nuggets, golden and heavy. Pockets of the stuff!

'Fish, here, come here! Look!' he cried.

Sampson Fish came out from his hole and walked over. 'Belsar you've made it. You're up in the stirrups now!' he shouted.

The gold trader at Kingower weighed and assessed Richard's nuggets. He looked efficacious, like an accountant inspecting financial records, as he meticulously measured the gold with his bronze balance scale. 'Eight-five ounces, and ninety-nine per cent pure,' he said. 'That's good quality gold, digger. Any idea what this is worth?'

'Not really. Maybe £100?'

'You'll get about £325. Maybe more.'

Richard's heart missed a beat.

'Here's my receipt of assessment. You can take it to a dealer in Melbourne for payment, if you want. Most diggers ride to Melbourne with the police escort with their gold and sell it to the government at the treasury building.'

'What if I don't want to go? Would you buy it?'

'Well,' the agent said, thinking about the risk. 'Maybe, I could strike some kind of deal. Not full price, mind you. But you'd need to sell your licence to me and sign a receipt of sale. I'd have to carry the risk of travel.'

'I'll sell it for £300. Not a penny less.'

The trader paused a moment, stroking his chin. He knew the deal was in his favour and wondered about bargaining further. Squeezing the digger some more. He knew he stood to make a quick £30 pounds. In the end, he decided not to haggle.

'Agreed,' the dealer said.

They shook hands and the dealer got to working scribbling out their agreement.

Richard collected his miner's right and returned to the trader's tent before he left, making sure his find was good and legal, and was paid in cash. Even with a retching cough, he walked out of the camp with a smile on his face.

Richard was a wealthy man with £300 in his pocket. Enough to leave the diggings, buy a good horse, a harness and new spring cart, get some decent clothes and have a long break to regain his health. Decide what to do next. First, he needed some rest. The coughing fits were worse. He felt hot with fever, like an infection was coming on.

He rolled his notes tightly into the whalebone he wore around his neck, packed up his swag and tools, and led his horse and cart out of the camp, back to Tyler's house. He couldn't get there fast enough, passing groups of diggers coming and going on the road to Dunolly. Yet he felt exposed, standing out to thieves and cutthroats – an easy mark, nervously thinking everyone was watching him, following him, smiling suspiciously, ready to steal his money.

He struggled on a few miles more, lying prone on the seat. Then he broke out in another coughing fit. Wave after wave of pain bent him over double. He struggled to breath. The whalebone seemed to burn around his neck. How he kept upright, he didn't know.

Just as he was about to collapse, Tyler's hotel appeared. Richard fell off the cart and crawled into his room at the barn, climbed on his hard bed, fainted, then went into blackness.

Elizabeth

March 1856

Elizabeth was busy cleaning rooms at Jackson's boarding house, removing bed sheets for washing in the copper in the outside laundry at the rear of the house.

She was hot from climbing the stairs for the fourth time with a basket of linen and wiped the perspiration from her forehead under her bonnet. Her work dress, apron, petticoat, stockings, and tight shoes restricted her when she carried the heavy loads up and down the narrow stairwell. The boarders had left for the day and the Jacksons had gone to Sandhurst for supplies. She was on her own.

She sat for a moment, idly wondering if she would stay with the Jacksons for another year, as her contract agreement was coming up for renewal. It would be another 12 months if she took it on. Not that she didn't like the job. In fact, she quite enjoyed talking to the boarders, and even some of the guests. She liked to hear their stories – the far places in the world they'd travelled to. But mostly they talked of gold; everything was about gold. Where they found it, how they mined it, who invested in it. The town lived and breathed gold. She didn't understand all they said; she only heard snippets from the kitchen or when they boasted and flirted with her at the table.

She was getting older. She was 23 now, rather plain, and although she'd had several proposals of marriage, she'd turned them down. One of the boarders, Reginald Smyth, usually very talkative, had become rather distant in his conversation. At first, he seemed all charm, smiling and making jokes, then he said right out, when no one else could hear, that she would never find a better suitor than him given her poor circumstance. He actually pushed her against the wall as he said it and held her firmly, insistent to the point of being threatening. While she might have been poor, and could not write or barely read, she had a way of knowing people. He was a dandy, with his sly looks and fancy clothes. She was never going to let him get under her dress, no way, nor catch her alone in the scullery again. She made sure of that.

Elizabeth wondered occasionally what happened to the man she'd helped that night. The tall one, with his deep blue eyes, who'd knocked on her window. He'd looked strong enough, but when she'd cleaned his head wound, he'd seemed lost, trying to laugh it off, not sure what to say. He'd held her hand, touched her shoulder. He'd looked at her in a different way. He said he'd be back soon.

That was three months ago.

Her life continued in the same routine with little time for herself. Each morning, rising early to fire the oven and prepare breakfast for the guests, serving up, cleaning pots and dishes afterwards. The heat of the oven in summer in the tight confines of the kitchen was atrocious.

During the day she washed sheets and clothes in the copper tub. She ironed, sewed dresses, mopped floors, tidied rooms, all the while harried by Mrs Jackson who watched over her like a hawk. Late afternoon, she usually worked with Mrs Jackson to prepare meals for dinner. Guests came and went – there was a constant flow of people, apart from the two regulars, Reginald Smyth and Simon Curruthers.

The only day to herself was Sunday and, even then, she usually attended church in the morning. This was an expectation by the Jacksons for her moral rectitude.

Jackson's boarding house, with its order and regimen, was about to be upturned by a man they vaguely recalled, one who stayed for a night several months ago. It came out of the blue, a surprise out of nowhere. Richard Belsar knocked on the front door and asked William Jackson if he could rent a room for several weeks.

Elizabeth was upstairs cleaning a room when she heard a knock on the door; another guest perhaps, then Mr Jackson's voice of welcome. Nothing out of the ordinary. She heard footsteps in the hallway to the sitting room, murmurs of a conversation, short laughter. Just another meal to serve, another room to clean.

She paused for a moment and listened. The visitor's voice sounded vaguely familiar, but there were so many lodgers coming and going that she wasn't sure. Curious, she put aside her dust cloth, closed the door of the room behind her and went down the stairs.

The door to the sitting room was open and she saw William Jackson by his desk. The visitor had his back to her, dressed in a clean linen shirt, jacket and trousers, his hair pulled back, tied in a short ponytail.

'You would be most welcome, sir,' she heard Mr Jackson say. 'We have a good room. The rate is 30 shillings a week, with breakfast and supper included five days a week. A week's payment in advance.' Then Jackson looked toward the door and saw her. 'Yes, Miss Carter?'

The man turned. It was Mr Belsar, the one she'd helped that night. He looked older, gaunt.

William Jackson broke the silence. 'Miss Carter, we have a new lodger, a Mr Belsar. You may recall him. Can you see him to his room, then assist my wife with the evening meal?'

Elizabeth bobbed her head and took a quick breath. 'I do recall, indeed. This way, Mr Belsar.'

They walked up the stairs, Mr Belsar carrying his bag, to the same room as before. 'Miss Carter, it's pleasing to see you again. I hoped you'd be here.'

'Where else would I be?' she replied, feeling a strange flutter at his words.

'Well, I'm not sure. Married, perhaps. All I'm saying ...' He cleared his throat. 'All I'm saying is, after all these months, I'm glad to see you. I hope we may talk some more now I'm here.'

'I'll consider it,' she said and left him standing at the door, unsure what was going on. What was causing this strange feeling within her?

Richard missed the evening meal that night. He still felt weak from the sickness, his appetite lost. He heard the lodgers downstairs, their voices, and their banter. What was the man's name again – something Smyth?

Richard lay in his bed and dozed on and off, wondering how long it would take to regain his health. Dysentery, the doctor had said. Fever and sweats from bad water from the camp. He needed rest, good food and purgatives like castor oil. After two weeks at Tyler's, he'd felt he had enough energy to take the coach ride to Sandhurst. He had enough money to last several months, if needed, to recover his health. Later on, he planned to buy a good horse and a new spring cart.

But most of all, he wanted to see Elizabeth. He wanted to marry her if she would have him.

The next day, coming downstairs for breakfast, he felt better. He'd slept like a log. He was washed and clean shaven and arrived on time, not wanting to upset the officious Mrs Jackson. He greeted her with a smile and cheerful voice. 'Good morning, Mrs Jackson.'

'Ah, Mr Belsar, I see. My husband told me you were back, and for some time, I believe?'

'Yes, Mrs Jackson. I'm pleased to say I'll have the pleasure of your establishment for a few weeks.'

She looked eager to establish her authority. 'Then you will recall the rules of the house. Temperance, timeliness, testaments. Follow those simple ways and I'm sure we will get along wonderfully. Good morning to you, Mr Belsar. Enjoy your breakfast.'

He recognised the two men sitting at the dining table, the same as before. 'Good morning gentlemen, Smyth wasn't it? And ...'

'Curruthers. Simon Curruthers.'

'Back from the diggings? I must say, you look somewhat yellow, Belsar,' said Reginald Smyth. 'Been with bush diggers? Rough and ready coves, rascals mostly, if you ask me. We read dreadful stories in the newspapers. And the diggers, here in town. Atrocious behaviour! Drunken revelry in most of the hotels here. Fights and profanity. That true where you're from, Belsar?'

'Mostly true, Smyth. Diggings can be rough on men, and on women. But then, rascals are everywhere, I suppose. I've seen them all over.'

'Been around, have you, Belsar?' Curruthers said. 'Looks like you have.'

'I've been around.'

'Well, like our good lady Mrs Jackson says, we can all improve ourselves. Wherever we come from, wherever we go. I myself have taken the temperance oath never to use as a beverage of any distilled or malt liquors.'

Curruthers and Smyth finished eating their bacon and eggs and excused themselves from the table, as they were heading to work for bank opening at 10 am. Richard sat and took his time, taking a second helping, drinking coffee, savouring fresh bread and butter. He waited at the table for Elizabeth to come in, to be in the same room together. He wanted to be alone with her just for a few minutes.

When she finally came in to pick up the plates, he said straight out, 'Elizabeth ... Eliza, if I may call you that. I have something to say to you. I won't beat around the bush. I intend on winning you over.'

She didn't seem put out by what he'd said but she didn't seem particularly excited either, except perhaps for the slight tremble of her hand as she reached for the plates. 'Well, Mr Belsar, you're forward, that's for sure. You'll find I'm not as easy as you think. You may talk to me; I'll allow that. And I'll have you know I have received another proposal.'

Richard looked at her, perplexed. 'Have you accepted? Who, may I ask?'

'Well, it's someone you know, that's all I can say. Now, I must clean up.'

Richard spent the day in town at Sandhurst's sale yard inspecting horses and carts. The were several fine work horses available. He planned to buy a strong two-wheeled cart he could use to hold his camp gear, tools and supplies, enough for one strong horse to pull. A mare, he thought. Something to handle rough roads, rocky tracks and creek crossings. And a cart big enough for two people, maybe more.

Yet all the time, while talking to the yardmen and cartwrights, he worried about what Elizabeth had said. Another proposal. One of the lodgers, Smyth or Curruthers, no doubt. They were younger men, perhaps wealthier, certainly more educated than he. But they were snobbish and patronising.

He left the sale yard disheartened and empty-handed, promising to return in a few days. By mid-afternoon, he felt exhausted and breathless, and struggled to walk back up the hill to his room to sleep for an hour. He slept for three.

The evening meal was strained. Smyth, Curruthers and the owner, William Jackson, talked constantly of Sandhurst's development now the town was a municipal district with impressive new buildings everywhere: the Golden Square, Colonial Bank, Gold Office, plans for a town hall. Gold was bringing wealth. There were parks and gardens, a new railway and bridges over creeks. Agents were advertising land sales. Local elections were being held. *The Argus* newspaper was touting that very soon, Sandhurst would be bigger than Melbourne! Public houses going up everywhere, big and small: the Criterion, the Albert, the Albion, the Shamrock.

'And Bendigo Hotel, nearby on Bridge, our very street!' railed William Jackson. 'A public house. A den of thieves. And, I must say, often walking past our boarding house, drunk as skunks.'

Richard, a drinker himself – ale, whiskey, rum, brandy, anything really – who'd been drinking since he was a boy in ports and on ships from Europe to the New World, kept quiet. He knew that one wrong word would condemn him and he'd be out on his ear, especially after signing the boarding house pledge book. Then where would he stand with Elizabeth?

After the evening meal, he brought his empty plate to the kitchen while Mrs Jackson was out, finding Eliza washing by the sink.

'Would you meet me in the park tomorrow, Eliza? Being Sunday and all. I'll buy you a lemonade,' he asked.

She didn't pause in her scrubbing. 'And do what, Mr Belsar?'

'Just talk.'

'About what?'

'I dunno. I could tell you about ships, where I've been. Perhaps Liverpool, where I grew up. Or Quebec. Anything, really.'

She hesitated, looking over her shoulder, perhaps at a sound from the hallway. Then she whispered, 'I'll meet you by the fountain at midday, after church. Now leave before we're seen.'

Richard declined William Jackson's offer for a cigar or pipe in the sitting room with Curruthers and Smyth. He pleaded tiredness and need for rest, as ordered by the doctor. In reality, he wanted little to do with them. He was conscious of Eliza in her small downstairs room, a thrilling presence moving below.

Sunday was bright and sunny, and the park, the only green area that remained in town, attracted hundreds of people who came out to picnic. They sat in the shade under trees and promenaded along the creek. Children splashed in the fountain and played games.

But all this went mostly unnoticed to Richard, searching the crowd for Eliza, expecting her to walk down Bridge Street from the boarding house. He was staring up the street and was taken by surprise when she said from behind, 'You look like a nervous cat, Mr Belsar.'

He turned and saw her standing in a printed grey calico dress, one piece with the skirt attached to the waistline. She smiled at him, white-faced under her bonnet.

'Please call me Richard.'

'I can here but not in the house.'

They walked to a park seat, in the shade. She jumped in first and broke the silence. 'You were a sailor, then? Where are you from?'

He was hesitant at first. Unsure what to say. He told her about Liverpool, its crowded streets, the bustling dock, the house he'd lived in with his family, the ropery, the ships on which he'd taken his first voyages. He talked of the seas he'd sailed, the world he'd seen: Canada, France, the Atlantic, the Pacific. He spoke of Van Diemen's Land and whaling.

'I grew up there. In Hobart Town,' said Eliza. 'My parents returned to England after I came here. I don't expect I'll ever see them again.'

It was then that he took her hand – not a touch this time, but a firm hold, like she'd had once before when she'd held his injured head. 'Eliza, we're both alone, here in this new place. I don't want to be on my own no more. I want to be with you.'

'Then keep talking to me.'

Two weeks passed at the Jacksons' boarding house with Richard and Elizabeth hiding their tentative relationship, stealing glances when they could, meeting in the park. There were hidden kisses, first on the cheek, then on their lips. In secret, they made an unspoken pact to be together.

Richard knew a confrontation was coming with Reginald Smyth, the boarder Elizabeth had said expected her to submit as his wife. He would speak to him, man to man. Then there were the Jacksons to deal with.

For the first time, Richard felt a sense of hope. Slowly his strength returned, buoyed more by desire than the foul-tasting powder the doctor gave him to bind his stomach and bowels. He remained a private man, determined, and kept to his room, coming downstairs only for meals, or to see Eliza. He purchased his spring cart and a horse at the sale yard, bought new clothes, canvas and rope, blankets, a hunting rifle, new carpentry tools. Everything he needed for the road.

He planned to say it out loud, in the open the next day, and declare his intentions, what had to be said, then take Elizabeth's hand in front of the Jacksons. He felt a sense of elation and wanted to celebrate with an ale or two at the Bendigo Hotel.

The bar was brimming with men at the end of the workday, miners and labourers, travellers up from Melbourne. He ordered a beer, then a whiskey, feeling a flush of euphoria.

'Another?' the barman said.

'Why not?' Richard replied, slapping a 10-shilling note on the bar.

He left sometime later that night, unsure how much whiskey he'd consumed, thinking he'd better get back before lock-up time, the dreaded nine o'clock curfew. In his hazy grog-filled head, a singular thought appeared and stayed with him while he staggered up the street, 'I'll sneak upstairs. Tomorrow is the big day.'

He passed the front gate, stepped quietly to the front door, hand on the door, pushing carefully, door opening, nearly there. Then, appearing in directly in front of him, was the face of Reginald Smyth, with an expression Richard had seen many times before, in taverns and saloons around the world. Furious, red-faced, bursting with anger. 'You lushy cove! You dirty dog!' Smyth lashed out and king-hit him, right on the jaw, knocking him over.

The Jacksons appeared from their sitting room where Elizabeth stood, crying.

'Mr Smyth, stop at once!' Mrs Jackson screamed. 'Not in this house! One degenerate is quite enough!'

Richard, looked up from the floor, his blood up, 'Coward's punch, is it, Smyth? I'll break you, man, if I have to.' He stood up in a crouch, head lowered, ready to attack. 'Here, or out front.'

'There'll be no more of that nonsense, Mr Belsar! One move from you and I'll call the police. You're drunk. In breach of our house agreement, signed and all,' William Jackson said.

'He struck me down,' Richard said. 'You saw it.'

'Hold there, Belsar,' Jackson said pointing his finger at him. 'It seems he had every right. You have seduced our Elizabeth. Mr Smyth says she has agreed to be married to him.'

'Liar!' Elizabeth yelled, looking at Smyth. She was in tears, but she stood firm. 'That's a lie. I did no such thing. He's been in their ears all night, saying that I accepted *his* proposal. Saying we were engaged. I never did.'

'And I say you did,' said Smyth. 'You gave me a promise.'

'I'd never say such a thing to the likes of you!'

Richard stood up and walked toward Smyth, who backed off down the hall. Although drunk, the rush of adrenaline cleared his head, a deep rage building within. 'If Eliza says there was no agreement, then there is none. Say anything different and I'll have you.' He then turned to the Jacksons. 'I'll be gone in the morning. And Eliza is coming with me.'

Mrs Jackson had the last word, of course. In fact, there were many words, of which he understood most, but not all. Certainly, he understood her harsh tone. Cursing him for drunkenness, his lack of moral decency, his uncouth behaviour, his breach of agreement. Worst of all, that he'd led poor Elizabeth astray, enticed her with 'God knows what' and as for him, demanding she go with him, 'She's under contact with us and will remain so.'

'You'll sleep outside tonight and collect your things in the morning,' she said finally.

He did sleep outside in his cart, under the stars. He wasn't worried about the incident at the house; he'd been through many scrapes before, much worse than this. He'd always known from the beginning what he was going to do. Money. It always worked.

Now he had cash, he could buy out Elizabeth's contract and keep quiet the Jacksons' moral preaching. In the morning, he would find out just how much Elizabeth was worth.

Getting Hitched

There are many ways couples get hitched. Most get married in a church, surrounded by friends and family, a big occasion. Others in a registry office with a witness. Some go unrecorded by a state or church registry; a common law marriage.

Until now Richard Belsar, former seaman now labourer, had known two types of hitches. He could tie ropes: painter hitches, mooring hitches, half-hitches. He could hitch horses to wagons. Now he was about to discover a new type of hitch, one more intricate than all. He was getting hitched to Elizabeth at Kingower, back at Tyler's Halfway House and Hotel.

Tyler welcomed him back, of course. Delighted to see his old friend in good health, smiling and happy for a change, with a young woman sitting next to him. Better dressed, clean shaven and riding in a spring cart of his own. They pulled up at Tyler's veranda, the one Richard had built, and hitched the horse to the rail, then came inside. When Tyler heard the news, he back-slapped Richard in congratulations and gave Eliza a kiss on the cheek.

'Good show, man, I say! The wedding must be held here, I insist. Leave it to me and the missus. We'll put on a good day for you. I'll write to the minister at once and invite him. We'll arrange it next Sunday, 18 September 1856.'

On the day Richard stood, clean-shaven, all spruced up, his hair tied in a short ponytail, stands of grey now appearing. Elizabeth wore a light blue linen dress she'd bought at Sandhurst. In her hands was a small bouquet of wildflowers. She had on a white veil, borrowed from a guest, and wore neat black shoes instead of her usual high-laced work boots. She had made sure she had the right clothes ready for travelling on the road before they left a week prior in Richard's cart and horse, with all their worldly possessions, ready to make a new life together.

'I will go with you, Richard Belsar, but on one condition. We must get hitched right away,' she had said. He was happy to oblige.

William Tyler was delighted to host the occasion. The hotel was cleaned and decorated with coloured paper rings and bunches of wildflowers on each table. There was a roast pig in a fire pit and bread in the oven; he even shouted drinks for local guests at his bar. There were bottles of wine and two gallons of ale for the festivities. A fiddler played jigs for some light dancing. Some of the guests gave presents – pots, pans, pewter plates, a wooden chair – to help the newlyweds get started.

The service was a typical affair, bride and groom, standing together before a minister; a travelling man named James Morish, an Independent Minister from

Avoca. He gave his sermon and they both promised to be true to each other in good times and in bad, in sickness and in health. Then he said, 'What God has joined, men must not divide' and it was done.

After, there was dancing and music and drinking and singing at the hotel. Even the minister, James Morish, partook in a glass or two of rum, then gave a toast to the couple's health. No one could dance properly, so they jigged and swung, trying to keep time with the fiddler.

A Scotsman stood up with his tankard of beer, overcome by the moment, and hit the bar hard with his fist. He shushed the crowd and said he wanted to sing. 'A know a poem by a man that knows the nature of women. Rabbie Burns. About a rose, like this lass here.'

His rich, deep baritone voice filled the room, his tone rhythmic and lilting. The crowd was stilled, not a dry eye among them, as they looked at Elizabeth.

My love is like a red red rose

That's newly sprung in June;

O my Love's like the melodie

That's sweetly play'd in tune;

As fair art thou, my bonnie lass,

So deep in love am I.

And I will love thee still, my dear,

Till a' the seas gang dry ...

After the ceremony and dancing, but before too much drink was had, the minister, James Morish, sat at a table with Richard and Elizabeth to register their marriage. He opened his ledger, took a pen from his coat pocket and then wrote the date and place of the marriage. He asked them where they were born, their ages, their parents' names. Richard lied and said he was 32 years old; he was actually 41. *Should I tell Elizabeth, he thought? Perhaps best not to, at least for now.* Then he took the minister's pen and signed his name twice in a flourish of scrawling letters, the first to declare he was a member of the Independent denomination, the next to identify himself as the husband of Elizabeth.

When the minister handed the pen to Elizabeth, she hesitated and made her mark 'X', looking embarrassed by her ineptitude. The minister, tender in his manner, smiled kindly at her to put her at ease. 'It's quite alright, my dear. What you may lack in letters, you more than make up in beauty.' He took the pen and wrote her name underneath her mark. Then William Tyler and his wife came over and signed their names as witnesses.

Richard and Elizabeth settled in the Kingower district for the next two years. He built a rough hut made of timber slabs, joined with wattle and daub to fill the cracks. Mud bricks for a fireplace, shutters on windows, bark and shingles on the roof, walls lined with canvas. He carved wooden stools from logs and a table from wooden planks. He dug a well lined with stone for water.

They used candles and a kerosene lamp at night while she sewed, snug and cosy. She cooked and cleaned with a washboard and tub. Occasionally, they went to restaurants in town for soup or stews or meat pies.

She found a café owned by a Chinese family and purchased cheap food: rice, vegetables, carrots, cabbage, beans. They bought sausages and cuts of horse meat from one of the hawkers in town.

Richard was happy with his circumstances. How could he not be? He loved her, the closeness of her presence, the warmth of her skin, the giving of her body. They shared intimate thoughts and spoke of mundane things: life in the goldfields, which vegetables to grow in the garden, where to buy blankets for winter. After years of restless wandering, he felt settled for the first time in his life. He was responsible for someone other than himself.

In the summer of 1857, on a warm evening after a day's work, Elizabeth sat down at the table. 'There's something you should know. I'm pregnant.'

There was a moment's disbelief, although it was never really a surprise. It was always a matter of when, not if. Richard looked at her across the table and took hold of her hands.

'When will it be?' he asked.

'Early August, if all goes well.'

There was delight in their happiness. Their lives had shifted, again. Now they had to think of their future, how they'd survive in the years ahead. There was still some savings left from his gold, but it was quickly running out.

At the back of his mind, gnawing away, he knew he'd eventually have to return to the goldfields. It was inevitable, given his poor prospects and opportunity. He'd been lucky once before. Gold fever still burned in his dreams, as it did with everyone, as much as he hated to admit it. Just imagine! Another lucky strike. It's what everyone spoke about, not just in the diggings, but everywhere. Walking along the roads, in public alehouses, around campfires, in hardware shops, on sheep stations. By every old shepherd or new immigrant. Where to next, lads? Strike ho! Get in early! The way a poor man could get rich was to find some golden glory and live like a king.

There was talk of another field opening at a place called Mount Korong, only 15 miles away. 'Nuggets still in gullies!' a group of ragged diggers called out to Richard one winter's morning, pushing their wheelbarrows and carts stacked with picks, shovels, pans, cradles, and canvass, carrying swags on their backs, heading north to Mount Korong. 'We're off, matey. Gold lyin' on the ground. Rich pickin's!'

He watched as they walked off, bantering in hopeful optimism, to disappear in the evening shadows. Days passed as he tossed thoughts around in his head. *What do I do? Ride around to stations? Knock on doors for casual labour here and there? Or throw the dice again and dig? Strike it lucky, settle down and build a house?*

'Maybe we could go, Eliza?' Richard asked that night, unable to contain the conflicting thoughts in his head. Yearning and trepidation mixed together. 'Diggers come back, all smiles and boast. You know they got their pockets full of the stuff.' They had seen them. It was impossible not to, as the track to the diggings camp passed right by their hut. Cheerful diggers on their way back to Sandhurst or Melbourne.

'I could push hard for a few months, digging, like before. Till the baby comes.'

'As I recall, last time nearly killed you,' Eliza said.

'Aye, but I didn't have you to look after me then. Things are different now.'

'So it's flippancy, is it?' She stared at him, waiting for an explanation, words of comfort to tell her how she and the baby would be safe. 'How are things different?'

'I'd take greater care. I know what to do. I can read the land, take it easier. Get more niceties for our camp. Now we've got a good cart with can bring more. I swear I'll look after you.' He was waiting for her to decide, to determine their fate.

'Let me think of it,' she said at last. 'First, you must swear off hard liquor. Then tell me how you'll look after me, in my confinement.'

In the end, they went to try their luck. They packed enough supplies to last them until Christmas, before the summer's intense heat arrived when creeks ran dry and water ran out. They harnessed the horse to the spring cart and rode to the Korong camp, where Richard purchased a mining licence at the police commissioner's tent, then staked a claim in a crowded gulley, close to their main camp. The gulley, a desolate field of mullock dirt and broken rock, had been stripped clean of all vegetation. Already, dozens of miners were working in sinkholes and puddling in mud in the lower reaches.

When they arrived, Richard rigged their canvas tent, hewed some remaining branches to make beds, unpacked their possessions, and rugged Elizabeth up with blankets to fend off the cold days and freezing nights. He built a mud brick fireplace, with a hearth and chimney, to cook their meals and boil their water.

He judged his claim as best he could, near a confluence of narrow channels, where he could wash his dirt. Then he began to dig. To pick and shovel and barrow and puddle and wash and pray. He dug and dug, with blistered hands and cut fingers and sunburned arms and neck. He found gold, some small flakes and pebbles. A few knuckle-sized nuggets. Enough to keep them going, enough to pay for food, enough to sustain hope.

Meanwhile, Eliza grew large with child. Each day, she kept busy around their camp, washing their muddy clothes, preparing food and meals, while trying to keep herself warm. She rested when she could, which was rare, with constant work about the place. Buying meat from a butcher, making damper, grinding oats, cutting wood to keep camp the fire burning, refilling buckets of water, stewing mutton, cleaning iron pots and pans.

She always worried about the water, if it was clean or contaminated. So many seemed to be getting sick. It was dysentery, going around the camp like wildfire, affecting old and young alike, killing infants. Elizabeth became fastidious with their drinking water, making sure Richard collected it upstream and boiled whatever they drank.

Richard worked with two other men, taking turns to dig with pick and shovel, or pan and wash dirt in half-cut wooden barrels. They took turns to dig. They put down four shafts about 10 feet deep, one sinking, one bailing water out of their catch holes, one puddling and panning in barrels. It was a three-way share arrangement. Whatever gold they found was divided in thirds. But it was small takings – only a few small nuggets, and a small jar of gold flakes. Not much, but enough to keep them going, to spur them harder to dig and pan and wash. Another shaft, another catch hole.

After four months of back-breaking labour, of sweat and mud and aching backs, from dawn till dusk, they found just over 30 ounces of gold, perhaps £130 worth, after being weighed and assayed. Still, it was better than a year's wage. When they split their takings three ways, they smiled meekly at each other and shook hands, hiding their disappointment. It was hard to always live on hope, especially when other diggers struck it rich.

In early August, Elizabeth told Richard that she was getting contractions, and he needed to find the camp midwife, a woman named Mrs Arnold. He hurried to the camp settlement, searching about, rushing to several tents and huts, asking where the midwife lived. He eventually found her in a hut treating a miner with a leg wound. Short and rotund, with a sunburned face unsuited to the harsh climate, Ms Arnold, was bending over and binding his leg with gauze, helped by an Aboriginal girl who looked to be no more than 15 years old.

'Are you the midwife?' Richard asked.

'I am. And the medical helper and apothecary. Everything from fixing wounds to relieving stomach rot, which we get much of around here. What do you need?' She got up to face Richard, then told the girl to finish binding the man's leg. 'Tie it off at the knee, Sally. Then give him a dose of carbonate of natron for his intestines.'

'My wife. She's having a baby.'

'Right now? Or just starting labour?'

'She's been in a labour a while.'

'Well, we better go see then. Lead the way. Come on, Sally.'

They arrived at Richard and Elizabeth's tent, huffing from walking up the gully, with Mrs Arnold carrying a black bag of swathing sheets and medicine bottles: castor oil, laudanum, Holloway's pills and ointment. Richard opened the tent flap and led them inside.

'Well now, lass,' Mrs Arnold asked Elizabeth, taking stock of their meagre furnishings, 'What have we got here? First time, is it?'

Elizabeth nodded, then grimaced as another contraction came on. 'Yes, my first.'

'Don't you fret none,' the midwife said, unpacking her bag. 'Me and Sally have helped bring many a new babe into this world, haven't we, Sal? As for myself, I worked at Melbourne's Lying-in Hospital, so lucky you.'

Mrs Arnold bent down and took out a small bottle. 'Here's a drop of willow bark to dull the pain.' She put a few drops of the bitter liquid on Elizabeth's tongue, then got to work, chatting as she went, boiling water, explaining each stage of birth, applying moist towels on Elizabeth's head and legs, encouraging her to breathe and push.

'Follow your urge to push. You're young and strong. Everything will be fine.'

Elizabeth's contractions became more frequent, more painful. When the baby's head began to appear, Mrs Arnold told Richard to leave and wait down in the camp. 'But no drinking' she ordered. 'I'll have no inebriated husband around here.'

Mrs Arnold turned to Elizabeth with a firm look of resolve.

'The child is moving now. Now lass, let's guide you through it.'

By late evening, Elizabeth heard the first cry of her baby.

Their child, a healthy girl, was born in the Korong goldfields on 4 August 1857. Her birth was registered two months later at Kingower, although she was officially unnamed. The district registrar, Charles Archibald Campbell, wrote the details: when and where born, father's name and occupation, mother's maiden name, name of nurse, accoucheur or witness. Richard took the registrar's pen and signed his name in a cursive, spidery flourish. The child was later baptised Ellen Jane Belsar, after Richard's sister.

Breaking into a Store

By the summer of 1862, Richard and Elizabeth were on the move. They left Kingower a year earlier and had travelled north for Richard to find work as a labourer in the Saint Arnaud, a flat, dryland of shallow stony soil and sheep stations.

He was down on his luck; savings had run out and there were more mouths to feed. A son, Richard Henry, had been born in 1859, and another daughter, Elizabeth Ann, in 1861, which kept Elizabeth fully occupied with their care. Ellen Jane had turned 5 and had become an active, inquisitive child always running about.

'I heard of a job further north,' Richard said one day while driving their spring cart along the rutted track from Saint Arnaud, a town they'd stopped to water the horse and to pick up a few supplies. 'Sinking tanks in the ground. Mostly driving horse teams, so I reckon I could do it. Six months contract.'

'What about us?' Elizabeth said.

'The station has huts for workers. Other families, too. We'd be settled for a while.'

Elizabeth was silent for a time, thinking about where they came from, where they'd once been. She looked over the flat brown plains and low hills, scattered with clumps of ironbark eucalypts and flocks of sheep. The grass was withered and bare. Even the sky seemed lurid. It held no promise.

'You know, I miss Kingower. Tyler's place, our little hut. This land here is so flat and barren and pitiless.'

'I know, Eliza. I miss it too. But it wasn't the same after Tyler sold up and left. Work dried up for me. A district full of jobless men. I'm too old for mining now. We agreed on that.'

'We did. And I'm happy about that. I'm just thinking of the littlun's. What's here for them?'

'We're together, at least. That's the main thing. I'll look after you, Eliza. I promised you that.'

'Where's the station?'

'It's called Cope Cope. I don't know what it means.'

'Ridiculous name. What kind of a name is Cope Cope?' Eliza muttered. It could have been anywhere.

'Don't fret, Eliza, we'll make do,' Richard told her, trying to lift her spirits. 'We'll save again. Get by like we always do. I'll earn a few quid and we'll find a better place. Move on if need be.'

'It's the young ones. Still babes, they are. And here we are, on the frontier.'

'I know. It just–'

'Can't we just settle? Build a little house again. In a town somewhere. Maybe near a school.' she stared at him, her voice lifted a pitch – not that she complained much – but now, having to re-establish again in the lonely bush, Elizabeth's temper flared.

'We will one day, I promise you, Eliza. I just need a job.' He'd run out of excuses.

'I've heard that before.'

'You could have stayed in Saint Arnaud. Rented a room while I work here.'

'And pay with what?' she asked. 'We're hard up. There's naught in your pocket.'

The Belsars joined the throng of itinerant labourers and failed miners moving back and forth on dusty tracks that linked sheep stations and mining towns in central Victoria. They often arrived at a squatter's homestead in their spring cart, where Richard asked for carpentry or labouring jobs. Sometimes on the road they had to forage for bush food and shoot kangaroos, wallabies and wild turkeys, and eat paddy melons growing along tracks. Earning just enough to survive day by day.

Cope Cope was a staging post and resting place 15 miles north-west of Saint Arnaud. It was a small settlement of stockyards, sheep washing facilities and a ramp for bullock drays to load wool bales. Passing drovers rested and watered their mobs of sheep. There was a small hotel, a general store, a blacksmith's shop, and a flour mill to grind grain. It was at the edge of Victoria's Wimmera district, near a watering hole, surrounded by flat, dry, hard scrub country.

There, on a 25,000-acre sheep property called Cope Cope Station, Richard was employed to sink tanks – using a team of work horses to dig wells and shallow dams. The station had a cluster of huts: a manager's house, a supply store, a kitchen, some stables, a shearers woolshed, shepherd huts, and fenced paddocks for sheep.

Cope Cope Station was owned by a squatter named Charles Williamson who leased the land to run his sheep, installing an overseer on-site to supervise operations. Like most squatters, he had no legal title but claimed it all, making it impossible for small, untitled settlers, certainly not lowly labourers, to purchase or lease small allotments of land for themselves.

The station manager, a young Scotsman named John Alexander Rose, offered Richard a six-month contract. They was given a hut to live in a mile or so away from the home station, roughly built from logs, with a fireplace and chimney, much like every other hut they'd lived in since they'd married. It was some distance away from the single men's quarters and they didn't have to bunk in next to the shearers.

They spent the day furnishing the bark hut with their few belongings, which they unloaded from their cart: a chest of cooking utensils, clothing, blankets, some food. Richard's carpentry tools. Rolls of canvas, kerosene lamps, medicine, candles, water bags, a harness. Elizabeth settled the three children, still toddlers, and began to explore their new home. If all went well, they'd be staying here for six months.

Richard joined a work crew of three men at a dry floodplain where John Rose explained the job. They were told surface water flowed there whenever it rained. Not that any had fallen in the last year; the land was dry as a bone, in the grip of severe drought. The cracks in barren soil were deep and pitiless as the sun.

The men harnessed a team of horses which they used to 'sink a tank' and create a more permanent water source for the sheep herd. The 10-horse team furrowed and ploughed the surface soil, first breaking it up. Then they re-harnessed the team to pull a large iron scoop to haul the broken soil out. Two men worked the horses – one walking behind guiding the scoop, the second leading the team with a rope. Back and forth they went, scooping up the ground, dumping dirt on either side, creating embankments to hold the water, when it came. Sometimes they had to break up rocks with a crowbar, hard sandstone boulders that couldn't be shifted by the scoop.

They worked 10-hour days in the sun, leading the horse teams, breaking rocks, changing harnesses and plough heads, then took the horses back to camp in the evening to feed and water them. Each afternoon, the sharp-tongued supervisor, John Rose, rode up to inspect their progress. One time, early in the New Year, he arrived to see them all sitting down.

'What's holding things up?' asked Rose.

The foreman said, 'Broken harness, boss. We had to repair the collar straps.'

Rose dismounted to inspect the collar break and new strapping job. 'Good job. That should do it.' He took off his hat and squinted up at the sun. 'Couple more hours left in the day, I reckon. Get back to work.'

One of the men, Paddy Conner, an Irishman from Limerick, leaned across and swore under his breath to Richard, 'Pretentious prick. Rides around like a flash rat. Like to see him put in a day's work.'

By day they sweated under a fierce Mallee sun, the wilting eucalypt trees providing little shade or respite. Two of their wives usually rode down to bring them lunch: billy tea, damper, jam, slices of boiled mutton. By evening, they washed their dust-caked bodies in canvas buckets and ate dinner, then spent their spare time repairing their clothes, smoking pipes, drinking warm beer, or gambling away their money playing cards. Sometimes, Richard wandered over to join the men, but mostly he spent evenings with Elizabeth looking after the children. Four weeks of labour ground on with insipid monotony, the daily grind sapping their energy. After they sank the first tank, they moved to sink another.

On 14 January, Richard rode to the station store hut to collect his rations for the next few days – tea, tobacco, flour, sugar – from the storekeeper, William Taylor. He'd been given strict orders about his weekly limit by John Rose. 'A pound of each, no more,' he said condescendingly. 'Then back to work. We haven't got all day.' He used his words like a whip, angered for some reason or another.

As he turned, Rose muttered something under his breath, a slur, just a whisper, barely a sound, 'Old lag.'

Richard heard the insult, offensive in its meaning. An ex-convict! Blood rose to his head and his face reddened, then something switched inside him. He watched in fury as the supervisor rode off. He thought of the back-breaking work ahead, his low wages, the burden of responsibility. There was an upwelling of anger and frustration, a deep feeling of being trapped by his poverty.

He walked into the station store hut, furious, eying bags of flour and sugar, chests of tea, plugs of tobacco, shelves of pannikins and blankets. Then he heard a reedy voice from behind the store counter. 'That right? You an old lag, then?'

'What did you say!' Richard shouted, his blood boiling.

The storekeeper, a small man called William Taylor, appeared, wrinkled and rake-like, his hands spread out in mock surrender. A lean man with a thin mouth. 'My apology, cobber. Merely enquired if your past was at the King's pleasure, as they say, given your –'

'My what?'

'Your countenance, my good man. Many lags pass through here. I myself had the honour.'

'One more word like that and you'll regret it, I swear. I'll cut out your tongue. Now my rations, if you please.'

Later that evening, Richard sat on his spring cart smoking his pipe, watching William Taylor as he locked up his store and left for the night. *Should I pack up and leave, or stay and keep digging dirt?* he thought. He knew he desperately needed the wage. But was there another way? An easier solution?

A decision was made, foolish and wildly impulsive. That evening Richard broke into the storeroom and stole some rations: 34 pounds of tea, 12 pounds of tobacco, and 84 pounds of sugar. He planned to sell them to the local hotel owner, Donald Murray, a well-known hawker and dealer of goods. He'd flinched a bag of flour before, and no one had noticed. Surely, no one would catch him. Goods were lifted from store huts all the time. He would pose as a trader and cover his tracks.

But he needed a go-between. Someone else to sell the rations, an unknowing 'fence'.

Hugh McKenzie was just another itinerant labourer, an old man in need of a job, one of many lone bushmen travelling through the district. McKenzie was camped nearby and happened to be walking past Richard's cart on his way to Cope Cope Station.

'Morning, friend. Heading the station, are you?' Richard said, walking up to shake his hand.

'Indeed, I am, mate. I'm told they're hiring.'

'They are. And it's grub work at that. Filthy labour sinking tanks. Killer work under the sun in this drought. A man could do better if he had a mind to.' Richard smiled, trying to read the man's expression of interest. 'I've a proposal in mind, if you're interested. There's a quid in it for you.'

'What is it?' McKenzie said.

'Go ask Donald Murray at the public house if wants to purchase some tea, tobacco and sugar at a good price from my cart. There's a pound for you if he agrees.'

After a moment's consideration and an inspection of the goods, Hugh McKenzie agreed to walk to the hotel and bargain with Donald Murray. A deal was struck with a handshake. Cash and bottles of rum were exchanged. Richard rewarded McKenzie with a one-pound note and a bottle of rum for his effort.

Donald Murray, curious where the good had come from, came out and saw the culprits by the cart. He laughed at the situation and said the deal called for some kind of celebration with a couple of tots of rum. A smirk passed between them as they enjoyed a glass of rum, then a few more, in the shade of a gum tree, leaning against Richard's cart.

'A toast to good labouring men and be damned to squatters,' said Murray, raising his glass. 'They don't work alongside us. They think they're gentry. We're as good as any man, and better than most!'

'Aye, I'll drink to that,' Richard said.

'I won't say a word. Me lips are sealed,' McKenzie said.

'I intend to chuck it in. You can take my job, McKenzie.'

They all drank rum, downing several bottles, got drunk and fell into a slumber that night propped against the cart, prone and uncovered on the ground. The first thing Richard heard upon waking from his stupor was, 'Get up, Belsar! You're under arrest!'

'What—?' A pair of hands gripped his arms, twisting him over in an armlock, holding him face down in the dirt. A knee in his back.

'Fuck off! What the hell's going on? Let me be!'

'I'm a policeman. Hold still, you dog. You've been accused. My name is Detective Secreton. You're under arrest for thievery, rogue. Hold or I'll beat you. Hold, I say!'

It became all too clear. Richard knew his guilt and surrendered to the detective as he stood, dropping his head, extending his arms so his wrists be shackled by a pair of heavy manacles. 'How'd you find out, copper?'

'The storekeeper, Taylor, found the store ransacked,' Secreton replied. 'Door lock broken, the supplies missing. Not a pound or two of flour and sugar, but whole bags of the stuff. Spilt flour and sugar all over the floor. Rose and Taylor named you. I must say, Belsar, you're a fool leaving easy tracks like that.'

'Could have been any of the station hands,' Richard said.

'Not for a drunk. Fencing the goods, sleeping near the crime for God's sake! Marked bags of flour, sugar and tea found inside Murray's hotel!' Secreton shook his head at the stupidity of the crime. 'Murray's been nabbed too, by the way. Get up, you're both going to gaol.'

Ararat Gaol

Elizabeth learnt of his arrest the following day. He hadn't returned that night, so something was up. She assumed he'd slept at the single men's hut after a night drinking, which he was known to do on occasion. Or at Murray's public house. She asked one of the wives at men's hut if they'd seen him that morning.

'No, not here. He didn't leave with the men this morning. Maybe he's on another job.'

She waited back in her hut. That's all she could do. Just wait with the children. No need to worry yet. He could be anywhere on the station; it was a vast property. She had her hands full anyway, baking bread and preparing stew, feeding the children; her youngest, Elizabeth Ann, still at her breast.

It was mid-afternoon when she heard a knock at the door. John Rose, the station manager, banging away. He pushed through, looking officious and curt, even before she could ask who was there.

He stood for a moment, red-faced, hands on each hip in a position of firm authority. 'Madam, your husband has been arrested for theft of station property. He's been taken to gaol at Ararat. You are hereby ordered to vacate this hut. You will be removed to Saint Arnaud this afternoon by one of my men. Please pack your belongings and be ready.' Then he turned and left.

Elizabeth was dumbstruck. She could hardly believe what he had said. Taken away? His words hit her like a hammer, and for a moment she felt entirely lost.

She cried in her small room, pacing back and forth around the children, 'What's the fool gone and done? The idiot!' Then the full weight of circumstance struck. What would become of her? Who would support the children if he was in gaol? For the first time in her 27 years, Elizabeth felt afraid.

The journey to Saint Arnaud seemed a blur. She packed their meagre belongings, fed the children, checked her purse, only to see one pound and five shillings, and left what she couldn't carry. The driver was courteous and helpful, and lifted her bags and the children up to the cart seat. 'Sorry about this, missus,' he said. 'I knew Belsar. Seemed a good enough bloke. A bad business, this. I got me orders to drop you at Saint Arnaud.'

They hardly spoke on the track. She clutched her youngest, Elizabeth, aged two, while Richard and Ellen sat quietly at the back, sensing something bad had happened. 'Where's Pa?' asked Ellen. 'Ain't he is comin' with us?'

On arrival, the driver stopped in front of a ramshackle building on Dundas Street, which he said was used as a police station, a courthouse, and for any legal business. 'You might find somethin' of it in there,' he said. Lifting Ellen and Richard down from the cart, he bade Elizabeth goodbye and left. 'Good luck, missus.'

She held her children and looked up and down the wide, dusty street, seeing familiar landmarks. A Cobb and Co. coaching station, a team of tired horses hitched to a rail, the rickety Royal Hotel with men drinking on the veranda steps, Struther's grocery and blacksmith's shop, a butcher she'd once bought meat from. She turned, gathered her strength and walked into the police station, young Elizabeth on her hip. Ellen sat on a bench and looked after the children while she approached a police constable at the counter.

'Yes?'

'I'm here about my husband, Richard Belsar.'

'What about him?'

'In gaol. That's all I know.'

'If he's in gaol, he's not here. I'll check the charge book.' His finger moved across a ledger, then pointed to a name. 'There he is. Breaking and entering. Stealing property. Left here this morning in the police wagon. Goes to court on the sixth of February. Charged by Detective Secreton.'

'Can I see him? My husband?'

'No way, missus. They're on the way south.'

'What can I do?'

'You can see the detective who nabbed him, now he's back.'

The constable got up and walked through the back door while she stood and waited for several minutes. Then he returned. 'He'll see you shortly. Wait here.'

She stood and waited, stiff backed, holding her head held high, trying not to appear daunted by the situation. Inside however, she felt afraid and uncertain. When Detective Frederick Secreton came out, she saw an imposing figure. A large man wearing a dark blue military-style uniform, his jacket buttoned to his neck. He had a serious expression, a zealous demeanour with dark, penetrating eyes.

'Madam, can I help you?'

She tried to appear undiminished by the power of his uniform Standing before him, her small hands clenched as fists on each hip, both elbows bent out. She leant forward and asked assertively. 'Are you the one who arrested my husband?'

He seemed momentarily confused. 'Who's that, then?'

'Richard Belsar's his name.'

'That thief. Stole bags of provisions. Fenced them for cash and rum. A prig, if you ask me.'

For a moment Elizabeth felt like slapping his face. But she knew the consequences of striking an officer, one who had the power to detain, even arrest her. Then where would her children be? She bit her tongue and tried another approach. Her arms dropped, her shoulders slumped, her head bowed in submission, her voice softened, eyes stared wide pleading.

'May I see him?' she whispered. 'Please?'

'No.'

Tears swelled in her eyes. There was no play-acting now. 'For mercy's sake! How am I to survive with the little money I have left?'

'The church, madam. The poor box at court. Have you no relatives?'

'None sir, all dead and gone. He's my only means of support.' Her voice quivered. 'And three small children to tend to. Look there.' She pointed to the children sitting on the floor. 'What's to become of them?'

The man looked at her children, their wind-blown hair and freckled faces. His look softened a bit, some of the arrogance slipping away. 'I'll go and ask the church minister. He may help.'

He deserved a smile for that. 'I'm grateful, sir. I really am.'

Elizabeth and her frightened children were allowed to sleep on the church floor that night until other arrangements could be made. She relied on the minister and his wife for charity – a few more shillings to feed children with bread and vegetables, which she made into broth. She slept on a blanket with young Elizabeth, while Ellen and Richard slept in their clothes on the bare floor.

By day they sheltered in the street, under shade, moving from place to place, using up her remaining savings to purchase food from a costermonger. It was a poor, sorrowful existence.

The minister's wife, a timid woman, checked each morning to make sure the hall was tidy and they were gone before any worshippers began to appear. Charity could only extend so far. She didn't want the church to turn into a hostel for the homeless. She encouraged Elizabeth to pray for salvation, 'The Lord will provide. He will help in your time of need.'

He won't pay my bills, Elizabeth thought.

After a week, the minister, looking uncomfortable, asked her if the court could find them more suitable accommodation. In other words, it was time to leave. They were back on the street, waiting.

Friday, 6 February 1863. Fifty-seven miles away, the Ararat Circuit Court opened inside a small weatherboard building with a tin roof. The court room was packed and hot as an oven. Some people sat on wooden benches, others stood, sweating in the heat. At the front sat Chief Justice William Foster Stawell wearing his wig and robes, an Irish judge who'd emigrated to Victoria and roamed the district on horseback delivering justice at key population centres outside Melbourne.

Circuit Courts heard both civil and criminal matters across Victoria and were modelled on British country courts. A jury of 12 local men sat opposite watching the clerk and barristers shuffle papers ready for the day's cases. At the other end, uniformed constables and detectives, including Detective Secreton. Court officers sat near a group of prisoners in handcuffs and foot shackles. In the gallery sat relatives of prisoners, a few curious onlookers, and a local newspaper reporter, all squeezed together.

The court dealt with serious crimes first: murders, robbery under arms with violence, cattle stealing, assault and robbery. Then came the case of theft at Cope Cope Station. Richard Belsar stood at the dock charged with breaking into a store and stealing, Donald Murray with receiving stolen property, knowing it to be stolen.

The jury listened as the witnesses answered each question: what was stolen, how food bags were recognised, the value of goods being £22, identification of prisoners, how the goods were sold. Justice Stawell listened intently as the accusations were made by the prosecutor. Only Murray had a lawyer in defence.

After a long and detailed account, the jury gave their verdict – guilty.

The story was published in the *Ararat and Pleasant Creek Advertiser*:

10 February 1863

Ararat Circuit Court

BREAKING INTO A STORE

Richard Belser was charged with breaking into a store and stealing therefrom; and Donald Murray was charged with receiving the stolen property, knowing it to be stolen – Murray was defended by Mr Lamont.

John Alexander Rose, on being sworn, said: I am the manager at Cope Cope Station, for Mr Charles Williamson. I know the Prisoner Belser; he was in my employment sinking tanks; John Murray is a publican; I saw the prisoner on the 14th January, at the home station, at the store; this was about 5 o'clock; Mr Taylor is my storekeeper; Belser came for rations; I gave instructions to the storekeeper to give him rations for a few days; he got them in my presence; I saw him leave the store; he was living at the station hut one and a half miles from the home station; Mr Taylor locked the store and came outside, and I went away; before I left all the property was in safety; tea, tobacco, flour, sugar, pannikins; Taylor resides at the home station; the door is fastened by the hasp and staple; I received information on the next morning from Taylor, and I went to the store and found the team chest nearly empty, and some bags of flour moved; the tea is worth about 3s per pound, tobacco 9s, sugar 5d, flour 50s per bag ...

Hugh McKenzie, a labourer, residing at Cope Cope Station: I remember the 14th of last month; know both prisoners at the bar; about the middle of the day I saw Belser at the cart belonging to him and his mate; he was in the company of his mate; I saw Belser afterwards between the stable and Murray's public house; Belser asked me where I was travelling to; I said I was looking for work; he said he and his mate had engaged at Cope Cope Station; he asked me if Murray would purchase some tea and tobacco; I said I did not know; he said will you ask him; I went down to Murray's and Belser said he would see me afterwards at a fence; I said where are the articles, he replied in the dray; I went to Murray's and asked him, he said yes; we made a bargain...he gave me £3 for all the tea and £9 for tobacco; when I gave the money to Belser he gave me £1... Murray eventually bought the sugar for three bottles of rum; so I got £1 and a bottle of rum from the whole affair.

Detective Secreton, examined: I know Cope Cope Station; I went there on the evening of the 14th January; I also know Murray; He is an hotel keeper; I went to his hotel with the witness Taylor, and found there articles which Taylor identified as belonging to the store at Cope Cope; I then asked Murray respecting the articles; he said he purchased them and given £4 for the tobacco and tea, and three bottles of rum for the sugar; I asked him for a description of the man from whom he had purchased the good; he replied he was an old man, about six feet high, with long hair; I arrested Belser afterwards from the information I received.

His Honor in summing up dwelt mainly on the evidence of McKenzie and directed the jury in considering their verdict, that they must regard McKenzie as an accomplice. The jury returned a verdict of guilty. Richard Belser and Donald Murray, the former guilty of stealing, and the latter of receiving, were sentenced to imprisonment in the Ararat Gaol for two years with hard labor.

Ararat Gaol was an imposing prison which had opened in 1861. High stone walls, large double-story cell blocks, officers' quarters and towers, the gaol was a solid mass of masonry and iron gates. It looked cold and heartless as the stone itself. After being taken from the police wagon, Richard marched in chains through the main gate with a group of prisoners. His home for the next two years. He walked past men in the stone yard, some chipping square blocks of bluestone. Uniformed guards stood next prisoners, looking bored, brandishing batons, ready to punish a disrespectful or lazy prisoner. There were 40 or so prisoners, and nearly as many turnkeys.

Richard was led into a room and stripped for hidden weapons and contraband – then changed into canvas prison clothes.

The Governor of Gaol, Mr Samuel Walker, read the rules. All prisoners must work. Gruel for breakfast. Twenty-six ounces of bread a day. Sixteen ounces of potato. Mutton in the cell kitchen. Hard labour meant breaking a cubic yard of rock a day. Muster rolls morning and evening. Group cells at night. Wash once a week. Empty and clean shit buckets each morning by the water pump. Sunday service to learn the Bible. Contraband would be punished.

Boys mixed with hardened criminals. Forgers, thieves and murderers were in there together. There was drudgery and boredom and only occasional changes of routine.

Sundays broke the monotony. A morning religious service where the prisoners could sit and sleep, the afternoon to rest, to yarn with other prisoners and, if you could risk it, secretly trade something or smoke tobacco in clay pipes. Plugs of tobacco were currency – they could buy anything, especially extra food.

Meanwhile, at Saint Arnaud, Elizabeth and the children struggled to survive, lost and alone and living outside. Life for them became desperate. They were noticed loitering by shop owners and local residents in town. They were seen sleeping in the streets.

Elizabeth's money ran out. She asked a grocer if he could spare some meat or vegetables. She returned to search in the church poor box, only to find a few copper pennies. Despondent, watching the children grow hungrier each day, she told Ellen to approach an elderly couple and ask if they could spare a few shillings, only to find them hiss and complain, saying town folk didn't abide with beggars and vagrants, even destitute women.

Elizabeth was miserable, lost in a cloud of helplessness, holding on to her confused, half-starved children.

In 1863, colonial law punished the poor. It was a crime to be on the street without visible means of support. Vagrancy was an offence. Poor, homeless people found wandering or sleeping rough were arrested by police. Destitute mothers were dealt with by magistrates responsible for adjudicating cases brought up under vagrancy laws and they had to deal with women who appeared before them. Many women were imprisoned, their children put in foster homes or institutions. Some brought before the bench on vagrancy charges managed to win the sympathy of the magistrate.

It was a police constable who eventually recognised her. The young man from Saint Arnaud station. Elizabeth watched him approach her while they sat in the shade of a gum tree at the end of Dundas Street, near the main road south. Fear rose inside her; she had a premonition of imminent disaster. She could sense it – they would take away her children.

Elizabeth was charged with vagrancy at Saint Arnaud's Circuit Court, one week after Richard's conviction. She tried to present herself as a respectable, married woman with three children but no means of support, not one 'succumbing to her own weakness' and making a living from her body, as some courts often found. The magistrate, the same Justice William Foster Stawell on his district circuit, decided to keep them together, the children being so young.

However, he followed the law under the Vagrancy Act. She was sentenced to two months' detention at Ararat Gaol. A court instruction was given to find a suitable benevolent society to accommodate them.

This appeared in the *Ararat and Pleasant Creek Advertiser* on 10 February 1863:

> *The wife and three children of Richard Belser, found guilty at the Circuit Court on Friday last week and sentenced to two years imprisonment with hard labour for breaking into a store and stealing therefrom, have been committed from St. Arnaud to the Ararat Gaol for two months, as destitute vagrants. The unfortunate woman is paralysed, and unable to do anything for the support of herself and family. We understand an effort is being made to get the woman and children into the Melbourne Benevolent Asylum.*

Elizabeth in Gaol

Elizabeth and the children arrived exhausted from their two-day coach journey, which left Saint Arnaud under a police escort. She didn't mind the bumpy ride to Ararat, 65 miles away, or the poor food they were served at a stop in Landsborough, or even the indifference shown by the constables escorting them – they were together. The magistrate allowed her to keep her children. She could endure any discomfort, she thought, any uncertainty as to their fate. If the court had taken her children, she'd have been broken.

'We're here, Mrs Belsar,' the constable announced as they arrived at Ararat gaol. 'Wait while I get your bag and inform the guard. I'll escort you in.'

She waited in the coach with the children, holding Elizabeth in her arms, with Richard Henry and Ellen Jane sitting silently beside her. She couldn't help but glance at the gaol's massive stone walls, looming bleakly, its grim presence bearing upon her like a heavy weight. She knew somewhere inside was her husband. Inside there'd be a reckoning.

The constable returned and ushered them through the gate. 'Follow me. Bring the children.'

They were admitted into a holding room where a guard halted her and explained the rules. She could care for the children but must help in the kitchen. She must keep away from the men as best she could. No fraternising or physical contact. 'I want no temptation, no fights, no outrage against your person,' the guard said. 'The only contact you may have is kitchen work or cutting men's hair, if instructed.'

He informed her that she and the children could share a cell with her husband. 'You may stay with your husband during lock-up,' the guard said. 'And remain so together until we find a benevolent home to accommodate you.'

Allowed to share a cell with Richard? she thought. *All of us in a cell?*

A guard escorted them to the cell block. They marched down several corridors, through a massive iron gate, and passed rows of cells with solid wood doors. They arrived at a cell and the guard opened the lock from a set of keys chained to his belt. There was a moment of disbelief as Elizabeth saw her husband standing there, haggard in his prison clothes.

The first thing she did was slap him across the face, hard. She kept hitting him, 'You fool! You idiot! Look what you've done!' Then she burst out crying. 'You've ruined us!'

Overcome by exhaustion and disgrace, she collapsed on the hard stone floor. The children wailed and cried, huddling against the wall. All Richard could do was go to them, put his arms around them and say, 'I'm sorry. I'm so sorry, little ones. There now, it will be all right. You'll get through this.'

But it would be a long time before their anxious fear subsided.

Elizabeth knew she needed to gather herself together. For the children's sake as much as her own. She got up and wiped the tears from her eyes and looked about. The cell they shared was dismal: little privacy, straw on a cold stone floor, a thin mattress, a slop bucket in the corner.

'They told me you were coming,' Richard said. 'They'll give us a bigger cell. And extra mattresses. Not so bad, considering.' He wanted to touch her, go to her, hold her, but she repelled him with a glaring look. All the while their children stood frozen, overwhelmed by the harshness of the cell and the tension rising between their parents.

'Why?' she railed. 'Why did you do it?' She pointed at him, accusingly, again and again. 'All for a few pounds and some grog? How could you!'

He couldn't say. He didn't know himself.

The first night was the worst. Huddled in the darkness, noises of men groaning, coughing, some crying. Men grunted and whispered and cried weird noises in their lunacy; every sound amplified in the darkness. The stench of slop buckets permeated across the bluestone floors and inside the cells. Locked cell doors creaked, and unknown ghosts haunted the darkness. No one slept that night.

In the cold dawn the next day, Richard rose to help Elizabeth, putting his hand on her shoulder. She recoiled saying, 'Get away! Don't touch me.' She went to the children and inspected their faces, their skin, their ragged clothes, looking for signs of fever or sickness like she always did. She had seen so many die young from influenza, fever, measles, whooping cough, any number of common ailments.

'We must prepare for the day,' Richard said. 'Breakfast, then our labour. I'm breaking stone. You are to go to the kitchen and help prepare breakfast. Ellen must look after the young ones here when we go. Wait for the guard.' He looked at their eldest daughter. 'Can you do that, my girl? When your ma's away, can you look after them here?'

'Yes, pa. I'll help.'

'That's my girl. Stay away from the men. Don't talk to them.'

The prison ran its routine each day regulated by a system of bells and punishments. They learnt to follow orders: clean their cell, scrub the slop bucket at the water pump, haul water buckets to the kitchen, eat in a cell block, wash clothes in a trough, remain silent, don't talk to the gaolers. Men and older boys sentenced to hard labour chipped stone in the yard, others dug drains to direct water and sewerage out from the cells. Women sewed, washed clothes and cooked in separate rooms. Mostly, they sat in their cells.

The relationship between Richard and Elizabeth remained strained and distant. They said little to each other. They were too tired at the end of each day, after work duties, then feeding and cleaning and settling the children to talk of things. The strain of incarceration sapped their interest and affinity. How could they plan a future?

Weeks of monotony rolled by. Then months. There was still no word as to where Elizabeth or the children might be sent. To a home or institution in Melbourne?

A benevolent asylum? Her only hope was that she would remain with the children and not have to give them up to a foster family.

After two months, the prison governor told Elizabeth that nothing had been found. After four months he called for her again and informed her they would be sent to a Benevolent Asylum in Ballarat. The *Ararat and Pleasant Creek Advertiser* reported on 12 May 1863:

> *A woman named Belser, who has with her three children, been contained for some time past in the Ararat Gaol, was sent down by escort to the Ballarat Benevolent Asylum. The woman's a fit inmate for such a place and is certainly an object of charity. The children are all young and unable to earn a living.*

Benevolent Asylum

Ballarat Benevolent Asylum in Ascot Street was an impressive and imposing building. Built in the Elizabethan style, it had ornate facades and turrets and large airy rooms to look after the sick, the infirm and the destitute. It accommodated society's leftovers who had been destroyed and discarded by the gold rush: the abandoned, the poor, the orphaned, the delinquent, the penniless, the chronically ill.

As Elizabeth, Ellen, Richard, and baby Elizabeth arrived at the asylum on a windy day in May 1863, at first she couldn't believe her eyes. After the journey by police coach from Ararat, rattling and bumping 60 miles on the south-east road to Ballarat, they were exhausted and hungry.

As the driver stopped at the asylum's gate, Elizabeth saw a grand two-story building and marvelled at its imposing presence. She had to ask the driver twice if this was the right place. From the dark gates of the hellish gaol, she felt like they'd arrived at a grand manor house. As they stepped from the coach, she did a quick inspection of the children: faces clean, clothes buttoned, boots on correctly. She quickly touched foreheads for temperature, alert for any fever or chills.

Cautiously, they walked to the entrance door.

They were met by the matron, a pleasant woman who introduced herself as Mrs Boughen, wife of the asylum's master.

'Name?' the matron asked when Elizabeth stepped inside.

'Mrs Elizabeth Belsar and children.'

'How do you spell it?'[1]

'Don't know. I never learnt my letters.'

'Well, let's get you and the littl'ns sorted,' said Mrs Boughen. 'I've been sent a letter from the court saying your husband is in gaol. No means of support, correct?'

'Yes, ma'am.'

'Here we strive to do good among our fallen sisters. Tell me, do you embrace God as a practicing Christian?'

'I'm a believer if that's what you mean. We haven't been to a proper church for many a year, living out bush.'

'We'll see about that. And some schooling for the older girl. Maybe the boy too. Now, one of our ladies, Miss Dixie, will show you to your room and sort you out. Good day.' She turned and walked back to her office, pausing with a final word, 'You'll be expected to earn your keep in the kitchen.'

---

1 *Elizabeth's name in the Register of Inmates is spelt as 'Elizabeth Belsor' (no number). It's one of the few records that remain from her time at the benevolent asylum, as nearly all personal records of inmates have been lost or destroyed over the ages.*

Miss Matilda Dixie, as it happened, was one of the teachers who took Elizabeth through the building to show them the rooms: kitchen and bakehouse, washroom, dormitories, classrooms, chapel, wards for laying-in mothers. They passed old frail men, children of all ages, young women with babies, smartly dressed helpers, tradesmen in overalls.

'You are to sleep in dormitories. Men and boys upstairs, women and children downstairs,' Miss Dixie said.

'Can we be together?' asked Elizabeth.

'I believe so. Little ones like yours are allowed to share a family room with mothers.'

'It's so big. How many people?'

'At present over 200 beds for inmates. Many of the needy come each day for bread and meat. We practice charity wherever we can,' Miss Dixie said.

Elizabeth studied the woman - her crinoline dress, braided hair and pale complexion, refined and reassuring. She wondered what Miss Dixie must think of her. Sent here from gaol, looking ragged, wearing a threadbare dress, a destitute woman.

'Now, I'll let you settle,' Miss Dixie said. 'Perhaps you can introduce yourself to the kitchen staff, Miss Elizabeth. They always need help.' Then she looked at Ellen. 'And I might see you in my classroom, Ellen. Would you like that?'

Ellen nodded enthusiastically. 'Yes.'

She had never known a school, never touched chalk or slate.

'Me too?' asked four-year-old Richard.

'I'm sure we can find something for you. Some picture books? Do you like toys?'

'He's never seen them,' Elizabeth said. 'He'd be thrilled, I'm sure.'

After they'd washed and rested, Elizabeth recalled where they'd come from. Prison. The farewell with Richard had been a cold affair. He had hugged each child, promising to see them again after his release. He tried to embrace her saying, 'I'm sorry Eliza. At least you're getting out. Away from the crooks and lags. I'll come for you when I'm free.'

She let him hold her but hadn't returned the embrace. She didn't know where she was going. She and the children were removed from the cell and taken out to the police escort. Alone in the gaol yard, about to be sent away to some strange new place, some kind of institution. She had no idea where she was heading.

Elizabeth settled into the daily regime at the asylum. It wasn't so much learning the strict discipline and asylum rules - she could understand her household chores well enough and follow instructions by the matron - it was a different feeling she got from being at the institution. A sense of certainty, an awareness of security that she welcomed. They were safe. Even cared for, for the time being. After months living in the punishing harshness of Ararat gaol, sleeping in a cold cell, eating poor food, always in constant fear of disease, they now had hearty meals, warm beds with blankets, large spacious rooms to live in, and could walk freely outside in the gardens.

She rose early each morning to help the cook make bread in the kitchen for sorry-looking women who came from town for rations. She'd seen many desperate souls before in her life – she'd been destitute herself so could understand their plight – and it gave her a measure of fulfilment that she could help.

Ragged-clothed boys sometimes ran up to collect loaves before school. She worked with several other asylum helpers in the kitchen who seemed to know those families who were most in need. People arrived at all times of the day, asking for some bread or any other charity handouts. Sometimes there'd be cuts of mutton, cups of sugar, or bags flour or vegetables to give away.

Then there were the inmates to feed. Elizabeth helped to prepare breakfast, and served bowls of gruel or porridge, always keeping an eye out for the safety of her children at the dining table. Watching if any of the diseased, especially old infirm men, sat near them. She kept them away from the sick as best she could.

Ellen was sent to attend school. She was one of the youngest of 60 children at the Common School, which had three lady teachers. She joined Miss Dixie's class and began to learn letters of the alphabet and some arithmetic. Not all, just the simple spelling and mathematic tables. She learnt to spell short words.

The master and matron, Mr and Mrs Boughen, an upright religious couple, ran the asylum like captains of a ship. Women inmates acted as servants and were instructed to clean floors, cook meals, sew clothing, do laundry, supervise children. Mrs Boughen was specific about children's education: they must be trained to labour. Girls were to be employed with domestic house duties and be fit for working men's wives. Boys learnt a trade according to their station.

Women were expected to attend Sunday service for their salvation. Matron constantly preached that intemperance, gambling and other vices were barriers to moral elevation.

Although the dormitories were cold and gloomy, Elizabeth was thankful she could share a room with her children. It slept 12 – three other women all with young children of their own. If hers had been older, they would have been made to sleep in separate dormitories. As it was, she took comfort knowing that she could work early in the kitchen each morning and leave Elizabeth Ann and Richard with one of the mothers, then go to serve inmates their breakfast. Ellen walked to Common School.

Winter turned to spring and the freezing westerly wind of Ballarat warmed, blowing over the plateau and through the asylum's large, airy rooms. Still, inmates got sick and were put in the infirmary. Some died quite casually. The elderly and infirm passed away in delirium. Single young mothers died in childbirth. The children caught things, of course. Coughs and colds, the usual childhood ailments, but Elizabeth's were a tough trio from tough stock, and they survived.

Elizabeth was sitting in the garden one morning, relaxing in the warmth of the sun after cleaning up dishes in the kitchen, watching Ellen and Richard play outside, when Miss Dixie walked over.

'May I sit with you a moment, Mrs Belsar?' Miss Dixie asked.

'Most certainly. I'm just enjoying a short break. A lovely day, isn't it?'

'Yes. Spring is delightful here in Ballarat. Especially after our bitter winter. I just wanted to say how well Ellen is going in class. She's bright, quite eager, in fact. Have you helped her before?'

'No. I don't know my letters.' Then Elizabeth smiled at the thought. 'I don't know where she gets it from. Certainly not from her father.'

'And where is he, if I may ask?'

'Ararat gaol. He's still there. I don't know when he gets out.'

'Well, I hope things work out so you all, Mrs Belsar. In the meantime, have a pleasant day.'

Miss Dixie stood up and adjusted her skirt, then tuned and waved to Ellen and several other children playing in the garden, before walking inside to her classroom.

Elizabeth looked at her children, Ellen and Richard, running about, playing some kind of game. She noticed they'd put on a little weight, no doubt from a better diet, and they seemed to have grown taller since they arrived. They'd lost all of their prison pallor. The five-acre property had become their playground, with a large vegetable garden, some shaded oak trees, milking cows in the barn, eggs to collect from the coop and other children to play with. They played simple games: skittle, hide and seek, hopscotch, tag, blind man's bluff. Ellen, in particular, had blossomed. She turned and saw her mother sitting there, then ran up, excited and skittish.

'What is it, Ellen dear? You look like a jumping jack.'

'Look ma, watch this,' Ellen said, holding a small piece of chalk between her fingers. She placed it on one of flagstones and scratched each letter: *Ellen*

'What's it say? Go on, ma. Take a guess.'

'I believe it's your name, sweetie.'

'Yes!' Then she rubbed the letters out with her hand. 'Now, what's this?' She wrote: *Ma*

Elizabeth smiled. She knew what it meant, and it brought a tear to her eye. She closed her eyes and raised her hands together to her face, as if in prayer. She didn't want to leave this place. There was an order to their lives. A sense of belonging. They didn't feel like inmates at all.

When she opened them, she looked down. Ellen had scratched more letters on the flagstone: *father*

Ellen asked her mother, 'When will pa be back?'

'I don't know.' There was no answer for that.

Elizabeth's regimented, controlled life changed in early June 1864, a full year after she arrived at the asylum. It was Matron Boughen who informed her that there was a man at the entrance claiming to be her husband.

Release

Whether or not Richard thought he was a good prisoner or not, he could not say. He followed the rules, at least in front of the guards and turnkeys, and did what he was told without question or complaint. Cleaning his slops bucket each morning at the water pump, washing the shit away. Eating meals quietly in the mess room with other prisoners, cleaning his cell before the day's labour. He washed his clothes and bathed once a week and attended religious sermons on Sunday. Most days, he laboured in the yard, moving bluestone or digging pits for latrines or sewage drains. The weeks ground on in relentless monotony.

It had been months since Elizabeth and the children had left. How many now he could not recall. Eight? Ten? He could only judge the passing of time by changes in the weather. The bitterly cold winter, the showers of spring, the sweltering heat of summer. The thick stone walls of his cell seemed to make each change of season more extreme.

Richard was digging a latrine trench, waist deep in dirt, when one of uniformed turnkey's, a corporal called Blyth, came over and stood by the pit.

'Get out and clean yourself, Belsar. The governor wants to see you,' Blyth said. 'I'm to escort you to his office. On the double. He wants you straight away.'

'Aye. Give me a break,' Richard said wiping the sweat from his brow, trying to catch his breath. 'What's it about?' There was no answer from the turnkey, only a look of distain as he stood waiting in silence. Richard lay the pickaxe down and climbed from the trench, then stretched his back. He was feeling his age, he thought. He shook the dirt from his clothes and boots and walked to the pump to sluice some water into a bucket to wash his face and arms. 'This clean enough?' he asked, 'Lead the way, boss.' He followed the guard, a step or two behind, to the governor's room.

The guard knocked on the governor's door, which was ajar, and said: 'Excuse me, Governor. Belsar's here, as ordered.'

'Enter!' The governor, Samual Walker, waved them in. He was sitting at his desk and instructed Richard to stand in front of him. His office was simply furnished with mahogany side tables and round back chairs, each wall crowded with files in locked bookshelves.

'Belsar,' the governor said, reading from several papers before him. 'I see you've served 17 months of a two-year sentence. Larceny of station goods.'

'Aye, sir. That sounds about right. I don't know the exact time.'

'I've just signed your release sign. You are to be pardoned, Belsar,' Walker said. 'You may collect your belongings from the police lock-up yard in town.'

'Leave early?' Richard said.

'That is my order. I have more prisoners to take in, and my cells are full. You may pick up your entitlement from the purser. And any personal cash upon incarceration. You will be released immediately.'

There was only one question on Richard's mind. 'Where's my family, sir?'

'Ballarat. The new asylum, I believe. You will find them there. Now, sign this.'

Richard took the quill awkwardly and inscribed his name in full on the discharge certificate.

'You are dismissed, Belsar. I hope you have reformed.'

One pound and ten shillings would barely cover food.

As the iron gate opened, he walked past the duty guard, away from the foul-smelling cells, the high bluestone walls and the sullen men, and into his freedom. He was out. Released early. The sense of liberation felt strange, walking alone down the road to town to the police yard. He expected any time he'd hear a command to halt, and he'd have to return. That it was a mistake. But no order came. He was truly free.

As he arrived at the police station a constable inspected his discharge certificate and took him to the yard to pick up his confiscated belongings; his cart, a swag, even his carpentry tools remained intact in the police lock-up. The thought crossed his mind how they'd been brought to Ararat, how they hadn't been stolen or sold, but he didn't bother to ask the constable. All he wanted to do was collect his gear and leave. Then he hit a snag.

'What about my horse?'

The constable looked at his register and stared back impassively. 'Horse? There's nothin' in my book about that.'

Dejected, Richard didn't know what to do. He was at an impasse. No horse meant he couldn't collect his cart. He'd have to walk away and leave everything. He had to find a solution. 'Where can I find a horse to purchase? Somethin' cheap?'

The constable scratched his head while he thought. 'Horse sales are over. Town butcher and abattoir, I suppose. You might find a nag there. One in for slaughter.'

The abattoir was on the outskirts of town. A dusty stock yard holding a mob of sheep, a few cattle, some pigs, and several broken down horses awaiting slaughter. Richard found the owner, a butcher named Charles Medcalfe, and asked if he was willing to sell him a horse, something decent enough to pull a cart. From what he'd seen, most looked broken down or lame, barely able to stand.

'There's one, maybe,' Medcalfe said. 'A mare's coming in from a property clearance. Good temperament. Still shoed. She'd do you. I could let her go cheap at five pounds. No less.'

It was several pounds more than Richard could afford. But he had to have a workhorse to pull his cart. It was the only way to carry his family. He thought for a moment, then decided.

'If you're willin', I can pay a deposit now,' He withdrew three pounds from his pocket. 'That's all I got. I can make up the rest labouring in your yard. I've slaughtered before, whales and cattle.'

The butcher looked at him, uncertain about accepting the offer. He a business to run. At five pounds, he knew he was ahead, but not by much. He could probably get more by butchering the horse and selling its meat. Then again, the mare was in fair condition and still had a few good years in her yet.

Richard continued, pleading. 'I haven't seen my family in over a year, Mr Medcalfe. Being just out of goal. And I can fix anything you need. Fences, gates, buildings. I need a horse to find my family. I really do. My cart, my tools, all my worldly possessions are all locked in the police yard.'

Charles Medcalfe felt sympathy and agreed to the deal with a handshake. He hired Richard for a week. 'Eat as much mutton as you want,' the butcher told him. 'You look like you could do with a good feed. Plenty of fresh meat here.'

'I appreciate that, Mr Medcalfe. Indeed, I do.'

'You can camp in the yard. Come on. Let's get your horse.'

The week passed quickly enough. Richard repaired several broken swing gates in the yard and replaced all the rotted floorboards in the meat storeroom. He was thankful he didn't have to join Medcalfe with the bloody job of killing and slaughtering the animals. After he finished the repairs, he collected his bill of sale from Medcalfe and bade him goodbye, then harnessed the horse, packed his tools and rode south.

Still gaunt from months of hard labour and poor food from being in gaol, Richard slowly made his way down the Western Road to Ballarat, stopping only once at a public house to drink a nobbler of whiskey; his first in over a year and a half. *That's to remind myself of my sin. It will be my last for some time, I swear*, he thought.

All his life he'd believed he was heading towards something better. That there was meaning. Becoming a sailor, leaving Liverpool, exploring the world, having a family, he had always carried a feeling that he was struggling towards some sense of purpose. That something positive was about to happen. A lucky break.

He believed other people saw that in him, would look past his poverty, his illiteracy, his social class. But they didn't. He felt he was destined to find contract labour wherever he could, to drink to escape, to wander. An itinerant soul. One with a conviction. Where could he wander now?

His eventual arrival at the outskirts of Ballarat caused him to pause and take stock of his current circumstance. He must look a right mess, he thought. Wild looking, desperate. He stopped by a small creek to bathe and shave his beard, then pulled his hair back, like he always did, and tied it back. There was nothing he do about his appearance, his boots and clothing, threadbare with holes in his jacket arms and trousers. He knew must look like a pauper, all skin and bone, emaciated from his incarceration. There was nothing he do about it now. He had to push on.

He found the Benevolent Asylum by asking directions from travellers he passed on the western road into town. He pulled up on Ascot Street but when he saw the imposing building, its towers and ornate brickwork, he lost all sense of self-confidence. *What am I doing?* he thought. *Released several months early for a start; an unexpected arrival. What kind of welcome will I get here?*

He hitched his horse and cart to the gate and walked up to the asylum's large entry portico.

'All charity's dispensed with from the rear building, old man,' someone called out. Richard turned to see a man, a gardener perhaps, digging by a side fence. 'Get ya victuals out back, not 'ere,' the man said.

'I'm not here for charity,' He lifted the iron knocker on the door and knocked.

Matron Boughen thought him to be just another destitute seeking food and shelter, which wasn't far from the truth. When Richard explained who he was and that he was seeking out his wife, she was taken aback. She asked him to wait and went to find her.

Elizabeth came to the door and saw the emaciated shape of her husband in a loose shirt and baggy trousers, torn and dirty, but clean-shaven. She looked shocked by his appearance.

'You're out,' was all she said.

'Last two weeks. Been on the road to find you. They said you and the children were here.' He was embarrassed and hesitant, not sure what to say, distracted by the imposing building and various groups of people moving about inside.

He stared at Elizabeth, then looked at the matron who, in her usual orderly way, took charge of the awkward situation. 'Well, come in, Mr Belsar. You look like you're in need of a good meal. You may join the inmates for dinner in the main hall, then I'll speak to the asylum president about what's to be done with you all. You can sleep in the men's dormitory tonight. Elizabeth will show you to your place.'

We know the family were reunited and left Ballarat. Elizabeth was discharged to her husband on 9 June 1864, and they were given £2 cash by order of the asylum's president. It was a charity donation to help them on their way. That's all we know from records by the *Ballarat Benevolent Asylum Register of Inmates*. Like so many public documents, all inmate records were destroyed over the last century and a half.

They travelled north, passing the familiar towns of Avoca and Saint Arnaud, to a small settlement of West Charlton on the Avoca River, where Richard found employment at a sheep station leased by a squatter named John Bell Chirnside. It was a huge property of 80,000 acres, some 17 miles long, adjacent to the river.

The cold winter of 1864 in northern Victoria bit hard into their lives. They did their best trying to keep warm in a slab and bark shepherd's hut. He worked as a contract labourer, month by month.

Richard, older, more reformed, sank wells – again – working horse teams to scoop dirt and dig dams to catch water once the Avoca River washed over the flood plains. But the river didn't flood that winter and the water never came; much of what they found was brackish. He cleared scrub and built stockyards.

Elizabeth did her best to look after the children and earn a few extra shillings helping the station cook. They struggled on and resolved their differences, mending their relationship, and 13 months later another son was born, James.

Tragedy

'Here's your wages, Belsar,' the Chirnside Station foreman said. 'We're laying off hands, given the drought.'

It was late October 1865 and there'd been scarcely a drop of rain for the last 18 months, and the Avoca River was almost dry. Sheep were scabby and working men looked almost as bad – downtrodden and exploited, dry as the bush, unemployed.

'There's work at Conover Station. I put in a word, and they'll have you,' the foreman told him.

Richard looked at the station homestead, its whitewashed brick walls and tin roof, a lean-to kitchen where Elizabeth worked. Nearby the shearer's huts, where hard men toiled from sunup to sundown shearing jumbucks, pressing wool, sleeping on wood floors. They kept their jobs and at better pay too. Crack shearers could earn £1 and 16 shillings a day. Chirnside station still ran a flock of 20,000. Overstocked the land while still in drought, so barely a blade of grass was left.

'Thanks, boss,' Richard said, 'I'll pack our things and head off in the morning.'

How would he break the news to Elizabeth? Another upheaval, another sheep station. They were living almost like a swagman, travelling from station to station, but by horse and cart instead of on foot. His small, poor family, their few possessions, his three children all under eight years, and now a two-month-old son.

'Eliza?' he called as he entered their hut. She was changing young James's nappy on the table. He didn't know to say it gently, so he came straight out with it. 'We're finished here and need to go. Half the hands just got knocked.'

'Leaving?' It was more her tone of resignation than a question.

'Boss said work's dried up. Only stockmen and shearers stay.'

'What will we do?' she asked.

'I got a job at Conover, a day's ride away. Carpentry and labour work again.'

There was no choice but to pack and get ready. Now with four children, she depended on him more than ever. She knew the bush was hard and unforgiving for women, away from towns, away from people. But she didn't have a choice. She had to make the best of things now they were on the road as casual labourers.

She recalled his words in Ballarat. He told her he needed to leave the goldfields district forever, the district around Ballarat and Sandhurst and Saint Arnaud. He said station owners would know of his conviction, his reputation for larceny. He'd been branded like a tattoo on his face. He'd never be offered labouring work in the district again.

'They gossip, don't they? Between themselves. My name's ruined. In the newspapers, in gazettes, on town notice boards. Yours too, Eliza. We're both marked now. We need to get away. Head further north.'

Richard had worked as a station hand at Chirnside Station on the Avoca River for a few months, where they lived with a few dozen men, some with families. Fencing and droving sheep. He rarely rode to another settlement, or saw other people, buying supplies they needed from the store hut.

Elizabeth's world was her children: keeping them safe, away from snakes or getting lost or hurting themselves, although even that was getting harder.

She let them run wild, now they were older. They ran in boots but mostly barefoot, making their own fun. After chores, they'd sneak to watch shearers with their shearing blades, swearing and shouting, cutting wool. They played with tarboys in the sheds, not much older than themselves, painting tar on sheep to stop a cut from bleeding, and watched the rousies pick up fleeces to sort. They saw ewes give birth and played with lambs, now it was late spring, and they climbed the yard fences to see drovers swing their horses in a muster.

Then, all of a sudden Richard was handed his notice, and they had to leave. Go to another place.

On 28 October, Richard, Elizabeth and the children were travelling in their spring cart on the south road to Conover Station and by mid-afternoon crossed a dry ford on Avoca River at West Charlton. Water hadn't flowed past the town for the last 12 months and they saw groups of hungry-looking men camped along its banks, swagmen and families on the move.

'How much longer?' Eliza asked. She was tired from the day's journey and looking forward to their arrival before dark, rather than having to set up camp beside the track, with so many single men on the move. She sat on the bench seat, holding James in her tired arms, next to Richard driving the cart, their son Richard Henry squeezed in between them. The two girls, Ellen and Elizabeth, were sitting on blankets in the back, almost asleep from the rhythmic motion of the cart.

'No far to go,' Richard said. 'Another four miles, I reckon.' They continued along the dirt track and by evening were close to their destination.

Then the grim reaper stepped in and dealt them a tragic blow.

Richard was driving at a moderate pace, half a mile from Conover Station, heading down a small hill, when his cart hit a log lying on the side of the track and bounced up with a sudden jolt.

'Whoa!' he cried out, pulling at the reins. 'Whoa, there!' He couldn't pull it in. The horse shied and bolted, and the cart tipped on its wheel and overturned, throwing off Richard and Elizabeth, still clutching the baby, together with Richard Henry, onto the ground. There were screams and twisted harness flying about. It was complete mayhem.

Richard fell and landed underneath the cart's shaft. The two girls, Ellen Jane and Elizabeth Ann, sitting in the back of the cart, landed underneath it as it rolled over on top of them.

The girls shrieked in terror. Elizabeth, crawling on the ground in a daze, frantically checked James to see if he was hurt. Face, arms, legs seemed fine, only some light scratches.

Richard struggled to his feet, 'Dear Lord!' he cried, and ran to the cart, taking hold of the reins as the horse pulled strained and bucked against its harness. He had to stop it dragging the cart. 'Lord, save us!' he shouted as he uncoupled the hitch.

He saw chaos everywhere. The tangled harness, the upturned cart, Elizabeth laying on the ground, holding James in her arms, frantically checking the baby's body for any sign of injury. She was dazed and white-faced from shock.

'The girls!' she screamed.

Richard ran to the cart and tried to lift it. It was too heavy. He stained and pulled and shouted: 'Ellen! Lisbeth! Can you hear me?' But no answer came.

Suddenly two men arrived, heaving and panting to where Richard was desperately trying to lift the cart. Men from Conover Station. They'd seen the accident and heard desperate cries for help.

'For God's sake, help!' Richard shouted when he saw them, straining at a wheel. 'There's children under.'

The men moved quickly to raise the cart and Richard reached under and pulled Ellen out, thankfully unharmed. 'Are you hurt? Tell me, are you injured?' he asked as he lifted her to her feet.

'No, I don't think so,' she said crying, then ran to her mother's side.

Staining muscles, they lifted the cart higher. 'Heave!' they yelled in unison and turned it upright. Then Richard saw her, Elizabeth Ann, lying still on her side. She was dead.

It was a miserable time. The tears that followed seemed endless. The men laid the small girl down by the track, her mother adjusting the little white cotton dress, holding her tiny hand, brushing away leaves from her hair.

Elizabeth wept in waves of sadness. 'My little one,' she kept saying again and again.

Richard stood stoically with the children, looking on in despair, fighting back his tears, remorse and guilt mixed with an overwhelming sense of disbelief.

Soon, other men arrived and began to steady the horse, refit the harness and clean up the scattered mess of boxes and supplies, leaving the family alone in their grief.

After an hour or so, Thomas Butter, one of the men from the station, said, 'It's getting dark. We better get back to the station. We'll help lift the child.' They picked up her broken body and carefully laid her on the cart, then walked slowly down the hill to the homestead.

Thomas Butter pointed to one of the huts. 'Take that one, Mr Belsar. We shall leave you in peace with your family. I'll have the missus bring you some hot tea and something to eat. I'll ask the foreman to see you later.'

A district coroner, Henry Radcliff, arrived three days later with a medical practitioner from Inglewood, George Crosland. They had been alerted to the accident by one of the station hands, who'd ridden out the following morning to inform them of the accident.

The foreman, Robert Nicholl, who employed Richard at Conover, led the coroner and doctor to the storeroom to see the child's body. By then she lay cold, discoloured, already starting to bloat from death. Elizabeth sat slumped outside the door, exhausted by her vigil. She had been by her daughter's side almost constantly for two days. Her face was gaunt, her eyes hollowed with dark circles underneath.

'When can I bury my child?' she asked. 'When can I bless her grave and send her to heaven?'

'My dear woman, you have our condolences,' Radcliff said. The men stood together, respectfully, their hats by their sides. 'We've come to determine the cause of death for the inquest report. The medical man here, Mr Crosland, needs to inspect the deceased.'

They walked inside. Radcliff came out a short time later and walked over to the men. 'I'll need to talk to witnesses and take statements,' he told the foreman, Robert Nicholl. 'I understand several men witnessed the accident and assisted the father.'

The coroner went about his job with grim determination. He asked each witness – Simon Cavanagh, Thomas Butter, Richard Belsar – what they'd seen and carefully wrote down their depositions, as they could not write well. He wrote quickly on his official papers and then asked each to sign their name underneath. Richard scratched his name in a shaky, labourer's hand.

Radcliff then wrote: *Taken and sworn before me on the first day of November AD1865 at Conover Station.*

Richard's statement:

I am a labouring man. I am usually employed at work on stations. I have no place of residence. I was at work at Chirnside Station, West Charlton. I was coming from West Charlton to Conover Station on last Sunday at about six of the clock in the evening. I was drawing my cart at a walk at about a quarter of a mile from the station. I struck the horse with the reins on the rump. This caused him to start suddenly forward at a canter.

I had my wife, one boy two months old, my son, a girl aged ten years, and the deceased aged four years with me in the cart. I noticed a log lying on the left hand side of the road. I endeavoured to pull the horse up but could not do so. The wheel struck the log and the cart impacted.

I was thrown on to the ground with my legs beneath the shaft of the cart. Upon freeing myself I tried to free my wife but could not but the foreman coming up I appointed him in doing so. The other men came up and lifted the cart up.

I found my daughter Ellen beneath the cart not hurt when the cart was removed. I saw Thomas Butler now present lift my second daughter from the cart. She was dead. I was sober. I cannot account for the accident otherwise than that the wheel struck the log and this impact the cart.

The remains of a female child now lying in the hut at the Home Station Conover is the body of my daughter Elizabeth Ann Belsar.

The medical practitioner, George Crosland, gave his findings.

I am a legally qualified medical practitioner at Inglewood. I found no external marks of violence except a depression of the lower jaw which is fractured and also the sixth vertebrae. The cause of death was fracture of the cervical vertebrae, which would have been immediate.

The coroner gave his final verdict for the Crown Law Office:

Elizabeth Ann Belsar was on the twenty ninth day of October accidentally, casually and by misfortune killed by fracture of the sixth vertebrae caused by the upsetting of a cart at about a quarter of a mile north of Conover Station.

Twelve station hands, 'good and lawful men', became jurors and swore an oath they had seen the body. Their names were added to the inquisition. The coroner and medical practitioner, Radcliff and Crosland, their work now complete, rode off late that afternoon, trying to reach an inn at Wedderburn town before nightfall. Permission was given to bury Elizabeth's body.

The day of Elizabeth's burial was the worst. Their final farewell. Richard didn't know what to say, standing by the grave with his distraught and shattered wife. She stood in a grey cotton dress, head bowed with hands clasped and watched as Richard gently lowered the small body of their daughter into ground, wrapped in a blanket. When he got up, he put an arm around her and stood with the children next to her.

'Do you want to say some words?' he asked.

Elizabeth was silent for a long time and then said: 'Dear Lord, take care of my child. So that one day when I leave this world, I may greet her again.'

Richard picked up a bible but didn't know what to say. So instead, he opened it, and recited words of the common prayer, words he's heard before while at sea: 'Lord, we commit this body to the ground, earth to earth, ashes to ashes, dust to dust, in sure and certain hope of the Resurrection to eternal life.'

The foreman at Conover Station, Robert Nicholl, had given them two days to mourn their loss in their quarters – an outhouse near the single men's shed. The station hands left them alone and kept their distance, silently nodding in respect when they passed. Elisabeth tried to keep herself busy, tried to tidy and organise their belongings, but often sat in silence and stared out the window into the distance.

Mrs Nicholl called in with their rations: hessian bags of flour, tea, salt, mutton, oats, potatoes. She brought a basket of freshly baked scones. 'Here you go, love. You must eat,' she said. 'Keep busy, is best. You've got littluns to look after. Come to the house when you're ready. I'll get you started.'

Richard was awkward in the silence and tried to make the best of things by taking care of Ellen Jane and Richard Henry, now eight and five years old. He showed them around the station, told them to keep away from the shearing sheds and horse yards. He gave them chores. 'You need to help your ma,' he said. 'Especially the next few days. Collect water from the well and eggs from the coop. Help out in the hut. Everything she asks for, no complaining.'

After two days Richard met the foreman, Robert Nicholl. 'Ready for work now, boss,' he said. 'What do you need?' He was given a list of jobs to do. The immediate task was to kill and butcher some cattle for the station's meat supply.

Richard worked with Thomas Butter and two Aboriginal boys in the cattle yard. The boys, lads of 14 or so, roped each beast by the legs so it fell to the ground on its side, then Richard jumped on its neck to hold its head down. After tying the animal's legs together, Butter moved in with his knife and cut its carotid artery. Then the butchering began. It was messy, bloody work.

By the end of the day Richard was covered with grime and blood and dirt. He estimated they'd killed and slaughtered 10 beasts, yearlings judging by their size. They tanned and dried each hide by staking it to the ground in the sun. As they walked to the creek to wash, he watched the boys run ahead and jump in, splashing and laughing with enjoyment. He asked Thomas how many Aboriginal people lived on the station.

'About a dozen, or so,' Thomas answered. 'They come and go. These two boys, Jarrah and Djalu, have been here a while. Strong lads, as you can see. Good workers.'

'They get paid?' Richard asked.

'They do. Same as us in the shearin' season. Not sure about after. Probably not. They can disappear for months at a time.'

When they reached the creek, they stood up to their knees in water, stripped off their shirts and used handfuls of long grass and water to wash their bodies. Richard scrubbed the blood from his arms and face with sand. *Reminds me of whale hunting*, he thought.

Elizabeth recovered and worked in the kitchen at the Nicholls' house. She cleaned rooms, prepared meals, laundered washing, and tended the garden. It was much like her work as a domestic servant at the boarding house in Sandhurst, only this time there were more mouths to feed. Hungry shepherds and stockmen, and ravenous children. It was always the same, lunch and supper. Mutton and damper, Johnny Cakes, potatoes and puddings, tea and scones for morning and afternoon smoko.

It took Elizabeth weeks to overcome Elizabeth Ann's death. The loss was unbearable, but she had little time to think of herself, to show any emotion in front of the men. It was only on Sundays, her day of rest, that she visited Elizabeth Ann's grave, often by herself, to pray and lay a bunch of wildflowers. She prayed for strength, reciting the only prayer she knew by heart, the twenty-third psalm, 'The Lord is my shepherd, I shall not be in want, he restoreth my soul …'

By December, the shearing season was in full swing. A gang of 12 shearers had arrived and taken over the shearing shed. They yelled and swore and gave orders to the flock masters, the shepherds and roustabouts, to pen the flock, draft them, push them up runs to be shorn, where they laboured with their blade shears. They cursed and competed among themselves, each shearer with his own pen behind him, capable of holding twenty sheep. They got paid well – four shillings a score of sheep. The crack shearers could shear a hundred a day.

Richard told Elizabeth he had to start work in the shearing shed. 'Everyone, man and boy, are expected to chip in, apart from women, who were unwelcome at the shed, as it upsets the men.'

'Even our boy?'

'Aye, him too. He'll be right. I'll watch him. You can come and bring us somethin' to eat, something' for smoko. You and Mrs Nicholl.'

'The shearers curse and swear most dreadfully. It's disgusting language. I've heard them.'

'The lad has to learn the hard facts of life sometime, one way or another. Least he'll be with me.'

The shearing shed was constantly noisy with sheep bleating and men yelling. Some days, Richard threw the fleeces on tables where sorters checked the fleece before he rolled and tied them up with wire. Other days, he worked at the pool, down by the creek, to wash the fleeces to remove mud and sheep shit. He tried hard to keep up with the younger, fitter men, the station hands and stockmen, but found he kept falling behind. His days of hard physical labour were reaching an end.

Although he was young, Richard Henry learned to work with Jarrah and Djalu as tar boys, standing by with pots of hot black tar, ready to apply on cuts on sheep made by the shears. 'Tar-boy!' the shearers shouted, and the boys scrambled to paint the wound. They had to move in and out quickly and be careful of the razor-sharp blades.

Each afternoon, Richard and his son returned to their hut, hand in hand, both tired from their day's labour, but happy being together. 'You like the work, Richie?' he asked. 'Bein' a tar boy? Earnin' some shillings?'

'Can I keep 'em?'

'Aye. They're yours. You earned them. You can save for something. Maybe a pocket knife.'

'What's fuckin' mean, pa?' Richard didn't know how to answer that.

After four weeks, the shearing finished and the gang left for their next job, thankful for a break. The shearers were well paid, more than any other worker at the time. Certainly, better than Richard and Elizabeth's wage, who worked six days a week, and were each paid only £40 a year, plus rations.

His next job was helping the bullocky load the pressed bales, to be stacked on his big dray for hauling to Avoca. That was the hardest work of all. Backbreaking for all the men. Lifting single bales with a baling hook, each man putting their hook into the corner of the bale, and stacking them onto the dray, six levels high. It was worse than any stevedoring he'd done on ships. Each bale seemed to weigh a ton, especially if it was wet. They strained their arms and backs and swore like navvies.

Richard was glad to see the end of the shearing season. See the bullocky walk lazily away along the track with his twelve-strong bullock team, his whip over his shoulder, singing alongside. He walked with an off-sider and a dog, who nipped the feet of the bullocks to keep them moving along the track.

After three weeks of heavy shearing, hauling fleeces, baling and lifting, Richard came home one evening, exhausted, bent over in back pain. He'd strained a muscle and could barely walk.

'Such hard yakka. Thank Christ it's over! I'm getting too old for this. My back aches something fierce.'

'You can talk,' replied Elizabeth. 'Here I am, on me feet all day in the kitchen. And now with child again. Four months gone, I reckon.'

He looked up at her, not knowing what to say. 'Well, then,' was all he could muster, too exhausted to celebrate. All he could think of was another child to care for, another mouth to feed.

Their child, a girl, was born in 1866. They named her Sophia. She died in infancy and was buried next to her sister, Ellen, at Conover Station. Her birth and her death were never registered with authorities.

Sophia's name is mentioned in the birth register of their next child, born in April 1868. The registration certificate lists the names all their children, their ages and their deaths.

By 1868, we find Richard and Elizabeth on the move again, this time along the Murray River, to a place near Echuca, in the colony of New South Wales.

Toorangabby Station

Toorangabby Station, a pastoral run of 100,000 acres, was owned by two wealthy English brothers, John and Samual Wilson. The station sat on the New South Wales side of the Murray River, about thirty miles from Echuca, and included 2000 acres of prime river frontage. The brothers ran a large herd – 400 cattle and 12,000 Lincoln sheep – plus 50 horses and a team of bullocks.

When Richard arrived there in early 1868, Elizabeth was six months pregnant. The journey had been an uncomfortable one – four days bouncing in their spring cart, packed with their worldly belongings, jolting on rutted bush tracks and rough dirt roads. After leaving Conover Station, they had travelled east, then north, averaging 30 miles a day, camping overnight, until they reached the northern road linking Melbourne to Echuca.

'It's a wealthy property, Eliza,' Richard had told her before they left. 'One of the finest in the district. Worth £23,000, they say!' He was excited about their prospects. He'd sent a letter for the job there, carefully handwritten over several nights, and he'd been given a reply. They could start upon arrival.

'It's closer to towns. Heaps of crops. Lucerne, oats, barley and wheat, and a steam engine to irrigate pastures,' he had told her. 'More families, too. You'd not be on your lonesome some much.'

'It's not so bad here. The Nicholl's have been good to us.'

'I can't take another shearin' season here, Eliza. I just can't do it.' He knew, more than anything, he needed a change. To get away from their closed, isolated world at Conover Station. Get away from shearing sheds and hard labour. Backbreaking donkeywork hauling wool bales.

Upon reaching Echuca, they found a river port full of passenger coaches, bullock wagons, steam trains, and steam-powered riverboats. Bustling traffic moved everywhere. A rail line to Melbourne shifted vast amounts of wool south for shipping overseas. Riverboats and barges of all shapes and sizes moved up and down the Murray River. They had never seen anything like it.

Richard pulled up on the outskirts and surveyed the town. 'We'll stop here tonight, Eliza. A hotel or guesthouse,' he said. 'With a decent meal and a soft bed.'

Elizabeth was exhausted. The strain of camping and the constant jolting on rough dusty broads and hills had taken their toll. 'I sorely need a rest. I'm tired and a little faint, and fearful for the baby,' she said. 'Find us a room.'

He pulled up at Bridge Hotel and went inside to ask the owner for a room, one large enough for his family. He negotiated a price, one with four beds, hot meals, a bath, plus a stable to secure his horse and cart. He tipped the young groom a florin to feed and water the horse, and keep a sharp eye on the cart overnight, particularly as it held his carpentry tools. 'There's another florin in it if you sleep in the cart, lad.' Then boy agreed and got busy unharnessing the horse. Richard wanted no repeat of the night at Sandhurst where thieves had stolen his goods.

After they'd unpacked, Elizabeth said she wanted time alone to bathe. 'To soak in a hot tub and lay on a soft bed.' As she sat on the eiderdown bed cover, fanning her face, she waved them off. 'I'll be fine. Go take the children to the river to watch the boats. Leave James here with me. Really, we'll be alright. Just give me an hour or so on my own. But no drinking!' she warned.

Richard walked the streets, holding the children's hands, in awe of the crowds of people moved about, bustling in stores and outside hotels. He pointed out various shops: coach builders, cordwainers, hardware traders, timber yards, stock agents, butteries and bakeries, abattoirs and butchers. A Wesleyan church and Cobb and Co. coach station. Further up the road, Hopewood's iron store. It was a cacophony: grinding sawmills cutting red-gum logs, people shouting everywhere, blacksmiths pounding on anvils, horse-led wagons rolling past, distant whistles of steam trains.

'The boats, pa! Show us the boats!' asked Ellen. They walked to the wharf and saw boats steaming up and down the river. Paddlewheel steamers, stacked high with wool bales, pulling barges laden with stacks of timber. Passengers waited to take punts over the river to Moama, the town opposite.

'Sit down here on the bank and watch,' he told them. The children were awestruck by the size and width of the river. He pointed out a large, flat wooden punt loaded with cattle, moored on the riverbank below where they sat.

'See that,' he said. 'That's a ferry. It takes people and stock across the river and back.'

'Are we crossing on that, pa?' Ellen said with a degree of trepidation. She couldn't understand how they could possibly cross such a wide stretch of water with their horse and cart.

'Tomorrow we'll take Hopwood's ferry. Don't worry, it'll be an adventure.' Richard studied it the same way as he would a ship. Judging its design and how it moved with the slow current. The pontoon punt sat heavy and low in the river, made of logs fastened together with ramps on either end so cattle and wagons could roll on and off. He saw the apprehension in Ellen's eyes.

'See how it floats and gets pulled by those chains?' he said, trying to distract her. 'Solid as any ship I know. How about you help me tomorrow? Can you take the reins and lead us onto the ferry? Keep the horse steady and calm. Could you do that?'

Ellen stared at him, unsure, then nodded.

Later that evening back at Bridge Hotel, they ate dinner in the downstairs lounge, busy with workmen and travellers coming and going. Elizabeth said she was feeling a lot better, and smiled as she watched the children fill their plates with piles of sausages, beans, mashed potato, carrots and peas. They drank tall glasses of lemonade and even ordered cream and peaches for dessert. It was a treat to just be served by someone else for a change. After the meal, they sat in wide squatter's chairs on the veranda and watched the river traffic slow for the evening, while Richard smoked his pipe.

Next morning, after they re-packed the cart and harnessed the horse, they crossed the Murray River on Hopwood's ferry, with Ellen at the reins. She expertly coached and cajoled their stubborn, stressed horse up the ramp and onto the punt. So attentive was she to the task, so focused on trying to control the fearful animal, she forgot all her apprehension.

After they'd traversed the river and were about to disembark, Richard invited her back up on the box seat next to him. 'Hey there, little driver! You can help take us to Toorangabby.'

It was a roundabout journey, crisscrossing tracks and dry billabongs, first north through lightly timbered forest of acacia wattles, passing shepherds' huts and Aboriginal gunyahs, before heading south to the station homestead, nestled among tall red gums close to the river. In the distance they saw the cluster of limewashed station buildings, low-set with angled rooves and wide verandahs.

The overseer, Robert Oliver, and his wife Elizabeth met them on arrival late that evening. He shook hands with Richard. 'You took the long way, I see. Overland. It's only three hours by river.'

'Yes, we have a heavy load. All my possessions and my precious cargo… my family.' Richard pointed at Eliza and the children. 'Let me introduce my wife, Eliza.'

She looked weary from the day's long journey and stood up holding James, smiling weakly. 'Pleased to meet you. Although I fear I am not in the best of spirits.'

Mrs Oliver immediately saw she was pregnant. 'Oh, you poor thing. You must be exhausted. Here, let me help you down. Straight to rest for you,' she ordered. 'Some warm Senna tea and scones for you. I can sympathise, my dear. I've seven of my own. Robert, sort everyone out and I'll deal with Mrs Belsar.' She led Eliza away to the homestead, leaving her husband to organise Richard and the children in their new home.

After unpacking, Robert Oliver sat with Richard and explained what he wanted done. They were expanding the herd, and Oliver would be away for several weeks, droving a flock of sheep down from Deniliquin. He explained work at Toorangabby in simple terms. 'Here, you're a shearer or shepherd, a stockman mustering cattle, a man irrigating and harvesting crops, or a timber man building fences and huts. What kind of man are you, Mr Belsar?'

'I work wood, Mr Oliver. I'm a carpenter.'

Oliver outlined what work he needed done. New pens at the shearer's shed, swing gates and fences for the stockyards, a new store hut.

'After those, I'd dearly like a side veranda at the homestead. Overlooking the river. Can you do that, Mr Belsar? And I need someone to supervise cargo being loading at the river. Once a week by the steamers.'

'I can build all that, Mr Oliver. I have my carpentry tools. And I grew up on the Liverpool docks, so I know how to load ships. I can organise loading and unloading for you.'

'Excellent. You start tomorrow. Now, I'll leave you to settle in. Please, join me this evening at the homestead. A glass or two of Harveys Cream sherry and a pipe of tobacco.'

In many ways Toorangabby Station was similar to Conover Station, only larger, more affluent, more productive. Thirty-five men – contract labourers, including a dozen *Yorta Yorta* Aboriginal men, did all kinds of work: shepherding, mustering, dipping sheep for parasites, wool rolling and pressing, loading bales on river steamers. Robert Oliver employed the *Yorta Yorta* for piecemeal work, often with minimal supervision by whites, which allowed them to maintain their traditional lifestyle. Cash payment in the busy season was the same rate as whites, unlike that of most other stations, who paid only with food, tobacco and clothing.

Everyone worked; the women just as hard. Wives divided their time between domestic chores – bread-baking, milking, churning butter, jam-making, vegetable gardening – and child-minding. Some occasionally taught children to read and write or gave religious instruction, although the classes were few and far between. Teaching was in learning a practical trade, a useful farm skill.

In the winter months of 1868, Richard built fences and gates and supervised loading by the river, where shallow-bottomed punts pulled up beside the riverbank. He ordered several cords of cut red gum hardwood from the timberyard at Moama and built a veranda on the homestead, his tough, hardened hands sawing and hewing the wood to frame the joists. He cut and sawed and shaved the timber, drilled holes with augers, chiselled mortise and tenon joints, laid decking timbers, and fixed support posts. When complete, the veranda flooring looked like a vibrant layer of brown-red carpet.

Elizabeth, in her pregnancy, was given light duties in the kitchen, helping to prepare the evening meals. Most afternoons, she sat in the kitchen, peeling vegetables, kneading flour to bake bread, frying johnny cakes, cooking stews and making puddings. In her confinement she worked fewer hours and spent more time in the sitting room, playing with the children. Cooking meals seemed a never-ending job when there were hungry men to feed, many of whom ate with the Olivers at the home station. Only shepherds and labourers in outstations took rations back to their huts.

Just as they'd settled, calamity struck. James died suddenly, barely two years old. We don't know how or exactly when. His death record appears lost. Although the Registration Act of 1853 ruled that all Victorian residents must register births and deaths with their local district registrar, many living in isolated stations didn't, or couldn't, and James's death certificate cannot be found. His death is mentioned in the registration of Richard and Elizabeth's other children.

James was buried at Toorangabby Station. He joined the countless thousands of infants who died in this era, often from common causes: fever, infection, measles, typhus, influenza. Medical practitioners often didn't know the actual cause; they recorded vague, unspecific terms such as dropsy, convulsions, paralysis, atrophy, debilitation, teething, diarrhoea, or simply 'taken by God'. It was a period of high infant mortality. The Registrar-General of Victoria reported the death rate in infants and young children under five as high as 60 percent.

The birth of Richard and Elizabeth's next child, a girl, on 8 April 1868, would have been a muted celebration, with the overseer's wife, Elizabeth Oliver, and a local midwife assisting the delivery. They named the child Elizabeth Ann in memory of the daughter they lost at Conover Station on the fateful day of the cart accident.

Four months later, Richard registered her birth with the district registrar, Donald Forbes, at Echuca Town Council, on the first day of August. Richard provided Forbes with all the details: his daughter's name (who was not present) and place of birth, 'Toorangabby'. He registered his and his wife's names as the parents, his age as 53, and named their other children, alive and dead. A witness, Emma Brown, was present.

When asked to sign the register, Richard scrawled his first name but made a messy job of it, the ink blotting the paper. The registrar crossed it out and re-wrote it more neatly underneath, and instructed Richard to make his mark with a cross.

Boundary Bend

By 1870, Richard was feeling his age. He was now 55. He struggled keep up with younger, stronger men; outdoor labour was a burden. His bones ached in winter frosts and the fierce heat knocked him breathless in summer. His eyesight was getting weak; he needed to wear glasses.

He dreamed of a slower pace, perhaps a small farm along the river where he could trade eggs and grow vegetables. Perhaps becoming a selector on a small block, getting a government land grant, growing fruit trees. The children could help farm now they were older. Ellen was 13, Richard 11. They still had a lot to learn.

In his spare time, he taught his son carpentry: how to cut wood, manage an axe, use a tape measure, sharpen a saw, split shingles, hew logs with an adze, join timber sections. Mostly it was small jobs around the homestead, but increasingly, he asked his son to help him with bigger jobs.

'I need Richie with me in the yards today,' he told Elizabeth one morning getting ready to leave. 'He can cut some fence posts and rails with me at the barn.'

'What about schooling?' Eliza said. 'Today is his class with Mrs Oliver. She's teaching arithmetic.' Elizabeth, not able to write herself, worried about her children's lack of education. It had been informal and random, broken by constant movement and upheaval, an occasional class with other station children – learning times tables, writing sentences on paper with an ink quill, readings from the bible. She was determined they would have more opportunities in life than she did. And a basic education was important.

It was becoming a bone of contention between them.

Richard knew Elizabeth wanted to live closer to a town, with more people around. She wanted a church, a school for the children. She never forgot how much they loved classes at the benevolent asylum in Ballarat. Learning from a real teacher, from someone sophisticated and educated, like Miss Dixie.

'They must read and write, learn their numbers!' she would admonish him. 'Read books, study the bible, learn about history, learn elocution. They can't get that here! I don't want them growing up illiterate! I'm worried!'

Richard worried too. But about something quite different. Mostly about money, or their lack of it. His employment contract was up for renewal, and he had to make a decision, very soon. Stay at Toorangabby Station or move again?

He'd had heard about a job at a pastoral run downstream on the Lower Murray, well past Swan Hill, on a property called Youngera Station. One of the stock agents had told him about it. Some gossip the owner, a wealthy Scotsman and squatter named Alexander McCallam, wanted to sell up and auction the station. It as an opportunity for him.

In the back of Richard's mind was the dream of becoming an overseer himself, putting himself forward, getting in sweet with the new squatter owner. It was a gamble, he knew that. He had little to no capital and no connections at all to the squattocracy. Most overseers he knew had been blood relatives of station owners and squatters.

There would be more responsibilities: buying a herd, keeping stock books and hiring men. But he had seen it done. He could manage a sheep run and find a partner, a better educated man than he, and share the burden. Someone who could keep the books and write letters. A business associate.

He quietly sent word down the river to the agent. He was willing to go and take a shot. He told the agent to put in a good word for him and to forward a letter of his interest to the overseer at Youngera Station.

'We should take it, Eliza,' he told her afterwards. 'Just a couple of years. Then we'll move closer to a town, I promise.'

Elizabeth looked at him squarely, but he could tell she didn't believe a word of it. 'We'll see,' was all she could muster. She would go, of course, and not complain. She was a battler, someone who refused to admit defeat. She had fought illness, struggled with physical hardship and isolation, overcome the deaths of her children, fought despair and imprisonment, and stuck by Richard in good times and bad. Then again, what choice did she have, really. All she could say was, 'I'll hold you to that.' But did she believe it?

They left Toorangabby Station in 1870. Richard's peripatetic spirit carried them 320 miles downriver, past Echuca, past Swan Hill, to a place called Youngera on the Lower Murray. It was a slow arduous journey, several days by steamer. They packed their meagre belongings – clothes, bedding, canvass, ropes, cooking gear, Richard's carpentry tools – and sold their spring cart and horse to one of the station hands.

After collecting his final wage from Robert Oliver, they bade him and his wife farewell and walked down to the riverbank, waiting for a punt to carry them to Echuca, where they would take a paddle steamer downriver to Swan Hill, then continue further downriver on to a place known as Boundary Bend.

As Elizabeth stood by the river's edge, she made a sign of the cross, her expression sad and mournful, staring up at the homestead, to tall gum tree with a small white cross underneath where they had buried their son, James. 'Lord have mercy,' she whispered. 'Wherever we go, we leave little graves behind.'

The steamer carried them downstream, meandering in the slow current, passing tranquil shaded billabongs and glassy lagoons, brimming with wildlife. It was almost hypnotic, gliding on water, listening to the steam engine thrumming and whirring along. Summer rain had been good, and the river had become swollen, its currents swirling with brown, silty water.

The steamer stopped occasionally to discharge passengers and cargo and to pick up wood from timber mills to feed its firebox. They drifted on, around oxbows, through narrow bends and high banks, past towering red-gum trees, beside wide sandy beaches and hidden creeks. They saw flat plains of rich grassland and lightly covered blackwood forests. Sometimes they passed floating logs, dangerous obstacles that could damage the paddlewheels. An ever-watchful deckhand alert at the bow signalled the captain when to avoid a hidden snag or submerged branch.

They passed other river boats coming upstream carrying every conceivable cargo of goods: flour, tobacco, tea, beer, stoves, galvanised iron, wire, dried fruit, cheese, pickles, pipes, drapery, sugar, hay, kerosene, and candles. Passengers hailed and waved at each other, yelled words of greeting, enquiring where they had come from, where they were going or the river conditions ahead. Along the banks, they saw poor run-down shanties, squatters' shacks, rough fishermen's huts, and timber mills. There were rustic landings on stilts and bark huts selling food and liquor.

All kinds of wildlife screeched in trees and flew overhead: flocks of wild ducks, white pelicans, parrots of bright rainbow colours. Occasionally, smoke drifted from Aboriginal camps at the river's edge. Groups of black-skinned children, swimming and glistening with water, waved and dived and somersaulted from the bank.

On the third day, they pulled in at Swan Hill. It was a small trading port and settlement. After they disembarked, a deckhand began to load firewood for the steam engine. The captain met several men to discuss loading cargo for the next day's journey to Mildura, then on to Renmark, across the state border in South Australia.

Richard set up camp nearby while Elizabeth wandered to the town, carrying her new baby, Elizabeth, in a sling.

She saw a bare trading outpost. It had a wide dusty street with a few weary bullock teams, some timber-clad buildings, a small bank. There was an Anglican church, Rains Royal Hotel, a post office and a general store. In the distance she saw a brick courthouse, a few timber-clad houses. A butcher shop and a bakery.

I might be comfortable here, she thought, *in a small place like this.* It wasn't much but they could carve out a living. The settlement would eventually grow. Perhaps lease a small farm, have close neighbours to meet, live near a doctor or a classroom for the children. She could imagine it, a small cottage of her own, morning tea with friends, trading goods with passing steamers. It might not be a city like Ballarat, but they'd make do.

It was late evening by the time she got back and saw Richard was frying meat and potatoes on the fire. She found it hard to hide her disappointment, her growing anger.

'How's the settlement?' Richard asked, not looking up. 'I hope to see it in the morning.'

'How far is our station? How far away will we be from here?' she demanded. 'Another day by boat! A week by horse, in the bush! How far!'

'The captain reckons Youngera's another 50 miles downriver.'

So far, she thought. *What will happen there in an emergency? If one of them gets sick and fevered again and needs a doctor?* She couldn't bear the thought of losing another child here, in this wild arid country, this primitive desert outback, on their own, at the end of the world.

The steamer continued downriver the next day, the water shining peacefully, the sky without a speck of cloud. Elizabeth sat in stoic silence. She found the river confounding, even frightening. She was bewildered by its direction. She had no idea where they were, how far they had travelled in the twisting, meandering waterway. One moment they seemed to head north, the sun on their faces, then they turned south, the sun on their backs.

She asked the boat captain when they might arrive at their destination.

'We're approaching Boundary Bend soon, missus,' the captain said. 'The bend where the boundary fence runs between Narrung and Youngera Stations. We're nearly there. Not far now.'

When the steamer stopped at Youngera, she saw a whitewashed homestead on the rise with a cluster of outhouses set next to a grove of majestic red gum and coolabah trees. Even Elizabeth was taken aback by its wild beauty. The land looked green and fertile. Cattle and sheep grazed in an expanse of silver and barley grassland, slightly elevated from the flood plain.

Not far away she saw an Aboriginal camp with its jumbled collection of bark huts and shelters, a dozen or so women and children clad in ragged clothes sitting on logs around cooking fires. Several black and white stockmen, wearing canvas trousers and wide-brimmed hats, were drafting sheep in the stockyards.

The overseer, Allan Roebuck, a middle-aged Englishman man wearing moleskins, tall leather boots and a cabbage tree hat, met them on arrival and introduced himself. He had a clipped English accent; another emigrant, who had come to make his fortune with sheep and wool. He had been expecting the Belsars.

'Hope you had a good journey, Mr and Mrs Belsar.'

'Indeed, we did, Mr Roebuck,' Richard said. 'Fascinatin' country here. Quite different to upriver at Echuca, where we came from. We're looking forward to getting to know the property. How it's run. How big it is. It's an impressive landholding.'

As they walked to the homestead, Allan Roebuck outlined Youngera Station's size. He pointed in each direction, east and west. 'Some 50,000 acres, with a tenure of 10 years,' he said. 'A river frontage of 30 miles. As you've seen, direct access to steamers and barges. Fenced on both sides from neighbouring properties. And well-watered by two large freshwater lakes.'

'Who are the neighbours?' Richard asked.

'It adjoins three other stations,' Allan said. 'Narrung, Mount Myall and Bambung.'

'Unusual names. Aboriginal, I assume. Do you know their meaning?'

'The first one, Narrung, might be from the cypress pines around here. I'm afraid I don't the others.'

They reached a log cottage which had four bedrooms, a dining room, a kitchen and a big cooking stove. A hundred yards from the cottage, in another paddock, there were stables, sheep yards, a shearing shed, shepherds' store hut, and some plant machinery.

Allan said: 'I'll have one of the men help with your kit. You can billet here in the cottage hut near the main house. Settle in and I'll show you around the property later. Meet me at the homestead for afternoon tea. Cheerio.'

Elizabeth inspected the small pine log hut, her home for the near future. *A good tidy will make it comfortable,* she thought. There were immediate practicalities: unpacking, settling the children and allocating chores, collecting water from the river, inspecting the outdoor privy, cutting wood for the stove. She knew how to organise; domestic duties were her second nature. But the thought of starting over again daunted her, especially as she was pregnant again. Housework wasn't as easy, especially when looking after one infant and carrying another, always tired with swollen feet. It seemed all she had done these last 14 years was bear children. And now, so far from anyone!

They met Allan Roebuck at the home station, took off their hats and came inside to see a large cedar table, a spread of tea, fresh scones and jam before them, served by an Aboriginal girl in a cotton dress and apron.

'Thank you, Dolly,' Allan said, who whispered after she left, 'Dolly's from the camp. She's learning kitchen duties. I hope you might assist in that regard, Mrs Belsar. After your own family obligations are met, that is.'

'I'd be happy to, Mr Roebuck.'

Richard studied Allan Roebuck, quickly assessing the man, his demeanour and firmness of handshake. He watched carefully as the overseer explained what needed to be done, jobs Richard was all too familiar with. Yard work, of course, stronger fences, an outhouse to build. Felling and cutting cypress pine or red gum for timber. Mustering and droving, shepherding in the busy season. Carting bales by wagon to the river for loading.

'I won't do no shearing,' said Richard, 'My back's too bad for that. No haulin' bales.' Then he asked outright, 'I heard Youngera's up for sale. There may be some changes in management. At least, that's what the stock agent said.'

Roebuck seemed doubtful. 'That may be true, Mr Belsar. Wealthy squatters in Melbourne buy and sell pastoral runs all the time. But here, overseers, head stockmen, boss cockies like me, they mostly remain. Are you familiar with the family that recently ran this place?'

Richard said he was not.

'A fine lady, a young woman from Melbourne, Jessie Hughan, and her brother, lived here. She married the squatter, Alexander McCallum; a much older man. He squatted tracts of land all around here, north and south of the Murray. Bought sheep overland and took out licences. The McCallums had children here too. She ran the property with her brother and her sister. After a time, she returned with old McCallum to visit his family estate in Scotland. The old bloke wanted to stay and sell everything here. Jessie didn't. So, she left him. Strange thing is, he died there soon after she left. She came back here and made a good go of it too, with her brother. She inherited Youngera. A brave woman, well-liked in the district. But she died from a lung infection in the winter of '65. Most of the men, like myself, stayed on.

'I'm here now, Mr Belsar. I'm the overseer. The station may be sold, but I'm staying.'

Richard swallowed hard. His dream of becoming an overseer lost. His hope of managing a pastoral run gone. He was back to being a general worker – a labourer, a bush carpenter, a hired hand. Hearding sheep, butchering meat, fencing, loading steamers, whatever he was ordered to do. Being told, no doing the telling.

'Would you excuse me a moment?' he said. 'I just need to use the privy.' He walked outside to gather himself, not wanting to show any sign of disappointment in front of Allan Roebuck.

He knew he would stay and make a go of it. He would survive and make the best of things with Elizabeth and the children, like always. He had to. What other choice did he have? Several minutes passed and he returned to the table, looking straight-faced and grim.

It was Elizabeth who jumped in to steer the conversation into a new direction. 'There are a number of blacks living nearby, Mr Roebuck. What's your responsibility to them? Some have been badly mistreated on stations. We've seen it.'

'Yes, Mrs Belsar. I'm aware of mistreatment at other stations, particularly near Swan Hill. We treat them well here as best we can. We provide rations each Monday. Medicine to alleviate injury or ailments. They hunt game extensively, and fish, of which there is an abundance.'

Elizabeth was wary of the thought of an Aboriginal camp being close to their hut. She had seen and heard of nasty things between blacks and whites most of her life. She felt unsettled, disoriented by their isolation, concerned for her children. She knew it was judgemental, an innate prejudice, but she had seen violence in outback camps and towns fuelled by intoxicating liquor.

'What of their health and vigour? And employment?' she asked.

'Ailments of a pulmonary nature can be alleviated by good measure from a plentiful supply of clothing and blankets,' said Roebuck. 'I ban liquor here and restrict its trade from passing steamers. Some settlers around here do sell sly grog. I have not known one instance of intoxication these past 12 months. I exert my utmost to deter those under my immediate control from going to public houses.'

'I'm most relieved to hear that, Mr Roebuck. As the mother of young children, I feel it my duty to know they are safe.'

'As for employment,' Roebuck went on, 'the men are excellent shearers and horse riders. We pay in wages and food during the busy season. And with trade, of course. Indeed, I gave a one pound note to the chief this morning for cutting me some canoe and bark, and he was much pleased. He bought flour for the camp. You should meet him, the chief. A man named King Jacky.'

When they returned to their hut, Elizabeth could sense Richard's bitter disappointment. She felt his frustration, blighted by the English class system. She hoped he wouldn't take it as a failing, either by their social status or opportunity.

'What will become of us now?' she asked. 'Will we stay? Would you be happy here?'

There was a long pause before he answered. 'We'll wait and see. Maybe it's for the best. Roebuck, at least, seems a decent bloke. We'll know soon enough.'

In the end, Richard, Elizabeth and their children would remain at Youngera, on and off, for many years. They settled and became people of the river. Mallee pioneers. They learned to live off the land, grow crops such as wheat and barley, cultivate paddocks, tend sheep, cut timber, slaughter cattle, fish for Murray cod, load wool on steamers, collect supplies from Swan Hill, trade goods, and befriend neighbours. They played a crucial role in the early settlement of the region.

They lived with the Wamba Wamba clan on their traditional land, led by a chief they called King Jacky. The Murray basin was home to numerous Aboriginal people and many family tribes. Pastoral stations had Aboriginal camps and shanties of varying quality. Some well cared for, but most suffered abuse, disease, and violence. Sickness, syphilis, smallpox, and drunkenness were rife. However, reports and eyewitness accounts at Youngara Station show it to be one of the better stations in this regard. However by today's viewpoint the conditions were atrocious.

At the time, Aboriginal people came under the dubious control of the Central Board for the Protection of Aborigines. The Central Board in Victoria, established in 1869, had the power to move Aboriginal people out of towns, set up managers, committees and local guardians (police, station managers, magistrates) for the reserves, control missions and prevent liquor being sold.

Youngera 'run' was located on the southern side of the Murray River in the colony of Victoria, approximately halfway between Swan Hill and Mildura. The land today lies east of Robinvale, between Bannerton in the west and Yungera (West Nurrung) in the east.

Youngera Station

Carrying his carpentry tools to the cattle yard, Richard set out to rebuild the enclosure with a new post and rail fence. He had been asked to replace the old 'brush fence' made from a tangle of cut trees pushed one on top of each other and filled with branches. A mob of cattle had escaped through gaps in the brush fence, including their milking cow, which had to rounded up by stockmen. It was time to fix the problem with a better fence.

Richard had worked the previous day to fell a number of Murray pines from a section of forest on the property. Tall and straight, the pines made excellent timber for fences. The Murray, or cypress pine, grew plentifully in the district and was prized for its wood. Fined grained and durable, it resisted termites and white ants due to its natural oils. He loved the feel of the pine in his hands, the ease of sawing and cutting it for various carpentry projects, such as cladding huts, or shaping posts and rails for fencing. He savoured the fragrance, its fresh, woody scent.

He set about the job with his son, Richard Henry, and one of the camp boys called Mudaree, a lad of about 15. Tall and rake thin, Mudaree looked all the part of a young jackaroo, wearing an old flannel shirt, some dusty canvass trousers and a broad-brimmed hat, stained with sweat. He was lean and strong, a keen worker around the station, and spoke English well. He and Richard Henry had become mates, being of similar age, and often played together, exploring the maze of creeks and waterways at Youngera.

'I'll mark out the post holes with pegs,' Richard told the boys. 'You dig. Each hole needs to be two foot deep, alright? Then we'll cut and measure the posts and rails, and shape the rail ends to fit. I'll show you how to use my cuttin' tools.'

'Good wood this *maroong*, make good glue,' Mudaree said.

'What do you mean, glue?' Richard asked.

'*Maroong* resin fix barbs to spears. Resin fix wood to axe. And to stone. Strong glue.'

'That, I didn't know, Mudaree. Can you show me?'

'Maybe.' Mudaree said after a while, looking away with indifference. 'Maybe.'

There seemed a reluctance with his answer. Richard didn't know whether it was the boy's nature or something about him, being a white man, something involving Mudaree's tribal family. He didn't push any further. He'd find out eventually. His son possibly knew more anyway, as they seemed to spend a lot of time together. Perhaps he'd ask him later.

They continued their fence work. After the holes were dug, they set about cutting logs for the rails, each nine feet long, to fit between each post. Richard took pride in his carpentry and kept his axes, saws, adzes and chisels clean and sharp, using a whetting stone to hone and sharpen the edges. He thinned each end of the rails, forming a tenon to slot into the post. He showed the boys how to cut mortice holes on each side of the posts with a hammer and chisel, or a mortising axe. It was exacting work, making sure each hole was cut to the right size, and required considerable skill to build properly, so that the posts and rails lined up squarely, and the fence was solid and looked masterly. Slowly, as they made their way down the line, the boys became proficient.

By the end of the day, they had completed 50 yards of fencing, three rails between each post.

'Good work, lads,' Richard said. 'Best post and rail fence in the colony, I reckon. Even a Mallee bull couldn't push it over. You can knock off. We'll finish the job tomorrow.' He collected his tools and watched the boys run off, yipping and hollering with youthful enthusiasm, and walked back to his hut. Back to his growing family.

Another pregnancy. Another birth. Richard and Elizabeth welcomed another daughter who they named Mary Ann, on 2 May 1870. As with their other children, no doctor attended the birth, although a local midwife, Mary Rhodes, had been there to assist.

'Congratulations Mr and Mrs Belsar,' Mary Rhodes said after the delivery. 'You've a healthy girl. You should celebrate and 'wet the baby's head' with a tot of sherry and a blessing for the child. I'll ask Dolly to rustle up tea and scones to bring down.'

There was a small gathering, outside their hut: the overseer, Alan Roebuck, station hands with their wives, the Belsar children. Childbirth in the outback always brought people together, especially in the outback. Cups were raised in a toast, Richard's back was patted, Elizabeth was congratulated for her strength and resilience, and the new baby fussed over. Some praised God for the wonder and joy of creation. All hoped and prayed the child would survive.

Mary Ann survived the critical period of infancy and six weeks later, on 28 June, Richard decided to travel upriver to Swan Hill to register her birth with the district deputy registrar, James Hickey. It was also an opportunity to pick up fresh supplies. Elizabeth gave him a list which he scribbled down onto a sheet of paper. 'And some needles and thread,' she said. 'And a roll of linen so I can make a new dress for the baby. If you can find any.'

It was a day's journey by paddle steamer, 50 miles upstream to Swan Hill, his constant companion being the loud thumping of the steam engine beating away as the boat pushed against the current. All the way he sat outside and watched as the murky brown water twisted and swirled in eddies, around log obstacles, and created small whirlpools. The river was high from good rains that year and the current flowed downriver at a respectable rate.

When Richard disembarked at the landing at Swan Hill, he walked to the courthouse and entered the door, seeing a clerk and a police constable sitting behind the counter. 'I'm here to see the registrar,' he said. 'About a birth.'

James Hickey came to the counter with a large book, slowly opened the page and picked up his quill. 'You the father?' he asked.

'Better be. I'd kill the man who said any different.'

Hickey went through each section with Richard carefully, writing down details with neat, cursive penmanship: Date of birth. Child's name. Father's name and occupation. Other children's names. Mother's maiden name and birthplace. Whether a medical practitioner was present.

When it was done, he closed the book and looked at Richard, seeing a man with weathered face, long greying hair tied back. He thought he looked older than his 50 years, which is what he wrote down. 'That all, Mr Belsar?' he asked.

'That's it, thank you. I might go over to Rains Hotel and stay for the night. Wet the baby's head again, now she's two months old.' He looked outside to the fading light. 'Too late to catch a steamer back to Youngera.'

'Good afternoon, then.' James Hickey turned and went back to his desk.

That night Richard got drunk. It's *an easy thing to rationalise*, he thought. *Let's give a toast.* It had been weeks since his last drink and he was celebrating, wasn't he? A few glasses of ale, a few whiskies. Smoke some tobacco, perhaps have a brandy or two. Have a yarn with the bullockies and stockmen at the bar. Maybe play a card game. Several men ended up patting him on the back and shouting him a drink, toasting the baby's good health. At closing time, he could barely make it to his room. He fell into oblivion.

He returned to Youngera the following day with a filthy hangover and faced Elizabeth's wrath. 'Fool of a man!' she said in a rage. 'You're hopeless! Spending what little we have on drink! Returned empty pocketed with no fresh supplies. You'll sleep in the shed tonight.'

'Here, Eliza. I got you something.' He took an object from his pocket and handed it to her. A delicate ivory comb to hold her hair. He had won it playing cards. 'I got your linen too.'

'This won't excuse you.' She stared at the comb, prettily curved with intricate scrimshaw of a ship on the shaft. There was a moment's awkward hesitation. Not forgiveness, but a measure of mollification at least. 'It's lovely. But you can't buy me off that easy.'

He still slept in the shed that night.

Their relationship was not always so fractious. There was affection, if not always love. They cared for and depended on each other, and took joy in watching their children grow. Most evenings, they sat together and gossiped about the goings on at the station: visits by neighbours, improvements needed with huts, planting seasonal crops, trading goods with paddle steamers, dispensing food and clothing at the Wamba Wamba.

camp. They organised events: bush christenings, Easter services, Sunday picnic lunches.

Their eldest children mixed easily enough. Ellen, 13, and Richard, 11, mostly ran wild. After work or chores, they explored shallow creeks and hidden billabongs, and caught river cod with Wamba Wamba children, who taught them to trap fish with cone-shaped, woven reed nets. They climbed hollow trees to find parrots' nests and made the young their pets. They fished the creeks for large yabbies, and on warm evenings sat, bare toes in the water, listening to the croak of frogs and the shrilling of crickets. They learnt to hunt wallabies and possums and make rugs from their skins. They collected wild fruit and nuts, quandong and yam daisy root, and swan eggs in the swamp.

Like other settlers in the Riverina and Mallee, the Belsars were isolated, miles from their neighbours – just a handful of people connected by the river. It was the Murray, that mighty riverine byway, that linked them. Winding, twisting through the landscape like a giant serpent. Aboriginal people had a name for it – *Dhargela*. Wide and deep in most parts or shallow enough to cross with a herd of sheep and oxen when the water was low. It connected settlers and travellers, upstream and downstream, between the Colony of Victoria and that of New South Wales. Allowing people to meet and trade, to socialise and share information. Settlers found out what was happening in the region at Echuca, Swan Hill, Meilman, Euroa, Mildura, Remark. Station owners got stock prices from markets in Melbourne or Adelaide.

News travelled in boats up and down the river like a telegraph; it was busy with the constant traffic of paddle steamers, barges, punts, small fishing and ferry boats. Hotels and public houses sprang up: Flynn's Hotel at Euston, Timothy Glynn's Hotel at Boundary Bend, William Reilley's at Narung. They were places to drink, discuss stock sales or hold public meetings, celebrate weddings or plan new business deals. Single men, tired drovers, station hands, shop merchants, shearers, loggers, sales agents could now catch a steamer and spend their wages to buy liquor within the hour.

Richard knew his neighbours, of course. He helped them out occasionally – moved stray sheep back, repaired boundary fences, looked after injured labourers. Social news between settler families travelled among adjoining properties, calling in by horse or cart, even on those with vast acreages.

On days Richard did not work, he explored the maze of creeks and wetlands connected to the Murray, walking or riding a horse. Among the debris washed down in a winter flood, he found an old punt, broken and semi-submerged in the mud. He dragged it out and repaired it, refitting new gunnels and side planks with fresh cut timber, and caulked the seams. He carved a set of oars and made it watertight, and began to explore the river and creeks, often rowing together with his son, Richard Henry, teaching him about boats, about the river's hidden currents, swirling eddies, how to read the wind.

The old man loved the water, even a flood-prone inland river like the Murray. Even with weakening eyesight, he could still row: drawing the oars to paddle upstream or simply drift, feeling the breeze and shimmering reflection on his weathered face, the sound of water splashing against the gunnels. The brown murky water, for all its difference, brought back memories of his days at sea.

They paddled and camped at night, he and his son, and fished for large, fat Murray cod or giant-clawed crays at a low-lying creek called *Nargooyia*, which meandered around Youngera's southern side to form a large, wooded island. Good land, part of the floodplain, lightly covered by black box and native grass. An island they felt separate from the station, one they felt as their own.

The island would later take their name. It would become known as Belsar's Island, although for many years officials spelled it as Belchers Island. After a lifetime of misspelling Richard's surname in public records and official ship registers, the island continued to be misspelt by forestry map makers for decades to come.

The Flood

In the months of September and October 1870, a great flood swept across the state, laying every district of Victoria underwater. The rain was relentless for weeks on end. A torrent of water surged into tributaries of the Riverina and Murray River, then flowed across the landscape like an inland sea. It was the greatest flood the burgeoning young colonial state had ever known.

'When will it ever stop,' bemoaned Elizabeth. 'Everything's sodden. The ground's like a sponge.' She was outside in the garden trying to save a crop of tomatoes, which had cracked and split. Richard was walking up from the river after having unloaded their weekly supplies from a steamer.

'I just got news from a riverboat captain,' he told her. 'It's the last boat passing through. Things are worse at Echuca, he told me. Floods have destroyed roads and bridges, swept away wharves and boats. It's inundated homes and buildings. A few people have drowned. Some small settlements wiped away. Tens of thousands of sheep, horses and cattle, all lost.'

'Are we safe here?' she asked.

'Aye, I believe so. We're on higher ground. It's a long way away from us.'

But the rain worsened. The deluge was immense, as if Mother Nature wanted to unleash her fury to cleanse the land of made-made and living things. In the Riverina, the inundation poured into the vast Murray basin and across floodplains, and then began flowing inexorably west, leaving a trail of havoc in its wake. It moved to the Lower Murray and beyond. It moved toward Boundary Bend and Youngera.

Richard and Elizabeth watched the heavy swollen clouds roll past them, again and again, dumping buckets of rain at Youngera, filling creeks and gullies until they overflowed. Their hut leaked, water seeped from the shingled roof, through the door and windows, and up through the slab floor. Their blankets and clothes and beds were damp. Richard dug channels around the hut to drain the water, but still it came in. Even the station horses and cattle looked miserable, huddled under gum trees which gave little respite.

'I want everyone inside, at least where I can see them,' Richard told Elizabeth. 'I'm going over to check with Allan Roebuck at the homestead. Stay with the children.'

In the distance, he saw the river rise to the top of its banks and start to spread across the plains like a creeping barrage. Several large trees swept downstream in the raging torrent. It was something beyond their experience.

'The river's rising fast,' cried Elizabeth. 'It's like a sea is approaching us.'

A meeting was held with the overseer, Allan Roebuck. He wanted all the men on ready to save their stock and move them to higher ground. By the time Richard arrived, the dining room was full of stockmen, shepherds and station hands.

'Men,' Roebuck said loudly, over the noise of rain beating down on the tin roof. 'We need to rescue a mob stranded with lambs in low-lying areas a mile or two from the homestead. If we leave now, we can make it. The river's still on the rise. But it's two thousand sheep, for God's sake!'

'Is it safe?' One of the stockmen asked. 'I mean, what are the chances? Movin' them in these conditions? Grounds are sodden. You know what they're like in heavy rain. Just stand there, too stupid to move.' The stockmen looked at each other, uncertain of the risk, as if they were being told to go on a fool's errand.

Roebuck quickly cut further questions. He said: 'I want every available person saddled up and ready within the hour. Get going! The mob will drown unless they're mustered to high ground.' He looked across at Richard, his intentions made clear. 'How about your two?'

Richard ran back to their hut, ever watchful of the river below them. Even Richard Henry and Ellen Jane were asked to join in, leaving Elizabeth alone with the toddler, Elizabeth Ann, and their newborn, Mary Ann, in the hut. When he told her about the meeting, the Roebuck's request, she was shocked.

'Don't fret, Eliza,' Richard said. 'I'll take care and watch them. If all goes well, we'll be back by mid-afternoon, I reckon.'

'If you think there's any risk, turn back, you hear! I don't care what Roebuck says. He can sack us, for all I care. Bring them back home safe. Forget the damn sheep.'

'I swear.' He looked at his son and daughter standing by with a confidence born from experience. Both agile and strong. They'd grown up on outback stations and could ride bareback or saddle with skill. 'Now Richie, Ellen, you ready for this?' he asked.

They both nodded. 'Yes, pa.' Then all ran off together to saddle up.

Elizabeth stood at the hut door and watched them ride off, gradually disappearing into the blanket of rain. She boiled water on the stove and brewed tea, then put Mary in her crib and lay on the bed to wait, listening to the constant drumming of rain on the roof. All she could do was wait and watch the river, hour by hour. After a time, fatigued by stress, she closed her eyes and dozed.

It was mid-afternoon when she woke, alerted by a sensation something was wrong. She turned to look at Mary, the baby still fast asleep. Then she looked across the room and saw Elizabeth Ann, sitting cross-legged on the wet floor wide-eyed in fear, staring at the door. A figure stood there, a silhouette of a tall, black man holding a spear and waddy.

Her reaction was one of instant dread, more for her children than herself. She jumped up. 'Go away! she shouted, 'Get out!'

But the man didn't move. He remained still, staring indifferently, neither coming forward nor withdrawing. Someone from the black's camp. Someone she didn't recognise.

Elizabeth pulled her daughter to her, clutching her protectively, fearing the worst. She heard stories of rape and killings at stations. If she made a sudden move, would he assault them, alone in the hut? 'What is it?' she yelled. 'What do you want?'

'Big water,' the man said, almost casually. It sounded more like *bigwaa*.

'What? What do you mean?'

'Big water come, missus.' She understood immediately.

She looked down at her feet, covered with water above her ankles. The flood had reached them; it was lapping around inside the hut. She glanced past him, out the door. A sweep of water had covered the yards and garden – a low, foamy wave was overturning everything in its path: chicken coops, horse troughs, dog kennels, picket fences. The river, usually a hundred yards below them, now stretched from their hut across to the other side, looking ominous and menacing, filled with branches and swirling debris. Dirty brown, full of mud, it looked like a monster, swallowing everything in its relentless wake.

We must leave quickly, she thought, *before we're caught in this deluge.*

There was little time to pack, just a pannier of what she could grab. Warm clothing, two blankets, a few possessions, a sling to carry Mary. She picked up both the girls and strode off with the man, splashing in the water. She saw Mudaree and a group of the Wamba Wamba making their way past the homestead, holding their young, carrying woven baskets and tools, heading toward the rise in the distant sand hills. She joined the evacuee party, praying to God for her family and hoping the stockmen, somewhere out there in the bush, were safe.

The men returned mid-afternoon, having mustered as many stranded sheep as they could find. It had been hard going on horseback in the sodden ground, the herd had become split all over, standing meekly in gullies, in thick scrub and on floodplains. The riders tried to push them onto high ground as best they could, but they knew it was hopeless. Only a few hundred were saved. It was heartbreaking watching lambs and ewes, bleating in fear and slowly drowning and being washed away. They couldn't reach half the heard. They knew most would become marooned in paddocks slowly filling with floodwaters. Even after the deluge receded it would be hard to save the surviving mob with enough food. Much of the grass had died, eroded or suffocated by layers of mud.

'What can we do, pa?' Ellen cried. 'They don't move!' She was sitting in her saddle watching the mob below them become engulfed in the raging floodwater. The river was getting dangerously high now, spilling over its banks, moving toward them like a creeping barrage.

"We must go now!' Richard yelled. "Or we'll get cut off. Ride back! I'll get your brother.' He swung his horse around and rode back to the stockmen, where his son was, mustering a small herd of sheep up a hill. Then he saw them turn and ride toward him. They were safe. Drenched with rain, but safe.

As the weary riders returned to the homestead, tired and wet, horses splashing in water over their hocks, they could not believe how quickly the river had risen. Richard and the children, each astride strong stock horses, rode to their hut and saw it empty. The whole station was deserted.

'Pa! Where's Ma and Mary?' asked Ellen, her voice rising in trepidation. 'Were they caught?'

Richard looked at them and spoke slowly and calmly. He knew Elizabeth would have escaped somehow. She was too sensible to wait. 'They'll be safe, I'm certain. She would have left, along with the others.' He turned and pointed inland at the sand hills. 'Over there. They'll be there somewhere. We'll find them.'

Then they heard a cooee, a call-out from near the homestead. One of the stockmen was waving his hat, signalling them to come. He was talking to an Aboriginal girl sitting on the roof, swinging her legs over the edge. It was Dolly.

'They all gone,' she said, wet through with but seeming unconcerned about the situation. She pointed, lifting her arm in a lazy arc. 'Up them hills. Your missus gone too, with the other station missus.'

'Thank you, Dolly,' said Richard. 'We're most relieved. Get down, we'll take you with us.'

Ellen moved the fastest, swinging her small pony around to the side of the homestead wall. 'Jump on, Dolly. You're riding with me!'

The riders found them. In the sand hills, huddled together, among a thicket of black box trees. Black men and women from the camp, white women with children, some sitting under tarpaulins, others standing in the rain. Relieved their loved ones had been saved, that no one had been lost in the maelstrom. They could only wait for the rain to stop and the floodwater to recede.

It would be three days before the flood subsided. They sat, huddled around smoky fires, trying to keep out of the rain under canvas awnings. Men rode back occasionally, wading in the muddy water to collect blankets, warm clothing, canvas for protection, food from the store, whatever they could salvage. As the floodwater receded, they returned to the station, all together, to begin the clean-up and repair. Mud and silt covered everything. Solid buildings were spared, but their hayshed, smokehouse and meat cellar had collapsed. Most of the Wamba Wamba huts and gunyah shelters were destroyed. They picked through their scattered belongings, washing away the dirt, hanging out clothes and bedding to dry.

The men butchered the carcasses of dead sheep so they could eat. For two days they laboured at the cluster of station homestead buildings, cleaning away the mud-splattered filth, repairing fences, drying the stores, shovelling mud from cellars and firepits. At night they came together to eat, Wamba Wamba clan members and white setters alike, and gave prayers of thanks for their survival.

Then they turned their attention to the loss of stock.

When the head stockmen and the overseer, Allan Roebuck, rode to inspect outlying flocks, they returned with grim news. 'Three thousand lost, I reckon,' said Roebuck. 'A third of our stock. A big hit to the station. Can't do nothin' about butchering neither.' It was a huge loss, just before the start of the shearing season. It would take another twelve months to recover and restock.

The great flood of November 1870 in Victoria devastated the state. The worst affected areas, in settlements along rivers and waterways, suffered the greatest. Lives were lost; bridges, roads and buildings and even small towns, swept away. Farms and livelihood destroyed. The economic impact was widespread and significant. Then the speculators began to appear, taking advantage of forced sales and bankruptcies.

In late 1870, Youngera Station was purchased by a wealthy banker and politician, Henry Miller, from Melbourne. The Honourable Henry Miller, member of Victoria's Legislative Council, was known a 'Money Miller'. He had fingers in many pies and had founded the Bank of Victoria and the Royal Mint. He owned large areas of real estate around the city of Melbourne and leased several squatting properties. He purchased Youngera and surrounding stations at public auction.

It's unlikely Henry Miller ever visited Youngera. His son Septimus Miller managed all his estate properties.

Allan Roebuck was right, after all. He remained overseer. After Miller's squatting purchase, little changed in Youngera Station's day-to-day operations. Itinerant labourers came and went. Overseers stayed for years. Richard Belsar never rose beyond being a station hand and bush carpenter.

Carwarp Station

Richard and Elizabeth arrived at Mildura Station by paddle steamer on a chilly winter's day in August 1872. They were in the arid Mallee region of Victoria, further west than they had ever been before, 100 miles from their home at Youngera Station. More isolated than ever.

Richard had taken a job fencing at a place called Carwarp Station until December, before the stifling heat of summer made such work unbearable – a contract to erect post and rail fences at one of the mustering yards. Carwarp Station was mostly arid land, a poor place for sheep. Loose sandy soil. Little more than a rough bush camp at a watering hole on the stock route south to Melbourne.

It would be hard, physical labour. Building stockyards. Cutting trees and hauling in logs by bullock teams for fencing. Trimming branches and shaping wood into fence posts. Posts had to be set and notched to take stout wood rails, then inside posts joined against them to hold the rails in place. Posts and rails were lashed together with raw cattle hides.

Young, strong men did the heavy lifting – tough station workers, white and Aboriginal stockmen alike.

Richard and Elizabeth arrived at Mildura Station and disembarked at the wharf where they were welcomed by the station owner, Hugh Jamison. They found him sitting casually by a gantry in shade away from the glaring intensity of the Mildura's winter sun. Jamison looked like a British officer. Tall, thin and wiry, he looked every bit the soldiery type and ran his property like a military operation.

Jamison stood to grab hold of the mooring line as Richard stepped off the boat. 'Good day to you, Mr Belsar,' he said in a crisp friendly tone, extending his hand. Then he saw Elizabeth and the children behind. 'I see you brought your young family.' His eyes immediately took in Elizabeth who held a baby in her arms. 'Sure that's wise? It's desolate country ahead.'

'My wife's a hardy woman, Mr Jamison. She knows what's ahead, Mr Jamison. I'm sure you'll find she's no burden.'

'Fair enough,' he replied. 'Come along now. You'll be leaving after lunch with the bullock wagon. Rations, tools and timber all loaded and packed. I'll walk you up to the homestead and explain the situation, and we can partake of some tea and refreshments. Your littluns looks like they'd enjoy a lemonade.'

'Can we have some, ma?' Lizzie asked.

'Thank you, Mr Jamison. That would be most appreciated,' Elizabeth said.

Richard already knew about Mildura Station, one of the largest and best-managed stations on the

Lower Murray. He knew Jamison ran a strict operation. Liquor, in particular, was rationed. There was a rule in place for all men to line up at the store at noon, where Jamieson served a tot of rum to each, and to Aboriginal workers a glass of wine. Other than that, no casual drinking was allowed, and drunkenness could lead to instant dismissal. He had a reputation for looking after workers and treating them well. He had done much to establish intercolonial trade on the Murray River between South Australia and Victoria.

As they sat drinking tea and mint-flavoured soda water on the veranda, Jamison outlined the job. 'I'm expanding things at Carwarp, my run further south. Wild cattle run everywhere. We can do more than just kill and skin them for hides. I want to expand the camp, build good mustering yards so we can drive the herd to Horsham and southern markets. I need bigger drafting yards.'

'How big is the run?' Richard asked.

'Carwarp's 64,000 acres,' Jamison replied. 'It's currently a grazing outstation for sheep and cattle. My stockmen kill and skin the wild cattle. Hides are stretched on the ground for drying, then folded and packed on carts. Meat's butchered, salted, and brought back here. But there's more profit in driving a herd down south. On to Melbourne.'

'So, you need holding yards? How big?'

'I need more fences at the stockyards,' Jamison said. 'Not much there now. Just men's huts and sheds. I need a strong, enclosed yard to hold a big herd. A hundred head. That means more timber and extra men.'

That would be around 20 yards by 17 yards, Richard thought, after doing the calculations in his mind. *I can get it done easy with some men to help me with the hard labour.*

They drank tea from pannikins while Jamison looked at Elizabeth, an expression of concern growing on his face. He often hired married men in the bush, many who were accompanied by their wives and children, but Carwarp camp was 25 miles from Mildura. It was hard arid county, Mallee scrub. Not a place for woman, he thought.

'Mrs Belsar, you'll be the only woman at the camp. How young are your children?'

Elizabeth felt the burden of responsibility upon her. It had been with her constantly since they'd left. She knew she would be on her own most of the time, alone during the day with three infant children to look after. She also knew they desperately needed the money.

'Lizzie is aged four,' she said. 'Mary's aged two. Our newborn you see in my arms, Margaret Annie, was born in July. She's one-month-old.'

'They're very young, Mrs Belsar, if you don't mind me saying. It's hard country down there.'

Elizabeth knew she had the courage to face adversity; she had overcome hardship many times before. She looked at Jamison and replied with a tone of firmness in her voice. 'I shan't be a burden, Mr Jamison. I'm quite capable of looking after myself. And my children. We'll keep clear, out of everyone's way. It's only a few months.'

'Well then,' Jamison said getting up from his chair. 'You better get ready. You will be travelling on the bollock wagon with one of my stockmen, Johnny Thompson.'

Their journey, hard enough in normal times, was all the more difficult for Elizabeth, with three infants to care for. She still felt the effects of her labour, recovering from the birth of another child. She now had eight pregnancies behind her. She would be caring for three infants, in desolate scrubland, living in a tent, on her own for most of the time. She knew hardship; she'd grown accustomed to it, but this journey would test her. They had only the bare essentials and were camping in arid desert country, surrounded by scrubby mallee eucalypts, spiky tufts of porcupine and spinifex grass. Living in a rough stock camp with rough men, ten or so, for at least four months.

They left the older children behind. Ellen, now 15, and Richard, 13, said they could look after themselves. Youngera was their home – a place of familiarity and certainty. Richard made sure to have a private word with the overseer, Allan Roebuck, about keeping a close eye on them while they were gone.

Johnny Thompson joined them on the wagon as it rolled slowly south, lumbering and jolting behind a team of bollocks, a bullocky leading them down the track; more a rutted stock route than a defined road. All the way Thompson chatted and jabbered about his time with the mounted police, mustering in South

Australia, killing and droving cattle at Kulkyne Station, which adjoined Carwarp. He was a talkative bloke, who took a fancy to wearing flashy clothes, and had on a bright red vest and polished leather boots. He said had explored most of the district and personally knew all the station managers.

Richard found him somewhat pretentious, tending to boast. He kept to himself, knowing they had to work closely together.

They arrived that evening at the camp. It looked spare and inhospitable, just a few canvas tents, several small cooking fires, a mustering yard under construction, a saw pit and skinning yard, a mob of weary cattle. 'One of 12 yards being built on Carwarp,' Thomson told them. 'Outstations and cottages will come later. I suggest you camp near the shallow lake, away from the stench. You'll have more privacy.'

They spent the next four weeks building fences and holding pens. The timber was cut and sawn and strapped together with strips of rawhide. Cypress pine logs, straight and pest-proof, proved best. Easy for the stockmen to cut and split and handle. Four-yard sections of post and rail fencing, one after the other. A race for drafting, a branding yard, two large pens to hold the cattle when caught. Timber cutters worked in outlying areas to load the bullock dray and bring in more logs to cut, strip and split. The men worked day after day.

The labour was tough on the men, especially for Richard, by then aged 57. Ten-hour days of sweating heat and red dust under a harsh sun. Even going slow, leaving the heavy lifting to younger men, he became exhausted by midday. His rest breaks and smokos took longer. Knocking off each afternoon, tired and beaten, he walked back to the tent doubled over with pain and stiffness. The only consolation was their food: hearty meals of mutton or beef stew, with lashings of damper and treacle, dried apples and sultanas, plenty of sugared tea. The camp was well supplied with bags of oats, sugar, flour, bacon, potatoes, and even a goat for milking. A camp cook prepared their meals and made sure they were well-supplied and properly fed.

Elizabeth did her best to settle into the monotonous isolation. She often visited the men's camp, sometimes helping the cook prepare meals or attend to an occasional injury for the workmen; there were frequent cuts to hands. She was always welcomed, and the workers polite, but it was a single men's camp, full of hardened bushmen who cussed, swore, and preferred to keep to themselves. Even Richard became isolated, being so much older.

Elizabeth felt it was hard enough to just look after the children, especially Lizzie and Mary, constantly running in the scrub. That, and the demands of the baby.

Lost

'Where's Mary?' Elizabeth asked Lizzie late one afternoon, coming outside from the tent. She had been breastfeeding Margaret and bathing her in a tub while the children played outside. She looked at Lizzie, sitting alone, humming, drawing in the sand with sticks.

'Where's Mary, Lizzie?' she asked more firmly. 'Where did she go?'

The child said nothing and kept humming a nursery rhyme.

'Mary!' Elizabeth called out again. 'Mary!' There was no answer in the silent bush.

She ran to the yards, looking behind each mound of saltbush, every tuft of high grass. *Surely, she's not far*, Elizabeth thought. *No need to panic.* She returned to the tent, searching everywhere, going over the same ground twice. *Maybe the dry lake, I'll find her there.* But Mary couldn't be found.

'Stay here, Lizzie,' she shouted. 'Stay with Margaret in the tent. I'm getting your pa.'

She ran and told him, becoming scared now, a knot of fear growing inside her chest. *If they acted quickly, they'll find her*, she thought. *Just a toddler on little legs. Surely, she couldn't go far.* Richard threw down his axe and asked several men nearby to help him search.

The search continued into the night without success. The men walked all over, spread out, calling Mary's name, stumbling over bushes in the rain until after midnight, searching with torches. By 1.30 am, Richard and Elizabeth were exhausted, depleted by a growing fear and overcome by adrenaline. Deep into the night they tried to sleep, to close their eyes, all the time praying to God for help.

But they couldn't sleep.

Another dreary day and stormy night passed, as the search parties split up and went in all directions, some accompanied Richard in the hope of attracting Mary's attention. They scoured the area around the dry lake, followed the track, the whole camp fully involved. Watchfires were kept burning, cooees echoed during the day and night. The search party, now full of anxiety, alternated between hope and despair, listening for the sound of an infant's voice or cry. Nothing.

On the fourth day, a muddy rider came back around midday and told them he had found her. She was dead.

Richard saw her, curled on her side behind a saltbush, looking like she was asleep. How had they missed her? How had she wandered so far? He picked up her small body, so slight and delicate, and carried her back to camp, crying in grief, not knowing what to say to his wife. The tired men walked behind in sorrowful silence.

'Oh God no, the pain's too much. My heart is broken,' Elizabeth cried when she first saw her, and rushed to see their child.

They sat and wept. There was nothing that could be said, really. They gently stroked her body, Elizabeth whispering over and over: 'Poor little darling.' Richard mumbled something about where they'd found her.

Eventually they returned to the tent where Elizabeth lay Mary's body on the bed. 'Leave me alone with her, please,' she said.

He stood looking, thinking about what to do. Should they bury her here? Her death should be reported. 'I'll ask someone to ride back and get a priest or constable,' he said. 'Get him to come here, consecrate the grave, say some words.'

'Leave me be.'

Elizabeth cleaned Mary's small body. Wiped the dirt off with a towel and dressed her in fresh clothes, all the while praying in a jumble of words. 'Merciful Lord, may she join the angels and saints, look after my little one. Bless her and keep her ... Oh God! Help me with my agony. Why did this happen? Take my Mary to Heaven. Lord, give me strength. Send me a sign, Lord, that our children, lost to us on earth, are with you.'

She blamed herself for Mary's death. In her grief she decried God and Richard for bringing them to this god-forsaken place. Her child, her little girl, lost and afraid, stumbling in the dark, seeing ghosts, becoming weaker, crying and alone.

She sat forlorn in the tent, looking out to the wilderness, gazing blankly into the distance, cradling Margaret and holding Lizzie's hand. She knew she had to feed them, breastfeed Margaret and do something for Lizzie. She hadn't eaten. She had no appetite, even after three days. Richard brought food from the camp and encouraged her, but she could only swallow a mouthful. After three days of worry, with little sleep, she looked gaunt and ancient, drowning in an ocean of despair.

Johnny Thompson came over to their tent. 'I sent a rider to fetch Constable Doherty from Kulkyne Station,' he said. 'Should be here in the morning. They may need to make a report of some kind.' He stood about awkwardly then turned to leave. 'Sorry for your loss, Mr Belsar.'

Constable William Doherty arrived the next day after a three-hour ride from Kulkyne, and got straight into questioning the circumstances of Mary's death. He spoke to Johnny Thompson, some of the search party, and was shown the spot where Mary had died. He spoke with Richard and then entered the tent, seeing Elizabeth slumped by Mary's lifeless body on a stretcher. She looked up, not really registering his uniform.

'My condolences, Mrs Belsar. I shan't take long. I just need to witness the body.' He drew away the sheet, glanced down, then covered her again. 'How old was the child?'

'She was two years old.'

'I'll prepare my report then I'll be off shortly,' he said. 'Or would you like me to stay for the burial? I assume you'll want to arrange that here. Perhaps I could attend and say a few words from the Bible. I have one with me.'

'Too late for that now,' she said. 'God has forsaken me in this desolate wilderness. You may leave.'

Constable William Doherty eventually submitted his official report. He registered Mary's death with the district registrar at Swan Hill on 7 January 1873. Doherty wrote that she'd died on about 2 October 1872 at Carwarp Lake. He wrote the cause of death: *Lost in the bush. Privations.* Five short words with so much meaning.

No inquest was needed; the circumstance of Mary's death required no further investigation. Constable Doherty authorised the burial and recorded Richard as the 'undertaker'. A registrar at Swan Hill named Leonard Fawssett recorded the details and signed his name on the death register with an illegible squiggle, then stored the ledger away in his office. This time, Richard didn't get to write or sign his name.

Richard's last job at Carwarp was to build a small coffin made of cypress pine and burying Mary near the shallow lake next to their camp. The grave had a small wooden cross with some wildflowers but was otherwise unmarked.

End of Watch

Mildura, 1888.

He had always enjoyed the ritual of smoking a pipe. Cleaning the bowel with his pocketknife, knocking the residual ash out on the heal of his shoe, packing the right blend of Capstan tobacco, lighting it with a match and puffing away. He could sit for an hour and smoke pleasantly. It always provided a feeling of pleasure and contemplation.

'What will we leave of ourselves when we're gone, do you think?' Richard asked Elizabeth one evening, sitting outside his tent under the shade of red gums on the bank the Murray River, as a blazing sunset lit up the sky above. He could barely see it now, the brilliant red and orange hues of a Wimmera sunset. His eyes, dull and foggy, hardly registered the colours of the sky or the bright glow of the sun's orb. His eyesight was poor and getting worse.

Elizabeth turned around to look at him, curious by the question.

'Our possessions for the children, some savings, I expect,' Elizabeth said. 'Your tools and clothing. Why do you ask?' She was busy fussing in the tent, tidying and cleaning up after their meal to consider the question too deeply. She had more to do now, looking after him with his poor eyesight.

'I don't mean possessions. I mean our lives. Will *we* be remembered, do you think? I know we haven't left a mark. I haven't much to show, at least.'

'The children will remember us, you silly thing. They'll have memories. What's this about, then? What do you mean?' She stared at him, more concerned than curious. He'd never spoken like this before. She came over and sat with him. 'Are you thinking of the hereafter?'

'No, I was just thinkin', that's all,' he paused to relight his pipe with a match. He could still do that, at least. 'They'll only remember us as being old. Me, a blind old man. They won't know what we did. When we had fire in our bellies. Who we were when we were young. Me, sailin' ships. You as a maiden. You and I in the goldfields.'

'Yes, and you in Ararat gaol. Me there too, then being sent away. You want them to remember that? What are you going on about?'

'I expect they know about that, Eliza. Whether we mentioned it or not. I'm not fussed about that. Apart from bein' a fool. Which, you know already.'

'If you feel so strongly about being remembered, you could tell them. Spend time with them. Tell them your stories at sea.'

He thought a moment, wondering what to do. Did it really matter, being remembered? Does their life have a meaning, other than to have survived and raised a family? Probably not, he decided.

'Ah, it's just a spell of melancholia, Eliza,' he said. 'I'm bein' maudlin.' He thought of his children, making their own lives. 'They don't care about a codger like me. Too busy with their own lives. Grownin' up. Richard chasin' girls. Ellen's still flirtin' herself, you noticed?' He puffed his pipe and tried to understand what it was making him feel this way, this contemplation on his life. Leaning over, he placed his hand on hers, rough and scarred as it was from a lifetime of seafaring and bush labour.

'You know, my greatest regret's not givin' you a cottage. One of your own. Here we are, livin' in a tent.' He paused a moment and squinted up to the sky. 'I'm sorry, Eliza. I really am. I know I made you a promise once.' As he said the words, a lump came to his throat. He could barely speak. 'I failed you.'

She shook her head and smiled, understanding and sharing his feelings better than he knew. She realised years back that her life would be one of hardship, living in the outback, moving from place to place. Ever since he took her away from Sandhurst. But she did not regret her choice to stay with him. Despite their poverty they had their children, now making lives on their own. 'You helped our Richard with his cottage though, didn't you?' she said. 'Helped them all out, where we could, within our means. What little savings we had, we gave them. Now, we're here. In Mildura. In a tent. Other families scattered about. At least it's warm and sunny. Mostly.'

He squeezed her hand. 'Thank you, Eliza. I ain't been much. Or given you much. But thank you for sticking with me.'

How strong were the bonds of Richard and Elizabeth's marriage? How close was their relationship? We will never know. The marriage survived – they remained together all their lives. After the death of Mary, they returned to Youngera and raised their family, living as best they could. Adapting to the seasons: the summer shearing, the quiet winter, the spring lambing. Life rolled on. They celebrated birthdays and Christmas, traded supplies with neighbours, travelled to Swan Hill or Balranald for church weddings. They recovered from the loss of four children but never forgot them.

They became grandparents. The first grandchild was born after a teenage wedding. The next arrived unexpectedly and was illegitimate.

Ellen Jane, their eldest, left to marry a station worker at Wentworth in New South Wales in December 1872 – a man named William Benjamin Bennett. She was 15 and he 21. Her marriage happened soon after Richard and Elizabeth returned from Carwarp so must have been a surprise. The circumstances are uncertain. How did the couple meet? Did they elope? Did her parents attend the wedding and bless the union?

Ellen returned to Youngera Station and gave birth in April 1875. A boy they named William Samual Bennett.

The next child arrived at Youngera Station when Richard Henry Belsar, now 22, returned in early 1881 accompanied a young woman and a newborn baby. It had been months since Richard and Elizabeth had heard from him, although this was a normal occurrence in the outback in those days. The child, their son said, had been born at Parramatta, near Sydney in New South Wales. The baby's name was James Belsar.

Officially, James's birth is a mystery. There is no record of birth, no registration in the New South Wales Register of Births, Deaths and Marriages. However, his death certificate provides an important clue – his father's name is recorded as Richard Belsar (seaman) and his mother's name is Elizabeth (formerly Carter). His grandfather and grandmother. Was his birth covered up to avoid the scandal of illegitimacy? It appears so. And why at Paramatta?

James was born out of wedlock, away from malicious gossip; the circumstances of his birth were covered up, as they were not in accordance with moral standards of the time. Did he grow up believing his grandparents were his real parents? Possibly.

Later in that year, in mid-1881, Richard Henry married 17-year-old Nellie Winifred Glynn, (likely James's real mother) at Balranald, a town 15 miles across the state border in New South Wales. Nellie Glynn came from Boundary Bend, near Youngera Station, where her parents owned a hotel. Richard and Nellie were neighbours. It seemed young Richard did more than just drink beer at the Glynn's hotel.

Richard Henry became a bush carpenter and labourer, just like his father, and worked on stations in the district. The following year, in September 1882, Richard and Nellie returned to Youngera Station for her to give birth to their (second) son, Herbert Richard. However, the grim shadow of death followed. Poor Nellie suffered from epilepsy. She had a seizure the day after giving birth and died. It was another tragic death, another bush burial, another lonely grave in the bush.

In the late 1880s, Richard and Elizebeth moved with meagre belongings to live next to the Murray River at Mildura. After a lifetime of travelling outback roads, living in rustic huts and bush camps from one season to the next, isolated from towns, you would hope poor Elizabeth, at least, might have found a small measure of comfort, in a cottage of their own, as she'd always wanted. Perhaps she did, from time to time. Perhaps, for a time, she lived at her son's house in Mildura, or her daughter's house at Swan Hill, and helped look after her grandchildren. Or did she always remain with Richard in his tent, looking after him? Of this, there are no clues.

They watched their children leave Youngera Station. Some stayed in the district, others moved away. Richard Henry worked on stations in Victoria and New South Wales. Tall, strong and athletic, he built stockyards and roads for shire councils. He leased land and became a selector – someone who took a licence to farm small land holdings that allowed freehold occupation of up to 360 acres. He became a contract worker, a prize-fight boxer and itinerant traveller, like his father.

He often left his family for months at a time, including a period with the 6th Australian Commonwealth Horse to serve in the South African War. By April 1902, when his contingent of horsemen arrived in Durban, the war was over, so their troop ship turned around and sailed home. Richard Henry Belsar had eight children and two wives.

James left home at 14 and became a deckhand on riverboats. He captained a paddle ship, PS *Success*, for the Murray River Steamship Company. In 1891, he moved with his family to live and farm on Belsar Island. He became famous for a while after rescuing two boys from drowning in the river at Echuca and received a medal for his bravery.

After river traffic ceased, James worked at the Murray Downs Station in Swan Hill and managed the irrigation pumping station for 20 years.

In 1886, Elizabeth Ann married a man named Henry Donovan, a butcher from Noorong Station near Balranald, at the district registry office, when she turned 22. Richard and Elizabeth both attended the wedding, and Richard acted as a witness. The couple went on to raise a large family and moved to live at Naracoorte in South Australia.

In 1890, their youngest daughter, Margaret Annie, also married a station worker, Joseph Mack, who worked nearby at Namung Station and later managed Bumbang Station. They remained in the Swan Hill district for the rest of their lives and also had a large family.

The Belsar family, who never cared how their surname was spelt – Belsar, Bulser, Belser, Belsor, Belcher – grew into a large clan and settled mostly in Victoria's Riverina and Western District. They survived and, in many ways, survive still.

In the winter of 1891, Richard and Elizabeth were still in Mildura on the river flat, a short distance from town, close to their eldest son, Richard, and his wife Jane, who owned a boarding house on Seventh Street.

Richard, the elder, now 76, had become frail after a lifetime of hardship. Blind, he depended on Elizabeth more than ever to look after him. Local doctors at the hospital had examined his eyes, which were cloudy and inflamed. He required specialist medical treatment, which could only be found in Melbourne.

Mildura town folk, showing true spirit, rallied to raise money to help him out. *The Mildura Cultivator* advertised a charity fundraiser.

Tuesday 7th July

Grand Minstrel and Variety Entertainment Evening in aid of R. Belsar, Sen., who is suffering from blindness
Fun, Frolic and Mystery
Look out for the Funnygraph
Prices 2s and 1s

Richard and Elizabeth travelled to Melbourne in late July 1891 – a long journey for the couple. There was no rail link to Mildura yet; the journey was either overland by a Cobb's coach or by riverboat to Echuca, then by train to Melbourne.

We don't know what the treatment was or whether it was successful. If it was trachoma or glaucoma, no specific treatment was available. Some doctors used crystalline alkaloids, including strychnine, administered hyperdermally to relieve the 'mental and physical depression'.

We do know while they were away, their tent was broken into on 29 July and items were stolen. The thief, Edward James Roberts, was eventually caught by police and charged with 'tent breaking and larceny'.

Richard and Elizabeth returned to a ransacked tent, more dejected than ever. It didn't matter that Roberts was found guilty and incarcerated for three months.

They remined at the river flat, in their tent, supported by good-hearted locals, and by their children. Grandchildren visited. Elizabeth helped as much as she could, telling them stories about her days as a girl in Tasmania or how she lived on the goldfields. Richard sat, smoking his pipe, drinking a glass or two of whiskey, much to Elizabeth's disapprobation. Their impoverished lives, spare and deprived, more limited than ever.

By this time, Richard was completely reliant on others. Blind, he lived by his other senses, his touch and smell, feeling for his things in his tent. In his thoughts, he often returned to Liverpool when he was a boy, playing at the docks and markets, running free in the streets. Of cherry trees by the well when the leaves turn green. His old house at Watkinson Steet. The first time he sailed in a boat. He thought of the sea, wild ocean swells, his ship slicing through foaming waves, wind in his hair, under a brace of canvas, heading to a new land as a young man, adventuring.

Things got worse for poor Elizabeth. Soon after they returned from Melbourne, she caught a dose of influenza. When it worsened, they called for a doctor, and she was taken to the small hospital in Mildura. There was no standard treatment for influenza then. Quinine and phenazone may have been used, as well as small doses of strychnine. Perhaps large doses of whisky.

Elizabeth died of influenza and bronchitis on 10 November 1891, aged 56.

The woman who had battled a lifetime of hardship and isolation, imprisonment and the death of her children, was laid to rest two days later at the Nichols Point Cemetery in Mildura.

The registrar at Mildura hospital asked Richard what religion Elizabeth was. For a moment, he was uncertain, lost in thought as he sat by himself in the small pine clad room, and hadn't realised anyone was talking to him.

'Your wife, Me Belsar. Her religion?' the registrar asked again.

'Catholic,' he replied. 'Make sure the priest buries her with the right Catholic words.'

'I don't think Father Costello is available at present, Mr Belsar,' the registrar said. 'He's away from the district. There is Reverend Thomas. I could ask him. A lovely man. He's a Wesleyan Minister. I'm sure he would be willing to undertake the service for your family.'

'He will have to do then,' Richard said. 'It's not like we're ardent believers.'

The following morning, the mourners gathered at the cemetery. A crowd dressed in black, looking formal and solemn, shaking hands and giving their condolences, even smiling in greeting, others standing in solemn silence. The extended Belsar family, a few friends from town, a nurse from the hospital.

Richard sat on a stool by her grave as they buried her, surrounded by his sons and daughters, and several grandchildren. He listened as Reverend Thomas began the committal. He could not see her coffin as it was lowered into the grave.

Richard barely heard the sermon, the words fading silently into the breeze. He sat, eyes shut tight. Images of Elizabeth, his Eliza, moved inside his mind – the young Eliza as she had been at 22 when he took her as his wife; the worn-out, furious Eliza he'd seen at Ararat Gaol with their three children; the shocked Eliza he'd seen upon their reunification in Ballarat at the Benevolent Society; the stricken Eliza, standing in lamentation by the graves of their dead children, all four of them. So many Elizas, none of which he would ever see again.

Frail and destitute, overwhelmed by loss, Richard was now alone. His family took him back to his eldest son's house at Seventh Street to work something out. They gathered around the kitchen table and spoke slowly so the old man could hear.

'What shall we do? Who's going to look after him now?' Richard Henry didn't think he and his family could bear the burden much longer. He was often away from home, he said, on contract labour jobs all over the district. It wasn't fair on his wife, given her duties at their boarding house.

What about Margaret? She was on a station near Swan Hill with her husband Joe and their family. Or perhaps Ellen could get down from Wentworth, although she had a tribe of young children of her own.

In the end, it was the old man who spoke. He stared at his son, his dull, inflamed eyes sightless. 'Go back to Youngera and claim the east section of the property for yourself. A few thousand acres around the island on the river. Go back and improve it. No one wants that floodplain. Farm it, build a cottage, stockyards and fences. Run cattle and sheep. Make it *your* run. Make it *Belsar's* run. The boys will help, won't you, lads?'

James and Herbert looked at each other and nodded.

In the meantime, the good people of Mildura organised another fund-raising event for him on 19 December 1891. This article appeared in the *Mildura Cultivator*:

The local amateurs are arranging a charity concert for Saturday evening, in aid of Mr. Richard Belsar, senior, who is totally blind, and who lately had the misfortune to lose his wife. The old man is in very reduced circumstances and sorely in need of assistance. The people of Mildura can, we hope, be trusted to assist this deserving case.

The amateurs are preparing a program and hope their efforts will be appreciated for the sake of the deserving cause in which they are working. Admission 2s and 1s.

The money raised helped to move Richard back to Swan Hill, back to Youngera, to be cared for by his family. He spent his final years in darkness, being moved here and there, fed and clothed and cleaned by others, listening to their conversations, living with his dreams. It is where he spent his final years.

He struggled on, a tough old bloke. He smoked his pipe and drank whiskey when someone would pour him a glass. Cursed and grumbled and swore, just like always. Told stories about the sea, about the old days, which became more and more incoherent and unintelligible.

Richard Belsar lived another seven years and died at Belsar's station at Youngera on 20 December 1898, aged 83, from heart failure.

The old sailor had finally crossed the bar. They buried him in a grave, but his soul went out to sea.

POSTSCRIPT

Richard Belsar Senior is my great-great-grandfather.

Richard appeared years ago in my family as a name – unidentified, featureless, nondescript, on my mother's maternal side. I saw his surname on a handwritten note my mother had written down. 'He was a sailor, I think,' she said. That was all.

She wrote it on a family tree, along with a few other ancestors, as she remembered them. I still have it. She knew their names, who married whom. Mum was a great one for telling stories about her family, especially in her final years, not that we children listened or appreciated them, uncaring as we were. She would have loved reading this story.

Years later, well after *Trove* appeared online – that amazing digital treasure portal of early Australian newspapers, but well before the current boom of all things ancestry – software, television programs, magazines, and DNA testing – I discovered a few facts about Richard Belsar. Where he was born, when he married, when some of his children were born, when he died.

My direct bloodline is through his eldest son, Richard Henry Belsar. He piqued my interest but remained in the shadows. Even more hidden were the women forebears like the long-suffering Elizabeth Carter. They go virtually unrecorded. They are mostly silent and, in the 19th century at least, were mostly poor and uneducated. What opportunities were there for women who wanted to work? Domestic servants, boarding house owners, barmaids, or governesses. Few, if any, public records exist to trace their heroic lives. Elizabeth, like so many women in the 19th century, was a wife, child-bearer, mother, dependent on a man. All too often they were domestic labourers for husbands and children.

I started digging in Victorian, Tasmanian and British archives. In shipping registers and crew lists, online in Lloyd's List and public registers of births, deaths and marriages. I contacted a several local historical societies and libraries. Ship arrival and departure timelines and ship names helped me piece together the jigsaw puzzle of Richard's early voyages to Canada and Africa and Portugal, and his seafaring days.

I discovered how he arrived in Australia. I unearthed his criminal records in government gazettes, in Australian and British newspaper archives. I read books about the Victorian goldfields and sheep stations, not only to trace Richard, but others in his family, and those he crossed paths with – all real people who'd once lived, experienced joy and hardship, loved, and ultimately died. It became a story too interesting to leave. I had to put flesh on their bones and give them a voice.

Life was generally very hard for most living in British cities in the mid-19th century, certainly for early Australian settlers in the bush. Even brutal, if we judge their lives by today's standards. I've tried to capture some of the hardship and brutality at sea and on land.

I haven't told the story of Richard Belsar and Elizabeth Carter because they were unique or extraordinary. They weren't. That's the reason I think their story is worth telling. They were commonplace and ordinary people, emigrants seeking a better life, like the hundreds of thousands of their time, who battled and survived great hardship. Men and women doing their best, with little to no education, opportunity or wealth. They searched for a small corner of the world where they could raise a family. Many drifted about, like Richard, with his adventurous spirit and itinerant soul, looking for a better place.

www.ingramcontent.com/pod-product-compliance
Lightning Source LLC
Chambersburg PA
CBHW030528190726
48283CB00006B/1822